The Dark Elf:

The Return of the Queen

Charlie-Lee Davies

Michael Terence
Publishing

This edition first published in paperback by
Michael Terence Publishing in 2021
www.mtp.agency

ISBN 9781800942233

Cover illustration
Grace Jolly

Cover design

1

The Dark Elf

In the year of 3019, different dimensions had formed a number of portals for the mortals and the magical folk to travel between. Different dimensions are in different eras, making the time travel more interesting.

***

The great old forest was a magical, beautiful and ancient forest that every magical being lived in. There was a beautiful, clear water stream that ran through the forest and at night, the stream would glow a beautiful electric blue.

The forest had trees that could touch the sky and go on for miles, grass, a rich green colour. There was a lovely cool breeze throughout the forest. At night, magic and magical creatures would glisten everywhere. In the great old forest, it was always summer.

Brunuhville was a beautiful, magical community village. It was in the middle of the great, old forest that was thousands of years old. If you looked down from the sky, you would see how beautiful and big the forest was and in the middle, you could see a medium size circle with a village community.

There were brown/yellow huts made out of wood and brick with wood, grass, leaves and moss on the roofs. There were huts with wooden stalls out the front of them, with pots, jewellery, food, wood, household items, anything you could think of was there.

There were pens, fences made out of wood, with horses in them that the farmers looked after for the riders.

There were different communities in this village. Each community was sectioned off to each elven family.

The village was such a beautiful place until most of it was burnt down after the battle.

The Brunuhville caves were sectioned off from the rest of the village. These caves held the dark elves. A powerful element was hidden in these caves and the dark elves thrived on it.

***

The days were getting darker and it was only the middle of July. The sky was dark, the air was thick and mist covered everywhere. This day was coming but no one knew that it would come so quick.

Alexa Snow, one-hundred and ninety nine years old, was a bright, young witch, with long blonde hair with blue tips, but had a traumatic childhood. Both her mother and father had been murdered but no one ever found the killer. She moved in with a family friend when she was only seven years old. She never remembered where she had came from. She couldn't remember where she was brought up or where her home was. She never understood what had happened that night or where she had got her powers from but all she knew was that she needed to find the person or thing that killed her parents.

Alexa was standing in a field surrounded by mist. Dressed in her blue jeans, black boots, a white shirt that she left the top two or three buttons undone with the laces hanging over her chest and her leather jacket along with a gold half of an eternity ring necklace that she had worn since her friend's birthday many years ago. With her hair blowing in the wind and the ring in her hand, she was looking around the field wandering what was going on. This mist was not like any mist she had ever seen before. Alexa was looking into the distance when a dog like shadow appeared. With magical sparks generating from her hands, she was ready to attack. As the figure moved closer to her she noticed something odd about the figure. She narrowed her eyes to focus on the shadow moving towards her when suddenly it changed into a human shadow. She readied her hands but as the figure became more clear, she cleared her head and the sparks disappeared.

"Alexa, you are early," a man's voice spoke.

"Leonard, I did not realise that was you," Alexa spoke, a hint of relief in her voice as she pulled her hand away from the necklace.

"No need to be ashamed of holding onto your necklace, my child. I know you miss her dearly."

Alexa smiled into her friend's eyes then looked away.

Leonard, an animagus was a great friend of Alexa's family. He had slightly scruffy, dark grey hair, wore black jeans, black shoes, a slightly off-white coloured shirt with a leather jacket to accompany it. Him and Alexa's mum and dad, Tamara and Leo Snow, grew up together. They knew everything about each other and did everything together until the day Tamara and Leo mysteriously passed away a few years back. From that day, Leonard had stuck by Alexa's side, took her in from a young age, teaching her everything she needs to know about what is about to happen to the world she lives in.

"Come, I must tell you something," the animagus announced. Alexa followed the man.

Alexa and Leonard walked what seemed to feel like ages until he came to a halt. The young witch stopped and the man turned around and looked Alexa in the eyes.

"There is something I must tell you, but I need you to stay calm," he spoke as the look on Alexa's face dropped to an emotionless look.

"Of course, Leonard, what is it?" she questioned.

Leonard took a deep breath, then started to speak. "Well, you know your mother and father had told you that the Snow family had something mysterious happen to them years before you were born?"

"Yes."

"Well that something was to do with your mother and father."

Leonard was hesitant. He knew Alexa needed to know as she will come face to face with this but there was something deep within telling him that he should wait until she was older.

He spoke again but this time with hesitation. "Well, to put it this way as I know you will have questions, it has something to do with your brother and what happened to him and who he has become."

Alexa's face suddenly became confused.

"What do you mean brother? I can't even remember what mum and dad look like, let alone remember that I have a brother. I don't remember much about my childhood. What is his name? Where is he? What happened to him?"

'So many questions, with all the answers you need in good time. Alexa sit and I will explain everything." They both sat on an old, broken tree trunk and Leonard began to explain everything.

***

After a while Alexa sat in silence, but then out of nowhere…

"So what you are saying is I have a brother called Link, who went missing after he killed our parents and Lena's parents and herself died along with them? But do you know where he is? And what do you mean by who he has become?" Alexa questioned, confused why she was being told all of this now.

"Yes and no. Me and a few other wizards have been looking for years but no one knows. Link is not a normal wizard Alexa. Something terribly horrible happened to your family that was caused by him. He possesses dark magic, the kind that takes years to learn, but somehow your brother was born with it in his blood," Leonard answered.

"How do you know all of this? Have you ever seen him?" Alexa was so confused but intrigued to know about this boy.

"I met him when he was about sixteen, a year before everything went bad. I have not seen him recently but three men that I know tracked him down a few years ago and only one came out alive," Leonard spoke with the hint of sadness in his voice.

Alexa knew not to press on but she knew there was something that Leonard was not telling her. So instead she decided to change the subject.

"Can you tell me about being an animagus?" she questioned.

"Of course." And from that Leonard began talking about being an animagus to Alexa but the thought of Link still managed to linger in Alexa's mind.

***

Several weeks later, the magical community noticed that the days were getting darker and everything was changing rapidly.

A young forest elf was walking through the small village of Brunuhville, creating magical, multicoloured sparks appear from her hands when someone bumped into her causing the young elf to fall to the ground and the sparks disappear.

"Yo what the…" The young elf went to finish until she saw Alexa laying on the floor in front of her.

"Oh hey, sorry I didn't mean to freak out, I was in my own world, better than the one we are in now." The elf gave a hand to Alexa and helped her up. Alexa brushed herself down and looked up at the elf. She smiled.

"Hi I'm Shadow," Shadow stated. There was a loud bang. Both of the girls jumped around seeing a younger elf walking out of a building with her brown hair all messed up and black marks on her face. She ran over to Shadow and Alexa and smiled.

"Hey I'm Shinara. Who's this Shadow?" the younger elf asked.

"Oh sorry, yeah, I'm Alexa. Are you sisters?" Alexa questioned.

"Yeah, Shinara is learning how to keep her magic under control, but does not seem to have grasped at that yet." Shadow laughed ruffling Shinara's hair up. Shinara gave her sister a look then smiled at the gorgeous girl in front of her, feeling slightly embarrassed.

"Well I will see you guys around. My friend is waiting for me." And with that Alexa turned on her heal and walked off into the distance.

Shadow watched as Alexa was no longer in sight then turned around to see that her sister was nowhere to be seen, again.

"Where has she gone?" Shadow muttered to herself as she started to wonder around the misty village in search of her sister.

***

Shadow was a seriously misunderstood forest elf. She and her younger sister, Shinara, were brought up in the village of Brunuhville by their mother and father, Willow and Legolas Ondovir. Brunuhville is a magical village for elves, where they can live peacefully.

Shadow had black, shoulder length hair that she always wore half up and half down with a braid hanging behind her ear. She wore a black top with a black hooded jacket over the top with the hood always over her head, blue jeans with blue converses. She wore a dragon necklace around her neck that shone when evil was near. She was independent and strong. The magic Shadow possessed was far stronger than the other elves within the village. And for a twenty-year-old elf, that was rare to come by. The people of the village wondered if she was truly a forest elf.

But what Shadow did not know was that her family have been lying to her since she was sixteen, the age where she was told what her magic had placed her as within the eleven community.

***

Shadow was walking through Brunuhville, swirling her fingers creating sparks when a voice called out to her.

"Shadow… Shadow… Shadow…"

She thought the voice was inside her head until a beautiful blue orb appeared in front of her. The orb started drifting through the air, making shadow want to follow it.

And so she did.

Shadow carried on following the orb until it vanished in front of her. All of a sudden she saw these grey shoes standing in front of her. She slowly looked up to see a elven man smiling at her.

"I see you got my message young Ondovir. It is nice to see you," the man spoke.

"Professor Elwin, you gave me quite a scare. I thought the voice was coming from within my mind," she spoke with relief.

"It was from within your mind my child, only elves who possess magic as strong as you can wield the gift of being telepathic." Elwin smiled. He moved aside, welcoming Shadow into his hut.

From the outside you would think that the hut was nothing special but the inside was quite magnificent. As soon as you walked in, there was a beautiful fireplace, with the fire burning, in front, there was a midnight blue sofa with two chairs next to it. There was a bed on the far right and on the left, there was a table with magical potions and viles hovering over it.

Shadow sat down, slowly followed by Elwin.

"Shadow there is something I must tell you. This lie has dragged on for too long and you need to know. Elwin stated and Shadow looked at him with plead in her eyes.

"Go on professor."

Elwin took a deep breath and began. "When you were sixteen, do you remember me telling you that you were a forest elf?"

"Yes, but you seemed odd that day when you told me."

"Well for good reason. When I conducted the ceremony, your mother and father did not like the elf that your magic placed you in. They told me to tell you that you had become a forest elf, like themselves, but that is not true." Elwin was emotionless.

"So what you are saying is that I am not a forest elf, I am something else?" Shadow questioned.

"Yes, your parents told me not to tell you but I know that this would be something you would need to know or you would be living a lie for the rest of your life."

"So what am I professor?"

With hesitation, he answered. "You are a dark elf."

"A dark elf? Aren't they immortal from the age of… Oh now I see why you are telling me." Shadow showed no anger but relief.

The professor smiled knowing that Shadow was happy being told the truth about who she really was. He knew that he could not keep lying to her and she would need to understand why she had lived for so long when forest elves don't live a full long life.

"My parents wanted me to be the same as them, forest elves, but I am stronger than them and they don't like that."

"No they don't but you understand why I have had to tell you?"

"Of course, professor, I am grateful for that. I need to ask, my sister's ceremony is tomorrow, can it be just me and her? I need to know what she becomes," Shadow asked with a look of mischief in her eyes.

Elwin noticed this look and swallowed hard. "O-of course Sh-Shadow."

Shadow smiled. She got up and turned to leave, but not before her last words. "We will see you at ten o'clock." And she left.

Elwin stood in shock. He swallowed hard trying to recover himself.

"I hope I did the right thing."

***

The next day arrived and Shadow and Shinara were making their way to Professor Elwin's hut to find out what Shinara's magic says about what elf she is.

They got to the hut and knocked on the door. The door opened, showing professor Elwin standing nervously.

"G-good m-morning girls," he stuttered. Elwin allowed the girls to walk in. They took a seat and waited for the professor to start the ceremony.

A few moments later Elwin came back. Shinara stood up and walked in front of Elwin so she was face to face. Elwin's hands started to glow and a blue orb appeared in front of Shinara's eyes. The sparks from Elwin's hands started to shot into the orb until the orb vanished. Elwin clicked is fingers and a piece of paper began to float through the air into Elwin's hand.

Elwin looked at the paper and sighed nervously.

"Shinara, you are a dark elf."

Shadow's eyes lit up and a slight smirk curved into her lips.

"Congratulations Shinara. We posses the same magic." Shadow hugged her younger sister, but the younger elf was not impressed.

"Go and wait outside, I just need to talk to the professor," Shadow told her sister. Shinara did as she was told, even though she hated this side of her sister, and walked outside.

Shadow looked at the professor and smiled.

"Thanks professor, for everything. But we won't be needing you now."

"W-what are you s-saying S-Shadow?" Elwin stuttered knowing where this was leading to.

"It would be a shame if someone where to find you dead in your hut," she smirked.

Shadow moved closer to the professor and whispered in his ear. "But don't worry, you will look peaceful dead in your bed."

Shadow stepped back and laughed. "Goodbye old fool."

Magic cards started to appear from the young elf's hands. Shadow was hesitant until she heard a voice.

"You know what to do, it's in your blood. Do it Shadow," a mysterious deep voice spoke.

All of a sudden she flung her hands forward and the cards created a forcefield around Elwin. She clicked her fingers and the cards flowed in mid air, moving the professor to his bed. The forcefield vanished and the professor fell to his bed. Suddenly rope started tying itself around Elwin's wrists and ankles.

Shadow walked closer to the bed. "I promise, this won't hurt." Shadow's hand went ice white as she pressed her hand against Elwin's chest.

Elwin started to go white and blue as the ice started to reach his heart. Elwin took his last breath and Shadow smiled. Removing her hand and then placing it on the professor's head, she closed her eyes. Within that moment, Shinara walked back in, seeing her sister standing over the dead body. She felt sick to her stomach.

"Is he dead?" she questioned.

"Yes, but now he would have died like an ordinary mortal. His magic is now mine." Shadow lifted her hand from his head and clicked her fingers. The hut started to change from looking like a high elf was living there, to someone that had no magical powers die in there.

The two dark elf sisters walked out of the hut, looking to see if anyone was watching, they started to walk back to their parent's home.

***

Shadow and Shinara reached their parent's hut. Shadow walked in, followed by her sister to see their mother and father, Willow and Legolas, talking in their living room.

"Guys you're home, how did it go?" their father spoke.

"Great, we have something we want to say to you," Shinara spoke, slightly sarcastic, hinted at her sister.

Both their mother and father looked at them, slightly nervous about the conversation to come.

"You lied to me." Shadow lifted her head as she spoke to look at her parents.

"What do you mean hunny?" their mother's voice shock.

"You told professor Elwin to tell me that I am a forest elf like you guys because you were to afraid of the magic inside of me. You knew I would become a dark elf, so you created a lie that only lasted four years." Anger rose in Shadow's voice. Legolas and Willow stood at this point and moved backwards until they hit their backs against their living room wall.

"And so you know, Shinara is a dark elf too." Shadow inched closer to her parents until she was centimetres away from them.

"You will pay." Shadow's hands started to glisten. Red and black sparks started to appear and Shadow's eyes turned black.

"Shadow, we are sorry, we never meant to lie to you. Please forgive us," Willow cried as she knew their time was up.

Willow placed her hand in her husbands and smiled at him as a tear rolled down her cheek.

"I love you Legolas."

"I love you too Willow."

"Enough!" shadow shouted. "Time to face your fate."

Shadow swirled her fingers, making the sparks grow bigger.

"Goodbye mother and father," Shadow spoke as she bent her hands back slightly and the sparks flew from her hands, towards her parents. The sparks hit right in the heart of her parents, their bodies turning to stone. Shadow turned on her heal and headed towards the door. Shinara watched as the bodies crumbled to the ground, then followed her sister out of the hut, tears running down her cheeks.

Both the girls put their hoods up on their jackets and started their journey of the legend of the high dark elf.

As they got to the edge of the village, they heard someone shouting.

"SHADOW! SHINARA!"

They looked behind to see Alexa running towards them. Shinara quickly wiped away the tears, making sure that Alexa didn't see her crying.

"Hey where are you guys off to?" Alexa questioned.

Shadow looked Alexa up and down to see that she had a rucksack packed. Then a plan came to mind.

"We are heading off on an adventure, care to join?" Shadow Smirked, noticing that Alexa didn't appear to have notice the smirk, she took that as a good sign.

"Sure let me just get my friend." Alexa smiled.

Alexa turned on her heal to look the opposite direction and began an incantation to call her friend. All of a sudden a black and white husky came running down the path. It came to a holt in front of Alexa.

"Who is that?" Shinara asked.

"This is my friend Leonard. Leo you can transform back now." Alexa smiled at the dog. All of a sudden the husky jumped up onto his hind legs and before their very eyes the husky turned into a man.

"Dude that was awesome! Are you a…?" Shinara questioned.

"An animagus? Yes," Leonard said looking back at Alexa.

"Alexa this is for you. I know you have always wanted one so here you go." Leonard knelt down, pulled out a black wolf cub from inside his jacket.

"Oh my god!! She's beautiful!" Alexa smiled as she crouched down to the wolf's level.

"I'm going to name you Kohana." And just as Alexa said the name, Kohana put her head on Alexa's shoulder to hug her.

"Thank you, Leo." Alexa hugged the man.

"You are very welcome." The man hugged back. They pulled apart and looked at the two sisters.

"Are we ready to head off?" Shadow asked. Everyone nodded and they set off. With Kohana at Alexa's side, her parent's friend and the two elves, Alexa couldn't be more happy.

Now the adventure started.

***

They were walking through the forest, sun setting, magic floating through the air when Kohana stopped in front of them. Everyone stopped, looking around.

"What is it K?" Alexa asked.

Rustling bushes and trees were heard all around them. All of a sudden Kohana flew into a bush. Everything went quiet until Kohana came out of the bush with blood down her side. Alexa ran to her wolf as Kohana collapsed.

Alexa put her hand over her wolf's side and began an incantation. The blood started to clear and the scratches started to scars.

Leonard was looking around when he saw a Canadian timber wolf running off into the distance. He narrowed his eyes and the wolf stopped in its tracks. It looked back and Leonard looked into its red eyes. The wolf ran off and Leonard join the group.

"Something is out there, we need to make camp," he mentioned and they all nodded.

Everyone but Leonard started to make camp. Shadow was making the fire, while Shinara was putting the tents up with Alexa.

"Alexa," Leonard called.

"I'll be back in a second," Alexa spoke and Shinara smiled at the young witch.

Alexa walked over to him and they sat down slightly further away from the camp.

"What's wrong?" she questioned.

"We aren't alone out here. When you were tending to Kohana, I noticed a Canadian timber wolf running away. As it turned to face me, I noticed it's red eyes. That wolf belongs to your brother." He thumbled with his hands until he felt a hand on his shoulder.

"Don't worry, as long as we have each other, we are safe, as long as we have each other, we can fight." Alexa smiled.

"That's what you think," Shadow whispered to herself behind a nearby tree, listening to the conversation that had just happened.

Alexa and Leonard both got up and sat by the fire, rubbing their hands together to keep warm. Kohana was laying by the fire watching the flames as she fell asleep.

Shinara noticed that Alexa kept fiddling with a necklace around her neck. Unsure of how open the witch was, she didn't want to question her about it.

***

It was the middle of the night when Shadow woke up to a voice calling her name.

"Shadow… Shadow… Shadow."

She got out of the tent and stood, looking around the camp, when she saw a red orb between two trees.

Shadow walked towards it and it vanished. She looked around but when she turned to face in front of her, a black figure was standing there.

"Link?" she questioned.

"Yes, good guess, Shadow," Link spoke as he took his hood down, showing his face. A tanned wolf walked up beside Link staring at Shadow.

"Sit Elsie, this is Shadow, she's one of us," Link told Elsie as she sat.

Shadow and Link walked over to a broken tree trunk and sat down.

"So what did you want from me?" Shadow asked.

"Your help to kill my sister. The last perfect witch in my family." Anger rose in his voice as he clenched his fist.

"What happened between you and your family?" Shadow asked. She looked back at Link waiting for an answer but he was in his own world.

***

FLASH BACK

Link was in the waiting room of the hospital with his father. His mother had just gone into labour with his brother or sister.

Link was only ten and had always wanted a sibling.

Someone had walked out of a room and Link looked up. A man walked over to Link and his father and smiled.

"Mr. Snow, you have a beautiful daughter." The man smiled.

"Can we see her? Please dad please?" Link question jumping up and down with excitement.

"Of course, son," Leo Snow said.

Link ran into the room to see his mother holding his baby sister.

"Link, this is Alexa, your baby sister," Tamara said as she handed Link Alexa to hold.

But little did he know, his life wouldn't be the same after that.

***

Through the seven years Alexa has been in this world, it was like Link didn't even exist. All the attention was on his sister.

Until he was 17.

When Link was told by the professor that he was a dark elf everything changed. He let the magic control him. He turned against everyone including his parents.

Alexa's best friend, Lena and her parents were standing in front of Link with his Parents.

"Son calm down, we can talk about this," his mother said.

"No! Why now? You never even wanted me! Since Alexa came into this family it was all about her! Did you ever think about how it would make me feel? No! You just thought about yourselves!!" Link shouted scaring his parents.

His parents, Lena and her parents backed up, leaving some space between them and Link.

"You won't even tell me how I became an elf when I am a wizard! None of you will tell me what has happened to me! Well if that's the case, I'll find out myself!"

"Son, we can talk about this," his father suggested.

"Link calm down," Lena's father spoke.

"No, I'm done talking! Now it's my time to take control and this time it's goodbye." Link lifted his hands up towards his parents and began muttering an incantation. They fell to their knees and looked at Link.

"We are sorry son," his father said.

And just then Alexa came into the living room.

"Mummy, daddy, what's going on? Lena what's happening?" Alexa cried.

"Nothing bunny, go to Leonard," Tamara told her daughter.

Alexa ran to Leonard and Tamara looked back at Link.

"One more thing, what's my name?" Link asked clenching his wand.

Silence filled the air and Link had had enough.

"You don't even know it." And with that, his parents, Lena and her parents were dead.

As Link turned to walk away, he saw Leonard running away with Alexa at his side until they vanished into the mist.

"I want to stay with mummy, Leo! I want Lena," cried Alexa.

And that was the last Link heard from his sister.

But when he turned back around to see his parents dead, there was a black and white mist cloud covering where his parents were.

FLASH BACK ENDS

***

Link came back into the real world and noticed Shadow sitting beside him and the sun coming up.

"Well, what happened?" Shadow asked.

"Well put it this way, it ended in my parent's death. I have to go but I will let you know when you are needed," Link said and with that he was gone.

Shadow walked back to the tent and laid back down as if she had been asleep the whole time.

"What was that all about?" she asked herself hoping she could see Link again to figure out what happened.

***

The next morning, Alexa woke to a screeching sound. She jumped out of the tent to see Leonard in his husky form and Kohana looking on edge.

"Leo, Kohana, what is it?" Alexa questioned.

The husky and wolf ran off. Alexa followed and came to a halt next to Leonard and Kohana to see this beautiful black and electric blue dragon sitting in the field.

Leonard changed back to his human self while Kohana sat inquisitive about what she was looking at.

"Where did he… she come from?" Alexa asked.

"I am am a he, young witch," the dragon spoke.

"I'm sorry. I'm Alexa, this is Leonard and this is my wolf, Kohana."

"I know who you are Alexa. My name is Smok. I have been following you since you started your adventure and I am here to help," Smok announced.

Alexa started to walk closer when Leonard grabbed her arm.

"Be careful," he sighed with concern.

Alexa carried on walking until she came face to face with the dragon. The dragon lowered his head so his electric blue eyes met with the young witch's blue eyes.

"Why are you here to help?" Alexa asked.

"I know you are looking for your brother. I know what your brother is capable of. You are not safe Alexa."

"Why am I not Smok? What do you mean?" Alexa started to worry.

"There is someone amongst you that can not be trusted. They do not want to help you. I will do everything I can to help Leonard keep you safe. While he is on the ground with your fellow wolf, I will fly high making sure the path ahead is clear." And after that, Smok took off into the air.

Alexa felt truth in what the dragon said and trusted him. She returned back to Leonard who was sat waiting for his young witch to return with Kohana next to him.

"Alexa, what colour were his eyes?" Leonard spoke with concern.

"Electric blue."

"Thank Merlin. He is one of us. Do you trust him?"

"I do. He said he knew what my brother was capable of but also someone amongst us doesn't want to help. They can't be trusted," Alexa stated.

"Me and Smok will keep you safe." And with that, Leonard and

Alexa walked back to camp with Kohana at their sides.

When they got back to camp they saw Shadow and Shinara finishing packing up the last of their stuff.

"We should head off while it's early. We can get as far as possible," Shadow said and started to walk off down the path through the forest.

***

As the morning went on, Alexa watched Smok glide smoothly through the sky while she held on to her necklace. She was amazed. She had read about dragons but not once had she ever seen one.

Leonard noticed Alexa's actions with her necklace and put a hand on her shoulder.

"I know how much you miss her."

"Not a day goes by that I don't think about her Leo. She was my best friend, you know? How could my brother do such a thing?" Alexa questioned, tears rolling down her cheeks.

Leonard wiped the tears away with his free hand and smiled.

"No one knows. She will always be in your heart."

Shadow and Shinara were walking behind the young witch and her guardian, talking.

"Where did you go last night?" Shinara questioned.

"Nowhere, I was asleep," Shadow lied.

"Don't lie to me Shadow. I woke up and you were gone," Shinara snapped. She hated when her sister lied to her.

Shadow stopped and pulled Shinara to a halt. "Fine. I heard my name being called. I got up to see what it was and Link was there," Shadow whispered.

"Why did you stay? He's not someone to mess with."

"Shinara you know I am like him. I'm not here to be friends with that witch!" Shadow slightly shouted, making Alexa and Leonard turn around.

"Whatever Shadow. I'm done playing games." Shinara went to join Alexa but a hand pulled her back.

"What do you mean done? I thought you enjoyed being evil? I thought you wanted to meet the high elf and for mum and dad to be dead?"

"No!! Why would I want any of that?! You made all the decisions for me. Now if you're not here to help Alexa then I suggest you leave and find someone else to follow," Shinara snapped and walked off leaving Shadow alone.

Shinara joined Alexa, Kohana and Leonard.

"Where's your sister?" Alexa asked.

The three of them turned around to see Shadow had gone.

"I don't know and I really don't care," Shinara stated, being true to her words.

Alexa looked at Leonard with a puzzled look. Leonard knew what had just happened, but he didn't want to worry Alexa at this point.

***

Later that day, Smok decided to come down and speak to Alexa. Shinara and Leonard were collecting wood for tonight's camp while Kohana was playing with a twig. The young witch walked over to the dragon and sat in between his leg and head.

"What is troubling you Alexa?" Smok's deep voice spoke.

"What happened to my best friend? Why are you really here? And where is Shadow?" Alexa questioned fumbling with her necklace.

"Your best friend, I can not say. It is not easy knowing where the dead go to. You have a destiny, my child, soon you will find out but now is not the time. And for the young elf, she had no business with you anymore. She had found what she was looking for. Is that correct Leonard?" The dragon looked at Leonard, who was currently standing in front of Alexa with Shinara.

"Yes. I had figured it out earlier. Shinara filled me in about the argument her and Shadow had. Shadow found your brother the other night. She wanted to portray you," Leonard explained.

"Well she portrayed my friendship," Alexa cracked. "Shinara, I am glad you are nothing like her and I am truly sorry for what she had done to your family."

"So am I. I'm just happy I can help you," Shinara smiled. Something about Alexa's words created butterflies within Shinara's stomach. Not knowing why, she pushed the thought aside and carried on with the conversation.

After the conversation, they all headed off, with Smok in the sky, Leonard on his four legs with Kohana and the two girls on foot.

***

Shadow walked the path through the forest alone. She had portrayed her sister and her friend. But she didn't care. She was listening to the nature around her when suddenly she heard a voice calling out her name.

"Shadow… Shadow… Shadow…"

Shadow followed the voice until she became face to face with the red eyes of Link's wolf. The wolf walked off and Shadow followed. They came to a halt when Elsie walked up to a hooded figure.

The figure turned around and walked closer to Shadow.

"I've been expecting you Shadow," Link's voice spoke as he took his hood down.

"What do you need me to do now?" Shadow questioned.

"Well as I now know where that little brat is, I need you to get them to meet me somewhere open and quiet," Link spoke.

"There may be a complication. Me and Shinara had an argument and I left as she never wanted to see me again."

"Well think of something. I know you will do what's best," Link spoke aggressively.

Shadow went and sat in a nearby hut and thought about how she would go about getting Alexa to meet her brother.

***

The next morning Alexa felt slightly off. Something was wrong and she could feel it within her.

She got up and walked out of her tent to see Kohana and Smok looking into the distance.

"Smok? Kohana? What is it?" Alexa asked.

"Come here Alexa, what do you see?" Smok questioned.

Alexa walked over to the wolf and dragon and looked into the distance.

"What is with all the mist?" Alexa looked at Smok. "Something bad is going to happen isn't it? And my brother is involved," Alexa sighed.

Smok closed his eyes and just gave a nod to his head. Kohana jumped to Alexa's side. She knew this wouldn't end well.

Leonard saw the young witch standing with the creatures and sighed. He knew what was happening. He walked up to Alexa and put his hand on her shoulder.

"It's time to head off," he said.

***

Two weeks had gone by and the mist had thickened. There was something different about this mist. It was like it was put there. There was nothing natural about it.

Alexa and Shinara walked side by side. Shinara noticed her friend holding onto her necklace.

"Alexa, if you don't mind me asking, why do you keep touching your necklace?" the young elf questioned.

"When I was younger, I gave one half of this necklace to my best friend on her birthday. A few months later, my brother killed her along with my parents and hers," Alexa stated, sighing hard while holding back the tears.

"I'm so sorry, I didn't know." Shinara felt guilty about the question she asked.

Alexa took Shinara's hand in her own, startling the girl. "Don't be. I know you have been meaning to ask the question."

Shinara smiled.

The two girls carried on walking as Alexa began to watch Smok fly swiftly through the air when she tripped over something.

"What the hell was that?" Alexa cried as she looked at the ground.

As Shinara ran over to help Alexa, Kohana started growling at the ground but Alexa and Shinara couldn't see anything as the mist was thick. Shinara placed her hand out over the mist, creating blue sparks, the mist cleared to reveal a red and black scaled oval shaped object.

Alexa went to pick it up but Leonard stopped her.

"Smok, I need you," Leo shouted.

The dragon swooped down and landed softly next to the man.

"What is this?" Leonard questioned.

Smok looked at the object on the ground and picked it up. He placed it in the centre of his paw and moved it so Alexa could see it.

"This my witch and shapeshifter is a dragon egg," Smok mentioned.

Alexa looked amazed.

"Alexa, you may take it. Dragon eggs appear to people when they open up their heart. To you may know them as dragon lords." Smok passed the egg to Alexa.

"Dragon lords? But I thought they were just a myth," Alexa stated.

"You, my child, have a lot to learn, as you, you are a dragon lord," Smok revealed.

As Alexa held the egg, it started to shake and rattle. Kohana started to growl at the egg when suddenly the top of the egg flew off and landed on top of the wolf's head. Alexa looked at her wolf as Kohana started to shake the shell off and she sighed.

Kohana walked closer and Alexa, Kohana and Shinara looked at the egg. Suddenly a baby dragon popped up. The dragon started to make screeching sounds and Kohana was moving her head in curiosity.

Alexa held her free hand out and the baby dragon walked onto her hand.

"Wow he is tiny!!" Alexa smiled. This was the most beautiful thing she had ever seen. Apart from her wolf of course.

Kohana looked at the dragon. She sniffed it a couple of times then gave him a big lick. The baby dragon walked across Alexa's hand and climbed onto Kohana's nose. Leonard, Shinara and Alexa both watched until Leo took the girls off guard.

"What will you name him?" he questioned.

"I think Draco." As Alexa called out the name, the baby dragon, who was now on top of Kohana's head, between her ears, made a screeching sound.

"I think he likes the name Alexa," Smok mentioned.

They all smiled and started to walk along the path again.

***

After walking most of the day, well and flying most of the day, they came to the end of their path.

Alexa, Shinara and Leonard stopped to take in the view before them. A field that went on for miles, covered in mist, laid before them.

Smok flew down and landed in front of Alexa, Leonard, Shinara, Kohana and Draco.

"We should set camp here, it will get too dark to travel soon."

Alexa looked at Kohana to see Draco playing with her ears. Alexa laughed then looked at Smok.

"Sounds good to me."

They set up camp and sat around the fire. Every now and then, Alexa would look at Shinara. She was extremely quiet and Alexa couldn't work out why.

Alexa scooted over to Shinara and put a hand on her shoulder.

"Hey are you alright?" Alexa questioned with concern.

Shinara sighed. "I have a bad feeling about this field."

Alexa knew what the young elf meant and she had been having the same feeling since they came face to face with it.

"Get some rest. We can play with Draco tomorrow."

Shinara smiled and walked over to her tent.

***

After a while, everyone was asleep. All except one. Alexa laid awake, holding onto her necklace. Alexa was used to her sleepless nights, thinking about her best friend and how her brother could kill her.

She looked into the dark sky wondering what will happen when she came face to face with her brother.

Alexa turned onto her front and snuggled up to Kohana.

***

The next day Alexa and Shinara had walked down to a beautiful, clear water lake. Draco was perched on Alexa's shoulder while Kohana was in the lake catching fish.

Kohana threw a fish at Shinara as she carried on fishing.

Alexa ripped a bit off and gave it to Draco. Draco snatched the piece of fish and ate it.

"I think someone is hungry," Shinara laughed.

Alexa put Draco down. He walked over to the fish and started munching on it.

After a while, Draco had eaten three fish, Kohana had eaten four and they had all returned to camp with enough fish to feed an army.

***

Later that day, the mist started to thicken. Alexa was playing fetch with Kohana with sticks while Shinara was feeding Draco some more fish.

Every now and then, Shinara would look up and watch Alexa.

Leonard and Smok were sat talking, leaving the girls to have some alone time.

"The girls are very uneasy Smok," Leo spoke.

"They know what will come," Smok mentioned.

Leonard looked back at the girls and sighed.

***

Shadow had gathered all of Link's followers. Some new, some that came after him a few years ago and some that were tortured into following him.

Shadow got the followers ready for the meet. Link was going to kill Alexa. He had enough of his little sister being happy in this world. He was going to make her pay for being the most important person in his family and making his parents forget him.

Link walked over to a few of the followers.

"Are you ready to meet the little brat and Leonard again Spike?" Link questioned one of the followers.

"Of course. This will be fun," Spike mentioned.

Spike turned around and looked at the other two men that were talking. Angel and Sparrow. These three men were friends with Leonard years ago. When Leonard sent them to find Link, the tables had turned when they did. Link had used dark magic to turn them into something evil.

Elsie was walking around getting agitated. She was unsettled. Shadow and Link walked up to Elsie and smiled.

"Everything will be okay girl. Just one more thing to do and then we are ready," Link said and nodded his head at Shadow.

Shadow clicked her fingers and suddenly Elsie turned into a girl.

"That's better. Now Alexa won't know what hit her," Elsie smirked.

***

All of a sudden there was a loud bang. Alexa and Shinara looked up to see smoke coming from the field.

All of them ran over to the smoke to see two hooded figures standing in front of them. One of the figures started to walk closer to them.

The figure took their hood down.

"Shadow you traitor!!" Alexa shouted and went to run at her but Leonard and Shinara held her back.

Shadow laughed. The second figure walked up to Shadow's side and spoke.

"We meet again Alexa."

"Link?" Leonard questioned.

Link took his hood down and smiled.

"Hi old man. Miss me?" Link sarcastically asked.

All of them looked shocked apart from Alexa. Alexa was angry.

"YOU KILLED MY PARENTS AND MY BEST FRIEND!!!"

"Our parents. And yes I did. They lied to me my whole life. Then when you came along, they forgot about me. It was all about you. They never wanted a son, well they never wanted me. It was always you! They had to pay! And well, Lena, I had the pleasure of killing her for no reason at all," Link spoke, anger filling his voice.

Alexa felt her eyes fill with water, but being the strong-willed girl she was, she held the tears back.

Kohana started to growl at Link and both Shinara and Leonard were ready to fight.

"I see nothing has changed old man. Always willing to save your loved ones and Shinara, your sister was right, so much fire within you. You could of joined us rather than this brat!" Link smirked.

"I'll never join you!!" Shinara aggressively spoke.

"Well so be it."

Suddenly more smoke appeared around them. Four more hooded figures came walking out through the smoke.

One figure walked up to Shadow and took her hood down. Alexa looked at the girl. She knew her but couldn't think of how she knew her.

The next three walked up to Link and took their hoods down. Spike, Angel and Sparrow looked at Leonard.

"What?!? What has he done to you? You were dead?" Leonard was shocked to see his three friends alive.

"We were never dead," Angel spoke.

"Link just gave us a new and better way of living," Sparrow continued after Angel.

Leonard was done. He was angry that his three friends turned against him.

"You'll pay for this Link!" Leonard spat.

Shinara got her magic at the ready and Alexa, sparks of magic surrounding her hands, she stared her brother down.

Shinara threw a fire bolt at Shadow causing her to be thrown backwards. Shadow got back up and started to make an energy ball. As she went to throw it at Shinara, Alexa blocked the attack and threw it at Elsie.

Elsie knelt down to the grass underneath her and put her hand on the ground. As she looked up, her eyes turned green. All of a sudden, the ground started to shake and two rock mounds flung up underneath Alexa and Shinara, making them fly into the air and land with a thud on their backs.

They both got back up and looked at each other. They walked closer to each other and joined their hands together. They started muttering a incantation and looked up. Their eyes had turned black and magic was sparking throughout their bodies.

All of a sudden, black sparks flung from their hands and hit Shadow and Elsie. Both of the girls went flying and landed on the ground.

Leonard was surrounded by the three men.

"Come on guys, can't we talk about this?" Leo asked, voice breaking.

"What's there to talk about? You sent us off to a better life," Spike said.

"We are forever grateful for that," Angel replied.

"But this isn't the life you want. I know there is still good left in you," Leonard begged.

"Whatever old man! After we have finished with you, there will be nothing left," Sparrow spat.

The three men readied their hands, Alexa and Shinara jumped to Leonard's side.

"Not on my watch. There will be nothing left of you!" Alexa spat at the three men.

This had got them angry, so all at once, the three men flicked their hands. Red magic flew from their fingertips and hit Leonard. Leonard fell to the ground.

"Leo!" Alexa shouted as she ran to his aid.

"Don't worry about me, I'll be fine. Go beat your brother's ass!" Leonard winced in pain. Kohana kept Leonard safe while he healed himself.

Alexa got up and walked to Shinara's side. She grabbed her hand and they looked at each other.

"Ready?" Alexa questioned.

"Always," Shinara replied.

At that moment, magic flew from their hands and hit all three of the men, making them go flying and land on their backs.

***

The fight went on for hours. None of them took notice of the sky turning dark.

Link laughed. Until he saw Kohana and Leo run to Alexa's side. Leonard looked Link in the eye.

"Where is Elsie?"

Leonard looked to the side of him, where Elsie laid in her human form.

"Dead."

"You'll pay for that."

All of a sudden Link screamed causing everyone but Alexa to be thrown backwards.

"Just me and you now," Link spoke.

"Bring it brother," Alexa spat.

Both Alexa and Link flicked their hands at each other. Red and blue magic appeared from each other's fingertips, both hitting the other person.

Shadow started to get up. She went to walk towards Alexa but Link pushed his hand in her direction. Without touching Shadow, she fell back to the floor.

"Stay out of this!! This is my fight elf!" Link shouted.

Kohana started to bark at Link. Alexa noticed. "Quiet, I'll be fine."

Smok flew down and with the tip of his wing, he smacked Link's followers that started the get up and help Link, flying.

As Smok landed, Kohana ran at Link. As Kohana got to Link, she bit his leg. Link kicked Kohana away.

"You'll pay for that beast!"

Link aimed his hand at Kohana.

"Oh! No you don't!" Alexa shouted.

And at that point, Alexa and Link aimed their hands at each other. Magic flew at both of them until the magic collided in the middle.

Suddenly there was a bang. Both Alexa and Link were thrown backwards. Alexa managed to land safely on her knees but Link was flung onto his back.

As he hit the ground, everyone walked over to him.

"He's close to death Alexa," Smok said.

Alexa bent down to his level.

"I'm sorry, Alexa," was all Link could manage to get out.

"Spare his and Elsie's life. I want to get to know my brother. He was young and stupid. Save him Smok, please?" Alexa cried.

Smok walked closer to Link and blew two rings from his nose onto Link's face and chest. And just like that, Link woke up.

As Link sat up, he smiled.

"Alexa, I am so sorry!" he spoke.

"Do you remember what happened?" Alexa questioned.

"Yeah." Link lowered his head, ashamed of what he had done. At this point, Elsie ran over to Link.

"You saved her! Thank you so much!!" Link hugged Elsie.

***

While they were all huddled together, Shadow started limping over to them.

"You are so weak!!! You used me!! Now it's my turn for revenge!" Shadow shouted.

Everyone looked at her as she started to create a fire ball.

"Not this time you don't," Link said.

And with a click of his fingers, Shadow was gone.

***

They all got up and dusted themselves off. They walked back to camp and made some food for all of them to share.

"Smok, what did you do to me?" Link questioned the dragon.

"I simply gave you your life back but made your heart good again."

"But why do I still remember everything I did?"

"You wouldn't be the person you are today without doing what you did," Smok reminded him.

Link looked at Alexa who suddenly look worried.

"Alexa are you okay?" Link asked.

"Where is Draco?" Alexa's voice shook.

Everyone looked around them. There was no sight of the baby dragon anywhere. Kohana and Elsie started barking at one of the tents.

Everyone got up to see what it was. When they got to the tent, Alexa pulled the material to look in. When she looked in, all she saw was Draco eating a fish. Everyone looked in and Draco stopped. He looked up, pulled the fish closer to him and started scoffing it down.

Everyone started to laugh. They all went back to the fire and sat down.

***

Link got up and walked over to Elsie. He sat on the ground and smirked.

"That dragon is such a fool. Nothing in this world could turn my heart good," Link muttered to Elsie.

Elsie growled.

"They don't know what's coming. They know nothing of what I've got in store for them."

***

As they were all telling stories and getting to know Link, there was a loud bang. Everyone but Link jumped up to see what it was.

This wasn't the end.

Leonard and Alexa looked at each other.

"Another adventure?" Leonard questioned as he saw the look on Alexa's face.

"Well with Link on our side now, we can beat anything." Alexa smiled at Link then turned back to the rest of the group.

"You know nothing Alexa Snow."

2
The Two Dragons

After the battle between the dark elves and Alexa's pack, Shinara had been feeling strange. Shinara and Alexa joined their powers together and after that, Shinara had been draw to her dragon lord friend.

Ever since the young elf and witch met, Shinara had been gathering feelings for her friend. But she wouldn't say a word as she didn't know what these feelings were and if Alexa felt the same way.

But the one thing Alexa and Shinara did feel the same for was they knew something hadn't changed with Link.

***

It was mid day. The sun was in the sky and the mist had cleared. Everything looked beautiful. The trees were green, the grass was soft, the sun glistened on the clear, water stream, birds were chirping and there was a cool breeze.

***

Alexa and her pack were walking back through the forest, heading back to Brunuhville. Leonard had shifted to his husky form and was up front with Kohana and Elsie while Link was walking behind the wolves.

Alexa was watching Smok fly through the air while Draco was sat on her shoulder and she held her necklace in her hand. Shinara caught up to Alexa and grabbed her free hand. Alexa flinched and looked at Shinara.

"Hey sorry, I didn't mean to scare you." Shinara choked on her words. Feeling guilty.

"Hey, don't worry, I was in my own world. Are you okay? Still worried about Link?" Alexa questioned as she grabbed the young elf's hand and squeezed it.

"Yeah, I'm still worried." Shinara hung her head.

***

Link listened into the conversation the two girls were having. He chuckled to himself knowing that they weren't stupid.

Link clicked his fingers and Elsie came running towards him.

"We have to make out we are good Elsie. The girls are on to us," Link whispered.

Elsie huffed and stayed at Links side.

***

Leonard looked up at Smok and barked. He ran behind a bush and shifted. He came back out and looked at Kohana.

"I have to go with Smok somewhere, run to Alexa's side," Leonard said.

Kohana nodded her head and ran to Alexa's side.

Smok flew down to the ground and Leonard got onto his back.

Alexa watched as the dragon flew off into the distance.

"I wonder where they are going," Alexa muttered to herself.

***

Smok flew off to Brunuhville castle. The only place he knew that the dragon caves would be empty.

As they got to the caves, Smok landed. Leonard jumped off the dragon and sat by his side.

"When will you tell the young dragon lord?" the dragon spoke.

"Soon. She's not ready," Leonard sighed.

The dragon's eyes changed to a darker blue. "You've been saying that her entire life. The girl is ready whether you feel she is or not. She needs to know."

Leonard backed down. He knew Smok was right. Alexa needed to be told who her family was.

The man let out a sigh and spoke. "I'll tell her when we get back to the village tonight."

And with that, Leonard jumped back onto Smok's back and they flew off to see how much further there was until they got to the village.

Smok was agitated. He knew Alexa had to be told. She had waited too long.

***

The day was growing darker as the sun was setting in the East and the moon was rising in the West.

Magic started to fill the air. The magical creatures were out shining their beautiful blue, red, green and yellow colours. The breeze was a little cooler, the trees swayed and made creaking noises as if they were talking to each other. The clouds were magically transforming into wolves and dragons.

The stream was glowing electric blue and certain spots changed to electric green as the water skaters and pixies danced across the stream.

***

Alexa and Shinara, with Kohana at their side and Draco on Alexa's shoulder, walked in front of Link and Elsie. Alexa looked up to see Smok and Leonard were flying overhead.

Draco started screeching. Alexa pulled a lump of fish out of her bag and gave it to her baby dragon.

"Soon enough you will be able to fly and get your own food

Draco." Alexa smiled at the dragon perched on her shoulder who had now scoffed the last bit of his fish.

Draco snuggled up into the crook of Alexa's neck and fell asleep. Shinara looked at him and smiled. Alexa looked at Shinara and felt butterflies in her stomach. Shinara felt eyes on her and she looked up. Alexa saw that Shinara had noticed her staring and looks away blushing.

***

Alexa couldn't describe what she was feeling but it was something she had never felt before.

"Is Shinara using dark magic on me? Why do I feel this way? Do I like women?" Alexa thought to herself.

Before she started to overthink her feelings any more than what she already has done, they come to an opening in the forest.

Shinara touches Alexa's hand and Alexa feels the same butterflies she had before.

"We are back," Shinara mutters.

***

Smok and Leonard fly down into the village and are welcomed by the whole community.

Alexa, Shinara, Link, Kohana and Elsie walk into the village and everyone goes silent.

"What's he doing here?"

"He's evil!"

"Why would you bring that here?!"

"Put him back in the cave! It's where he belongs!"

"He don't belong here!"

Moon, fire, sun and ice elves shout as they see Link.

"Please, I'm sorry. I am good again. Smok healed my dark heart and it's now good. I won't hurt any of you," Link says as he starts getting dirty looks.

"Like to see that. Link Snow good? You're having us on," a middle-aged moon elf shouts.

Link hangs his head as they all walk to a hut that was built for them all to stay in.

The village had changed since the last time the pack was there. The last that they all saw of the village was after the battle and it was up in smoke.

When they got to the village that night, some of the huts were being rebuilt, some elves were putting the fires out and some were gathering up the resources that didn't get damaged.

***

The hut looked small on the outside by when you walked in, it was like magic.

Opposite the door there was the living room with a fireplace, two single chairs, a sofa and a coffee table. To the right there was a beautiful red and blue tiled kitchen with a sink, stove, cups, plates, bowls, cutlery and a fridge. To the right of the kitchen there was a bedroom with a double bed with an animal fur cover, a wooden wardrobe and chest of draws and a animal fur wolf's bed. To the left of the kitchen, you had the same as the right.

To the left of the living room there was another two bedrooms, just the same as the other two.

***

When the pack got into their hut, Leonard put the fire on. Kohana and Elsie curled up by the fire while Leonard and Link sat on the two separate chairs and Alexa and Shinara shared the sofa. Shinara kept edging her way closer to Alexa, but to her disliking, Alexa got up.

"I need some air," Alexa mutters. She got up and walked out of the hut leaving Leonard and Shinara confused.

***

Alexa walked around the village looking at all the destruction. She saw a elf with blue hair struggling to lift a fence up so she went over and helped him.

"Hey what happened here?" Alexa asked the elf.

"I'm not sure any of us know how to answer that. All we know is that we were all enjoying a peaceful night when we all heard a massive explosion. A few of us ran out of our huts and saw that the majority of the village was on fire," the elf explained.

Alexa finished helping the man and started walking back to the hut. She was just about to reach for the door when it flew open showing Shinara's figure. Alexa turned on her heal and went to walk off until she felt a hand on her arm.

"Alexa we really need to talk," the young elf spoke.

"I don't want to talk. Leave me alone," Alexa shouted as she stormed off.

Shinara ran after the young dragon lord and stood in front of her, blocking her path.

"No Alexa, we need to talk. You can't keep avoiding me."

"I can and I will. Now get out of my way." Alexa pushed Shinara aside and carried on walking. She didn't want to talk to someone who used dark magic to get what they wanted.

Alexa thought she had got rid of the girl but then she was dragged into a nearby hut. Alexa turned around to see Shinara locking the door behind them.

"What are you doing? This is ridiculous," Alexa spoke, anger in her voice.

"Alexa, stop. We really need to talk. This is stupid. We can't keep doing this." The young elf walked closer to her friend.

"Don't come any closer." Alexa backed away.

Shinara sighed then looked into Alexa's beautiful blue eyes. "Alexa what's wrong? You keep avoiding me."

"I'm so confused. Ever since we connected our magic I have had these weird feelings. I don't understand them."

"I know that feeling. I don't understand what's happening either." Shinara looked down, twiddling with her fingers.

"So you're saying you're not using dark magic on me to make me feel this way towards you?" Alexa questioned.

"God no. Why on earth would I do that? I don't even possess that and even if I did, I wouldn't use it to make you fall in love with me," Shinara spat.

Alexa sighed in relief but then realised that she still had these feelings.

"Well what are we going to do now? I don't understand these feelings and I'm scared. I've never felt like this before and never towards a woman before." Alexa hung her head. She was telling the truth. She didn't understand why this was happening to her.

Shinara walked up to Alexa. She tilted her friend's head up with her finger to make them see eye to eye and rested her other hand on Alexa's shoulder.

"We will work this out together. Just no more avoiding me. We can't help each other if we avoid each other." Shinara smiled.

Alexa smiled back. She looked into Shinara's blue eyes and got a tingling feeling in her stomach as if something was telling her to kiss her friend. She pulled away slightly making Shinara look confused.

Alexa grabbed her friend's hand and smiled. "Let's go back to the others. It's getting late, I'm hungry and they are probably wondering where we are."

Shinara nodded and unlocked the door. The girls walked hand in hand back to the hut.

***

They reached the hut and let go of each other's hands. Alexa walked in first with Shinara at her heal.

"Where have you been?" Leonard spoke. Words filled with worry.

"Sorry Leo, I needed some air and Shinara came to see if I was okay," Alexa answered.

***

The pack were sat in front of the fire, eating an amazing roast dinner that Shinara made. She had cooked a big lump of juicy beef, roast potatoes, carrots, peas, broccoli, Yorkshire puddings (home made of course) and home made beef gravy. She had even made some for the wolves.

Alexa finished the last bit of Yorkshire pudding and sat her plate aside.

"That was the best roast dinner I have ever eaten. Where did you learn to cook? You're amazing." Alexa smiled while discreetly putting a hand on Shinara's thigh.

"My mum taught me." Shinara's voice filled with sadness.

"I'm sorry Shinara, I didn't know." Alexa rubbed her friend's leg and changed the subject. "Well at least we know that the wolves love your cooking." They all looked over at Elsie and Kohana who had managed to get the majority of their dinner over each other. Kohana looked up at them after licking her plate clean. She nudged the plate towards Shinara, asking for more.

"Yep, they definitely loved it," Shinara giggled.

The whole hut filled with laughter.

***

After they had all finished their dinner, they all said good night and headed to bed. Apart from Link and Elsie who stayed in the living room by the fire.

Alexa took the bedroom to the right of the kitchen, Shinara took the one left to the kitchen and Leonard took the one opposite Alexa's.

***

As they all closed their doors, Leonard shifted into his husky form. He nudged his door back open to listen to see if anyone was still awake.

There was no sound and no movement so he jogged to where Link was in the living room and both him and Elsie were asleep. He ran to the door, nudged it open and ran to the caves to find Smok.

When he reached the caves, Smok was sat with an angry expression on his face. Leonard shifted back to his human figure.

"Smok lo…" Leonard went to speak when he got cut off.

"No you said you'd tell her when you get to the village and you didn't. You will tell her first thing tomorrow morning," Smok snapped. He hates when people say they will do something but never do.

"I will." Leonard shifted to his husky form and went to leave but not until Smok had his final words.

"If you don't, I will." And Leonard ran off.

***

Alexa couldn't sleep. She had a lot on her mind. She was missing her best friend more than anything right now, she had these feelings she didn't understand, Leo had been off since they have arrived at the village and there is something going on with Link.

Just then there was a knock at the door. She got up and opened it to find Shinara standing in the doorway.

"Hey what's up?" Alexa questioned.

"I can't sleep, are you okay if I join you?"

"Sure. I can't sleep either." Alexa closed the door and turned and walked to the bed.

Alexa laid down and shifted over so Shinara had room. They put the covers over themselves and laid staring at the ceiling.

Shinara turned around and snuggled up closer to Alexa.

"Are you okay if I cuddle up to you?" Shinara's sleep voice was heard.

Alexa smiled. "I, uh, yeah of course," Alexa stuttered as she let her friend cuddle up to her and she stroked her friend's hair to help her fall asleep.

"Good night." And with that, both girls drifted to sleep.

***

The next morning, Alexa and Shinara were awoken by the sun shining through the window and the smell of bacon and eggs. Alexa looked down next to her to see blue eyes staring up at her.

"Good morning." Shinara smiled and jumped out of bed. She snuck back into her own room to change into something more comfortable.

Alexa got out of bed and changed into a blue, oversized shirt that she left undone so the laces hung over her chest, denim, skinny jeans that was accompanied by a pair of black boots. She walked out of her room while putting her hair up in a ponytail. Alexa sat in the living room and started to eat her breakfast that was left on the coffee table.

Shinara joined her friend after she had changed into a pair of black skinny jeans that were accompanied by a pair of white boots and a black shirt that was done up all the way.

Leonard and Link joined while the wolves had their breakfast.

***

Everyone finished their breakfast and cleaned up. Link walked out of the hut with Elsie at his side.

"Shinara do you mind giving me and Alexa a few minutes? I need to tell her something important," Leonard spoke.

"Yeah of course." Shinara left the hut to leaving Alexa and Leonard alone.

Leonard and Alexa sat down on the sofas.

The man sighed knowing what he has to tell the young witch. So he began. "You know you have always wondered who your parents were, where you lived and where you come from?"

"Yes. Where is this going?" Alexa asked confused.

And just then Smok landed outside. The witch and the shapeshifter went outside and stood in front of the dragon.

"Have you told her?" Smok spoke.

"No, I am now, before you interrupted," Leo snapped. "As I was saying, your parents were royal. You lived in Brunuhville Castle before I had to take you away. You lived in a small hut in this very village. Your parents didn't want you tube treated differently compared to the others."

Alexa looked shocked. She looked up at Smok. "Is this true?"

"Yes young witch, you are the royal princess. You are the royal baby of queen and king Snow. Your mother and father," Smok said.

Just then Alexa started to get dizzy and before she knew it, everything went black.

***

While Shinara left her friend's to talk, she wondered off to take a dip in the stream. She walked into the forest and a few more minutes of walking and she was at the stream.

Shinara dipped her feet into the water to feel how warm the water was. She jumped into the stream and swam away.

***

Link and Elsie followed Shinara to the stream. They hid behind a bush and watched what she was doing.

They planned what they would do to her when she come back for her towel.

They waited till she came back.

***

A few hours passed and Shinara came back to the edge of the stream to dry herself off with her towel but her head was pushed back under the water.

Shinara struggled trying to get back up to the surface as she was running out of air. The hand moved and Shinara jump back up.

"What… the… hell…" She struggled. She looked up to see that Link and Elsie were sat looking at her.

"I knew you were still bad. Nothing could ever change your heart good!" Link smirked.

"Alexa should have left you to die!" Shinara shouted as she jump out of the stream and stood on the warm grass.

Link laughed. "Yeah she should of."

Just as Shinara clicked her fingers, Link pushed her back in and held her head back under. But what he didn't know was that Shinara just called for Alexa to help her.

***

After a while, Alexa came too. She looked around to see that she was still outside her hut.

"Are you okay?" Leonard questioned, concerned about his young witch.

"Yeah. Just a bit overwhelmed," she spoke.

Kohana came running up to her barking and going crazy. She looked around to see that Shinara and Link were still gone.

"Where's Shinara?" Worry filled her voice.

Just then Kohana pulled her up and pointed in the direction of the stream.

***

The pack ran into the forest, towards the stream. Alexa knew her friend was in trouble and it had something to do with Link.

They got to the stream to see that Link was holding something under water. Smok swatted Link away as Alexa ran to the stream and helped Shinara out. Shinara was unconscious and wasn't breathing.

Kohana had pinned Elsie down and Leonard had Link pinned to a tree.

Alexa pumped down on her friend's chest, hoping that she would start breathing again.

"Come on Shinara, don't leave me, not now," Alexa muttered.

She carried on pumping her chest. Link started to laugh and Leonard tightened his grip around his neck.

Alexa heard him laughing and got angry.

"Kohana, kill his wolf now!" Alexa shouted.

Kohana did as she was commanded. She snarled down at Elsie and scratched at her eyes. Elsie winced in pain. Kohana scratched at her face so much that she had made deep gash marks. Elsie struggled, trying to get the black wolf off of her.

"Please stop! Don't kill her!" Link shouted. He was watching everything.

Kohana had had enough of torturing the wolf that she had clenched down on her neck and ripped her throat out.

"NOOOOO!!!" Link screamed.

Alexa was still pumping at her friend's chest.

"Come on Shinara, I love you." And just then Shinara started coughing up water.

She looked up at Alexa and smiled. "I love you too."

***

Alexa helped Shinara up and they walked over to where Leonard had Link pinned to a tree.

"What do you want me to do with him?" the man asked.

Shinara cling to her friend's arm, trembling.

"Smok you know what to do," Alexa said.

Leonard removed his hand and let Link fall to the ground. They all walked off and left Link and Smok alone.

***

Smok walked closer to Link, making him walk backwards and hitting his back against the tree he was just pinned against.

"What are you going to do to me, you disgusting creature?" Link spat.

Smok took one look at the dark elf and blew rings from his nose. The rings wrapped around Links body and tightened against the tree so he couldn't move.

Smok looked at him and smirked. "Any last words?"

"I hope you all die," Link spat. And with that there was a grumble in the dragon's tummy and then fire erupted from his mouth, burning Link alive.

As the fire was burning Link, Link screamed. Smok smirked then took off into the air.

***

The pack walked back to the village and back to their hut. Alexa felt a shooting pain go through her chest.

“Are you okay?” Leonard questioned.

“Yeah, just a twinge,” Alexa answered.

“What the bloody hell was that?” she thought to herself.

Shinara was still trembling from the events that have just happened. Alexa knew her friend was scared and took her inside their hut and to her room.

Alexa helped Shinara change and get into bed.

“I’ll be just outside if you need anything,” Alexa whispered as she got off the bed and went to walk out.

“Did you mean what you said? That you love me?” Shinara asked.

“Sleep, we will talk later.” And with that Alexa left and rejoined Leonard outside.

As Alexa walked out of their hut, Smok landed. “Link and Elsie are no more, your grace,” Smok said. Well so he thought Link was dead.

***

Back at the stream, Link’s body was burning its last flame. The body was as black as coal and started to smell of rotten flesh.

As the last flame went out, red and black sparks started to sore around the body. A mass of dark energy has formed into an electrifying red and black ball. The ball flew into the body and the black mess glided up into the air.

The body started to spin and a dark forcefield generated around the body. The body started to glow and the forcefield grew bigger.

Suddenly there was a loud bang. The forcefield exploded causing trees to be thrown back. The body fell to the ground and landed on one knee and both hands.

The body got up slowly. As the body stood up, the black mass fell off and turned to ash when it touched the ground.

After all the black mass had fallen off, the body started to look human again. But something was different. Link looked at his body and clicked his fingers. Suddenly black and red clothes started to form on his body, his hair changed to black, neck length and his eyes went a deep red.

He let out a laugh. "It's not that easy to kill the most powerful dark elf."

He walked over to Elsie's body and knelt down. He started to twirl his fingers, making magical sparks appear. He put his hand down onto the wolf's body and gave it a shock.

The body started to transform into a human. All of the blood was gone and the gash marks had turned to scars.

"Welcome back, Elsie, now let's get you some clothes," Link said as he clicked his fingers and a white top with a black leather jacket, black jeans and converses formed on her body.

"Let's get out of here. I know where to go," Link said. And with that they walked off, heading towards the caves.

***

Back at the village, Alexa was sat on the edge of Shinara's bed, watching her sleep. Shinara started to stir and soon her eyes fluttered open to show her beautiful blue eyes.

"Hey how are you feeling?" Alexa asked as she noticed her friend was awake.

"I'm okay thanks. Can we talk?" Shinara questioned as she sat up.

Alexa nodded her head. "If it's about what you asked me before you fell asleep, then yes, I meant it. I do love you but I need time to figure out everything."

Shinara reaches for Alexa's hand and took it in her own. "Whatever you need, I'll stand by you."

***

Alexa walked into the living room to see Leonard sat with Kohana. There was a knock at the door. Alexa and Leonard looked confused at each other. Leonard got up and opened the door to find a man in armour holding a green scaled egg.

"Leonard, I am…"

"Sam, it's good to see you. What brings you here?" Leonard stopped the man as he knew who he was.

"We heard the princess was here and had one of the three dragons. This is our gift. The second dragon," Sam spoke. He handed Leonard the egg, turned on his heal and headed towards the castle.

Leonard walked back into the living room and handing Alexa the egg.

"Another one? Who by? How many left?" Alexa questioned.

"You have one more and one of the guards at your castle heard that you were here so they brought you a gift. Your second dragon, and you are the dragon lord Alexa," Leonard explained.

Just as he finished talking, the egg started to hatch in Alexa's hand. Draco climbed up Alexa's back and sat on her shoulder, watching the egg hatch. The top of the egg flew off and a green dragon popped out and climbed onto her hand.

"I think I'll call you Spitze," Alexa said and both the green dragon and Draco screeched with happiness.

"I think you chose the right name for him," Shinara spoke as she walked in and leant against the wall.

Alexa smiled and put the two dragons in a cage that she had in the living room. The cage was big enough for twenty dragons their size.

Alexa never kept Draco in there. She would let him out so he could stretch his wings. Now he would have a brother to do that with.

***

While on their travels to the Dark Elf caves, Link and Elsie have been hearing a lot of whispers around the forest. Link wasn't interested in them until he heard the a few elves say,

"Have you heard that the princess is back?"

"Yeah, I heard she's been gone for almost ten years now."

"Yeah after her parents were murdered, she must have seeked revenge and decided to come back."

Link stopped in his tracks and listened in a bit closer to hear what else these elves were talking about.

"Do you think she knows she is the princess?"

"I'm not sure. If she doesn't, she probably will now with the castle guards going to find her."

"Yeah true but she was only ten when everything happened. This might be a shock to her."

Link continued walking to the caves with Elsie. He was trying to figure out who this princess was and why she was so important.

There were another two elves having a conversation and this time, Link sat on a nearby bench and listened in.

"I hope the princess seeked the revenge she needed. If it was my parents that got murdered by someone, I'd seek revenge."

"Me too. I hope she has. Even if she hasn't, I heard that the castle guards have three gifts for her."

"Wow they must really miss their princess, or should I say, Queen."

"Well, I miss her. After all she is the most powerful woman in Brunuhville."

Link got up and carried on with his journey.

"Who do you think they are talking about?" Link questioned.

"I'm not sure but this princess must be someone amazing and powerful," Elsie replied.

"Hmmm, that would explain it. Brunuhville has been a mess since the king and queen died," he muttered.

They carried on walking. Link tried to think of who this princess was and who were her parents.

***

Link and Elsie had reached the caves. When they walked in, they were welcomed by other dark elves.

"Hey Link, is the bitch dead?" one shouted.

"Hey I heard she was the princess!" another shouted.

Link ran up to him and pinned him against the cave wall.

"What did you say?" he spat in the elf's face.

"I… I heard she was the p… princess," the elf said.

Link let him go and walked off to the back of the cave to his room with Elsie.

"How does everyone know about my family? Alexa never even knew she was the princess. Mother and Father never told her. But of course, that stupid old man has told her," Link snapped.

"I'll kill her for you," Elsie spat.

"No, she's mine. The time will come when she will die. And it will be at my hands," Link said.

He laid down on his bed and muttered to himself.

"I will kill her. I'll kill her like I killed our stupid parents. I will be the rightful King to Brunuhville." And with that he fell asleep.

***

Link woke up during the night. He got out of bed and walked through the fire lit cave until he reached the exit. He noticed Elsie was sat looking up at the stars and moon.

"Why didn't you tell me you were the prince?" Elsie questioned indicating that she knew of Link's presents.

"I don't know. I am sorry. I just wanted to forget everything like my parents forgot who I was when she came into this world," Link spat as he sat next to Elsie.

They both looked up at the moon then something caught their eye. They both looked over to Brunuhville village to see fire burning and elves shouting.

"What's going on down there?" Link questioned.

Elsie shrugged her shoulders and both her and Link jumped when they heard something behind them.

"Sorry I didn't mean to scare you," A young dark elf boy said. "They are having a party. Moon elves and fire elves always party at night. The moon elves like to worship the moon and the fire elves just like a good party so they help out. Sorry I overheard what you said." The boy sat down next to Link and smiled.

"What is your name?" Link questioned the boy.

"I'm Jasper, you must be Elsie and Link?" Jasper said as he stuck his hand out for the two to shake and they kindly accepted.

All three sat and watched the party down in the village all night until the sun rose, the fires burnt out and the shouting became whispers.

Link stood up and went to grab some food with Elsie and Jasper.

"Jasper, what do you know about King and Queen Snow?" Link asked.

"Oh, a lot. I did a lot of research on your family Link," Jasper smirked.

Link smiled and looked at Elsie then back at Jasper. "You'll definitely be useful."

They all smirked at each other and took their food into Link's room and Jasper filled Elsie and Link in with what they needed to know about Link and Alexa's parents.

***

Alexa was sat in front of her hut, feeding Draco and Spitze some beef chunks when someone touched her shoulder. She spun her head around to see Shinara smirking.

"Hey, don't do that, you scared me," Alexa laughed, patting the spot next to her, indicating for Shinara to sit down next to her.

"I'm sorry, I didn't mean to." Shinara sat down next to Alexa and helped feed the dragons.

Shinara picked up a beef chunk and held it out to Spitze. Spitze sniffed the elf's fingers and then took the food. After Spitze had finished scoffing the beef chunk down, he walked over to Shinara, climbed up her back to her shoulder and perched himself there.

"I think he likes you," Alexa said as she smiled at her friend and dragon.

"Both your dragons seem to like me," Shinara stated as Draco climbed up to the girl's other shoulder and perched himself there just like his brother.

***

Alexa had been teaching the dragons commands and it had been going really well. Shinara was sat admiring the work her friend had been doing with the boys.

"Tine." And the dragons blew fire.

"Iasc." And the dragons got some fish.

"Smután mairteola." And the dragons got a beef chunk.

Alexa tired teaching the dragons some battle commands but there was still a long way to go until the dragons listened.

"Sruthán." But Spitze ran off and hid behind Shinara and Draco sat there and blew rings through his nose.

"God you're a little bugger," Alexa said to Draco. This wasn't the first time he had acted childish. Most of the time it was because he was being watched by Shinara and she liked to laugh at him.

"Give him a break. He's only young," Shinara laughed.

"He does this to show off in front of you. He's an attention seeking little bugger." Alexa smiled.

Alexa never got frustrated which was something Shinara loved.

"Right guys, one more time," Alexa said as Spitze returned next to his brother.

Alexa put pieces of small wood in front of them and began to command her dragons.

"Sruthán." And both the dragons blew fire and burnt the wood.

"Well done boys." Alexa gave the dragons a beef chunk each. She looked at Kohana who was sat there with puppy dog eyes.

"Here you go K," Alexa said as she gave her wolf two whole fish.

Kohana was sat next to Alexa watching the whole time. Every time the dragons did a great job, she would bark at them and lick them.

Alexa and Shinara shared a smile when Leonard walked over with Smok, both holding a serious look upon their faces. Alexa stood to her feet and looked at her friend.

"I'll be back soon."

Shinara nodded and with that, the witch walked with the shapeshifter and the dragon into the forest. The three of them sat by the stream as Smok's deep voice was heard.

"You and the elf seem to be getting rather close, your grace."

"Yeah, we are." Alexa smiled, but then became more serious. "I don't believe she is a dark elf. The high elf was under so much pressure with Shadow that he said whatever he could to make her happy but it back lashed on him," Alexa contined.

"Do you love this girl?" Leonard questioned as he put his hand on the girl's shoulder.

For a short time Alexa thought to herself. Did she really love Shinara? Were these feelings true? And then it hit her.

"I think so, but I am still so confused about all of this. But I will do anything to help my friend out." She smiled warmly at Leonard.

"Then there is one thing you need to do," Smok began. "There is a high elf in the village. Take Shinara to him. You two cannot love each other to the fullest knowing there maybe bad with in your friend."

"Okay I will," Alexa smiled.

"Oh, and young witch," Smok began.

Alexa turned on her heal and looked at her guardian.

"Take your time. If you feel that you are indeed in love with young Shinara, everything will fall into place in due course."

Alexa smiled, and with that, they all left to go to the village.

***

When they got back to the village, Alexa noticed that Shinara and the dragons weren't outside. She started to panic.

"Something bad must have happened. Shinara was here when we left. So were my dragons!" Alexa panicked.

"Alexa, calm down, nothing would have happened," Leonard spoke.

"You don't know that! Link could have got her again!"

"Link is dead, your grace. He couldn't come back after what I had done to him," Smok replied.

Alexa started to breath heavily. She couldn't calm her breathing down until the door to her hut opened.

"What's all the commotion about?" Shinara's figure was standing in the doorway with the two dragons on her shoulders.

"Thank god!" Alexa let out a deep sigh of relief.

Alexa walked over to Shinara as Draco and Spitze cried for her.

"Shh shh, I'm here," the witch soothed as her dragons climbed onto her and she cradled them in her arms. Alexa smiled then looked into the blue eyes of her friend.

"I want to take you somewhere. A friend of Smok would like to meet you."

"Okay. Who is it?" the elf asked.

"He is a high elf. I believe that you are not a dark elf like your sister. Your professor was under a lot of pressure from Shadow that he just said that you were a dark elf to make her happy." Alexa stated.

"Well, that got him killed."

"Yes well, this high elf is under no pressure and would love to meet you." Draco moved to Alexa's shoulder as she held her hand out for her friend to take.

"Okay." Shinara took Alexa's hand and they walked across the village to the high elf, leaving Leonard and Smok waiting.

***

When they got outside the high elf's hut, Alexa went to knock but the door slowly opened. The two girls walked in to see the beautiful hut.

The hut wasn't like professor Elwin's, it was much neater and magical. There were two fireplaces, one with an ordinary fire and another with a purple flame burning within the beautiful brick sculpture. Above the fireplaces there was a picture of an elf with a girl.

In front of the fireplaces, there was a round wooden table, with three single chairs around it. To the left, there was a rectangular wooden table, with books that had spells, enchantments, ruin symbols and many other magical things in them, potion vials with different colours in them that were being held in a glass rack. Hanging above the table, there were dried elves ears, Howlet's wing, Hemlock root, etc and to the right of the wooden table, there was another, just like the first one but this one had vials filled with ingredients such as Eye of Newt, Toe of Frog, Tongue of Dog, etc, along with neat bundles of Wool of Bat, Gale of Goat, Slips of Yew etc. To the right, there was a kitchen and a bedroom.

"This place really is something special. Both like professor Elwin's hut," Shinara whispered to Alexa as shed looked over to the picture and smiled.

"I should hope it's not anything like his hut." The girls heard a deep voice making them jump. "And that is me with my daughter," A man's voice spoke.

Alexa and Shinara turned to see aN elf with a long white beard and long white hair standing next to them.

"I am professor Lorny, you must be Alexa and Shinara," Lorny spoke as he looked at the two girls.

"Yes, we are. Thank you for seeing us, it's just that Shinara was told she was a dark elf and we all believe that she is something different," Alexa spoke.

"Of course. I will begin the ceremony. Shinara, I'm sure you know what to do." Lorny winked at the young elf as she walked to the centre of a blue and purple carpet on the floor.

The high elf took a needle from his table and walked up to Shinara. "I need a drop of blood."

Shinara nodded and Lorny pricked her finger. He went back to the table and picked up a vile with a clear liquid in it, then walked back to Shinara. He held her finger above the vile and squeezed it gently, letting a drop of blood fall into the clear liquid.

He walked back to his table and swirled the vile, mixing the blood and liquid together. The high elf started to swirl his fingers, making magical sparks appear and then clicked his fingers. The liquid then started to change colour from clear to red, then red to blue, then blue to green then back to blue.

He walked back over to the young elf with the vile and held it out to her. "Drink this and we will see what your true elf is."

Shinara took the vile and looked and Alexa nervously. She put the vile to her lips and drank the liquid.

Nothing happened at first but then her hair and eyes started to change colour. Alexa looked at Shinara nervously, hoping that she truly isn't a dark elf. Draco and Spitze watched from Alexa's arms. Their faces nervous at first and then they calmed.

Then suddenly Shinara's hair and eyes stopped. Alexa stood up with both dragons in her arms and walked over to her friend. The elf's eyes were ice blue and her hair was an electric blue.

"You are an ice elf, Shinara." Lorny spoke and both the girls smiled.

"Thank you so much, professor Lorny," Alexa spoke as she walked up to him with Shinara at her side.

"You're most welcome. Now go and enjoy the rest of you day. You will be journeying back to your castle, your grace, soon." And with that the girls left and walked back to their hut, hand in hand, to rejoin their friends.

***

When the girls and the dragons got back to their hut, Alexa walked into the hut and put the dragons in their cage, letting them rest. She rejoined her friends outside. Alexa stood at Shinara's side and took her hand in hers. The girls smiled at each other and then looked at the dragon and man.

"Well?" Leonard questioned.

"I am an ice elf," Shinara grinned. Happy that she wasn't something bad.

Alexa looked at Shinara, then turned so that their faces were centimetres apart. The girls smiled.

"I'm so happy that you did this for me. Knowing that I am nothing like my sister is amazing and I have you to thank for it," Shinara smiled.

Alexa closed that gap between them and hugged her friend.

"I am glad that I could help."

The girls pulled away and looked at Smok.

"Now we begin our journey to your castle, your grace," Smok spoke.

And with that, Alexa picked up her dragons, wolves and her belongings along with Shinara's and Leonard's. She put all of the belongings onto Smok's back and they started their journey to Brunuhville castle, the home to princess Alexa Snow and her friend Shinara Ondovir and her dragons.

***

As they walked through the forest, the sun started setting. The magical creatures were making themselves known, magic was flying through the air and the trees swayed in the breeze. Kohana started to chase some of the magical creatures as they started tormenting her. Every now and then she came so close to catching some but failed in doing so.

Alexa laughed, then looked around the forest, taking in the beautiful sight. She looked down at her dragons in the cage. They looked distressed. She let them out and they scurried off behind a bush.

"What are they doing?" Shinara questioned. Leonard and the girls watched as the bush started to russell and the dragons began to screeched. Kohana started barking as she didn't understand what was happening.

Suddenly the noise stopped and the bushes stopped moving. The Three watched as both the little dragons walked out from behind the bush, not so little anymore.

Alexa smiled. "Wow, they have growing up so fast."

"Your grace, you have had Draco for just under a month which means that when Spitze hatch, he and his brother took hold of the same age," Smok began.

Draco and Spitze walked over to Alexa. Alexa gave them both a whole fish. Both the black and green dragon as if asking permission to go and fly with the old dragon.

"Dul." And the dragons took off, flying up into the beautiful clear, blue sky to fly with their fellow dragon.

"Wow Draco listened," Shinara said as she was shocked at the dragon's actions.

"Don't get used to it," Alexa smirked and carried on walking, watching her dragons fly.

Shinara watched as Kohana and Leonard were playing chase in front of her.

***

Elsie and Jasper were getting quite close. They would spend sleepless nights together, looking up at the stars and they would watch the moon and fire elves party, they would eat together and they would go to the stream together. Link was happy that she had found someone but jealous that she wasn't all for him anymore.

Elsie and Jasper were down by the stream dipping their feet in and enjoying each other's company and talking about what Elsie had been through.

"So what you're saying is you used to be a wolf but Alexa's wolf killed you and Link brought you back to life and changed you into an elf?" Jasper questioned making sure that he heard what Elsie said correctly.

"Yeah. If he had kept me as a wolf I would have been deformed and I would be weak, but as an elf, I am more powerful and have so much magic to explore," Elsie spoke.

"That explains your fluffy blonde hair and sharp K-9s," Jasper and Elsie laughed.

Jasper jumped around, nervous of something. "Did you hear that?"

"Hear what?" Elsie questioned. Just then a rustle was heard from the bushes opposite them.

Elsie and Jasper jumped out of the water and went to investigate. With magic sparks forming at their hands, they walked closer to the sound as it got louder and louder.

The sound stopped and the elves stopped in their tracks.

"What do you think it is?" Jasper asked.

"Or who," Elsie said as a hooded figure walked out from behind the bushes.

The figure approached Elsie and Jasper and stopped. The figure pulled down their hood and revealed a familiar face.

"Shadow? I thought you were dead?" Elsie questioned, shocked at who was standing before her.

"No. Link teleported me to a safe cave so no one would know I was alive. But I heard about princess Alexa Snow and had to come and help my friends out," Shadow mentioned.

"He'll be happy to see you again," Elsie huffed.

The three of them walked back to the caves.

***

After the long walk, Alexa saw the three dragons swoop down and not rise back up. Kohana ran over to Leonard.

"Where did they go?" Alexa and Shinara ran up to Leonard who had stopped at an opening in the forest.

Alexa looked at the beautiful sight. She was speechless. Shinara took her hand and smiled.

"It's stunning," Shinara spoke as she squeezed the princess's hand.

"Princess Alexa, welcome to Brunuhville Castle, your home," Leonard spoke.

Alexa smiled and they all made their way up the pebble path, through the kingdom village.

***

Elsie and Jasper walked up to Link nervously when they got to the cave. Elsie tapped Link's should and he turned around to face them.

"Link, we have something you need to see," Elsie's words shook.

"What?" Link spat.

Elsie and Jasper parted as Shadow walked forward and stopped in front of Link.

"Miss me?"

3

The Queen of Brunuhville

"Miss me?" Was all that Link could think about. Him and Shadow walked off into his room so they could be alone.

"What are you going to do about Alexa?" Shadow questioned.

"I am going to kill her," Link spat.

There was a comfortable silence that filled the air. Link thought about the different ways to kill his sister. The hatred for her grew bigger and bigger after knowing she will be taking his place on his throne.

Elsie and Jasper were standing outside his room listening to everything they were saying.

"This doesn't seem right. Killing his sister so he can have the throne," Elsie sadly spoke.

Jasper stayed quiet for a while then spoke. "I need to tell you something but you have to keep it between us, okay?"

"Sure. What's up?" Elsie asked.

Jasper looked around the cave to make sure that no one was listening. After seeing that the coast was clear, her turned back to Elsie and began.

"Well, you know I told you that I am a dark elf? Well, I'm not. I am an ice elf. I'm one of the good guys," he nervously said.

Elsie smiled at him then went in for a hug. "Thank you for telling me. So what have you been doing? Lying to him?"

"Well yeah, I don't want my queen to get hurt."

They both smiled and walked away from the door.

***

As the pack walked through the village, Alexa and Shinara were amazed by the sight. They came to the end of the pebble path and was faced with the castle doors. Alexa looked around to see that her dragons and Smok were no longer flying in the sky.

"Your dragons have gone to the dragon caves under the castle and Smok had to leave to go to the ice mountains," Leonard spoke. He looked up at a familiar guard and gestured for him to open the doors.

Once the doors were open, the pack walked into the castle. Alexa was amazed. There was a beautiful gold chandelier hanging from the ceiling with candles burning, the walls were black with red and electric blue dragon silhouettes over the black and the floor was tiled.

Alexa walked around the castle and looked into every room. There was a room with loads of books, new and old in it, a room that had a long wooden table in, that Leonard said was where meetings were held, there were five bedrooms that Alexa counted. The first bedroom was the master bedroom. It had a queen size bed with animal fur covers, a wooden wardrobe and a wooden chest of draws with a mirror hanging on the wall above it. The other rooms were slightly different. They still had the wardrobe and the chest of draws but the beds were king size with animal fur covers.

The last room Alexa got to, the doors were closed and guarded. Leonard asked the guards to open the doors and they did. When the doors opened Alexa was met with a large room with tables around the sides and in front was a set of steps leading up to Alexa's throne. Alexa walked down the middle of the room and up the steps with Shinara and Leonard behind her. The throne was made out of stone and carved into a dragon. She put her hand on the throne and walked around it.

"It's beautiful. I can't believe this is all mine," Alexa spoke with excitement. When she got back to the front of the throne, she sat down with Kohana at her side.

"It suits you," Shinara said, winking at her friend.

All of a sudden, footsteps were heard walking down the throne room. Leonard and Shinara moved to the side as they saw it was Sam with two other guards by his side.

"Your grace, I am Sam, your guard. We are so grateful that you are home," Sam spoke as he bowed slightly and stood up straight again.

"It's nice to be home," Alexa smiled.

"I would like to show you something, your grace. Do you mind?" Sam questioned.

"Of course. lead the way," Alexa smiled and followed Sam through the castle, leaving Leonard and Shinara to settle in with Kohana.

Sam took Alexa down a part of the castle she hadn't explored yet. When they got to the end, there was a metal door with a dragon engravement on it and two guards at both sides.

"This must be the dragon caves Leonard was telling me about," Alexa smiled.

The guards unlocked the door, allowing Alexa and Sam to walk down the stone steps to the cave.

***

When they reached the bottom, Alexa saw Draco and Spitze playing. They turned around to see that Alexa was standing there. Alexa then noticed a yellow scaled, teenage dragon walking towards her.

"Is this one the third dragon?" Alexa asked.

"Yes, your grace."

Alexa held her hand out to the dragon as he walked closer to her. As he approached her hand, he sniffed it first. He was unsure at first but then the realisation hit him and he allowed Alexa to stroke him.

"I think Zepter would be a great name for you," Alexa spoke, smiling as all three of her dragons screeched in happiness.

"Can they hear me call them?" Alexa asked.

"Yes, but you can only call them in your mind and thoughts," Sam replied within his mind.

"You must teach me how to do that," Alexa spoke.

"Just say something within your mind and you will know if I can hear you."

"I think I am falling for Shinara."

Sam looked at his princess and smiled.

"Tell her, your grace."

Alexa smiled as she allowed her dragons to play as her and Sam walked back up to the castle. When they got back to the top, Alexa watched as the guards closed the door and saw something written at the top.

"Tiarna Dragon. Dragon Lord, if I'm correct," Alexa spoke.

"You know our native tongue?" Sam questioned.

"Yeah, I heard it around the village and started teaching my dragons."

They both smiled then walked back to the throne room. Sam walked Alexa in and smiled. "I will leave you now, but if you ever need me just say Sam and I will be there."

"Okay. Thank you, Sam," Alexa smiled.

Sam bowed slightly then left Alexa in the throne room. Kohana came running in and sat in front of Alexa.

"Kohana, I have been thinking about this a lot and I think it would be best if you became a witch. You'll be more powerful than you are now and you will also be an animagus."

Kohana nodded her head. Alexa placed her hand against the wolf's chest. She started to draw circles with her fingers as blue sparks started to appear. Suddenly Kohana started to change. She started to lose all her fur, her legs changed into arms, hands, legs and feet and her face changed to a human face.

She sat on the floor looking at the new body she had been given. "Wow, I'm glad I'm not the only one who has been thinking about doing this," Kohana said.

Alexa smiled and handed her friend some clothes. Kohana changed into them and stood to her feet.

"Leonard will teach you everything you need know about being an animagus. He will teach you how to change into your wolf, but first we need a good nights' sleep."

Both girls got up and walked to their rooms. The day had fallen to night and it was getting late. The girls bid each other goodnight and walked into their rooms.

Alexa sat on her bed and looked around while playing with her necklace. "I can't believe this is my home. I wish you were here to see all of this Lena," she said to herself.

She laid down on the bed and just looked up at the ceiling. There was a knock at the door. "Come in."

The door opened and revealed Shinara's figure. Shinara walked over to the bed and cuddled up to Alexa.

"So, this is going to be our home?" she questioned.

"Yep, and in a couple of days' time, I will be crowned queen and become two-hundred," Alexa smiled.

Both of the girls snuggled down in bed and let darkness take over.

***

Back at the cave, Elsie and Jasper were talking. "So you want me to come and live with you in the kingdom village?" Elsie asked.

"Yes, but only if you want to. I know the guards and I can even talk to Alexa about you. Get you in her good books," Jasper laughed.

Elsie thought for a while. She would be leaving everything behind. Her friend, her home and then it hit her. She never wanted to be bad, Link just controlled her and made her do things she didn't want to do.

"Yes, I will come with you. When do we leave?"

"Well, I was kind of hoping you would say yes so I have packed all of our stuff and we can leave now."

Elsie laughed. They both stood to their feet and they walked out of the cave and into the forest, making their way to the kingdom.

***

The walk wasn't long. Jasper lead the way down the pebble path of the kingdom village with Elsie behind him. Jasper stopped in front of a brick hut and smiled at Elsie.

"Welcome home."

Elsie walked in and smiled. The hut had two bedrooms, both with a double bed with animal fur covers, a wardrobe and a chest of draws. The living room and two single chairs and a sofa with a wooden table in the middle. There was a fireplace that Jasper had just started and a kitchen.

"Wow it's beautiful," Elsie smiled.

***

Link and Shadow had been looking around the cave for ages, trying to find Elsie and Jasper.

"Where could they be?" Link spat, getting angry.

"They may just be out on a walk," Shadow suggested.

***

The next day, Alexa woke up to see her friend still asleep next to her. She crawled about of bed carefully and snuck out of the room. She closed the door behind her quietly, making sure she didn't wake Shinara.

She walked to Kohana's room and knocked on the door. "Come in." Alexa walked in to see her friend changed and ready for the day ahead of her.

"Come on then. Let's get this show on a road," Alexa smiled, leading Kohana out of the room and to the throne room.

When they walked in, they saw Leonard standing there waiting. "Good morning girls. Are you ready Kohana?"

"Yeah, let's do this." Kohana walked over to Leonard and they started their training.

Alexa walked over to her throne and sat down, watching her two friends.

A little while later, Shinara walked into the room and saw Leonard training with a girl. She walked up to Alexa. "Who is that?"

"Kohana," Alexa spoke bluntly, keeping her attention on her friends.

"What? When did that happen?"

"Yesterday. We had both been thinking of doing this so I did. Now Leonard is training her as she is an animagus," Alexa said turning her attention to her friend. ""I actually need to ask you something."

"Sure, what's up?" Shinara questioned.

"Well, you know that we have been friends now for just over three months and we have caught feelings for each other?"

"Yeah?"

"Well, I was wondering, would you be my princess?" Alexa asked.

The question took Shinara by surprise but it didn't take her long to answer her friend.

"Of course, I will!" And with that, Shinara jumped onto Alexa's lap, cupped her face and kissed her gently on the lips.

Both of the girls smiled once they had pulled away, the turned their attention to watch their friends train when the suddenly stopped. Alexa and Shinara got up and Alexa walked over to her friend.

"That was fast," Alexa laughed.

"She is the only person I have trained that only took half a day," Leonard spoke. "But she is ready."

Leonard had taught Kohana how to calm her inner and outer self, clear her mind, talk to her wolf through her thoughts and how to change into her wolf. He had also helped her change her name.

Leonard changed in front of the girls then back to his human self. "Aria, now it's your turn."

"I don't know."

"You are ready. Just clear your mind."

Aria smiled and then closed her eyes. She cleared her mind then started talk to Kohana. "Are you ready?"

"Yeah, let's do this."

Suddenly Aria's eyes changed to a dark yellow. She went down on all fours and fur started to grow out of her skin. Her body started to change from a human to a wolf.

Alexa looked at Kohana and smiled. "Damn that was amazing. Now I need you to do something. I need to see if the dragons will still be happy around you."

Kohana nodded her head. Alexa walked out of the room with Kohana at her side. They walked to the end of the hallway then stopped. The guards opened the doors and Alexa and the wolf walked down the steps.

When they got to the bottom, Draco and Spitze walked up to Kohana and started playing with her. Zepter looked at the wolf and his brothers and joined in. Alexa let them play for a little while then called Kohana back.

"Kohana, it's time to change."

Kohana ran over to Alexa and changed into her human self. The three dragons looked at Aria in confusion. The girl held her hand out as Draco walked up to her. He sniffed her hand then let her stroke him. The other two dragons joined in with a group hug.

"I'm guessing that means they still like me?" Aria questioned.

Alexa just laughed and gave a nod to her head. She left her friend and her dragons to play while she walked back up to the castle.

***

Alexa walked back to the throne room and sat down on the throne. Suddenly the doors opened to reveal Jasper and Elsie.

"What is she doing here?" Alexa spat.

"Your grace, I am Jasper, I am an ice elf. I have brought Elsie here because I have saved her. If we could just talk in private then everything will be explained."

Alexa waved off the guards and Jasper and Elsie walked closer to Alexa.

"What do you mean saved?" she questioned.

Jasper Explained how Link controlled her and that whatever he said she had to do because he would hurt her. She never wanted to be bad, she has always liked Alexa. She even liked Kohana.

"Well, I am glad you came to me about this. Elsie you can stay here as long as you want. I will keep you safe from that brother of mine," Alexa spoke.

Jasper and Elsie went to walk out when Alexa stopped them. "And Kohana is now Aria. I changed her to become a human."

Jasper and Elsie smiled and continued out of the castle.

"See I told you after talking to her she will be okay with you," Jasper smiled.

"I know, I just get nervous sometimes."

After the two left, Alexa called upon Sam.

"Your grace," Sam spoke.

"Keep an eye on them two. Something seems off with them."

"Yes, your grace."

As Sam turned to leave, Alexa began to speak.

"Oh, and make sure it is discreet. I don't want them finding out."

"Of course." And with that, Sam was gone.

***

Alexa was sat in her room thinking about the language this kingdom speaks.

"Sam," she called and suddenly he teleported into her room.

"Yes, your grace?"

"Would you mind teaching me the native language?" she asked.

"Of course."

Sam sat down on her bed and started teaching her the language. Everything he said, he got Alexa to repeat in.

***

A few hours had past and Alexa had managed to learn the language.

"Now repeat after me, Ich bin die Drachen Lord. Ich verspreche, Sie zu schützen, und lassen Sie niemals zu, dass Schaden in Ihre Nähe kommt, mein Volk."

"Is mise an Dragan Tiarna. Geallaim duit tú a chosaint, agus ní ligfidh mé do dhochar teacht gar duitse, mo dhaoine," Alexa spoke fluently.

"Well done, I am impressed with you." Sam smiled.

There was a knock at the door. "Come in." Alexa commanded. Two men walked in and closed the door behind them.

"Your grace, Sam, I am Maester Logan and this is Dorian, my apprentice. Your grace, if we could have a minute of your time?" Logan spoke.

"I will leave you to it your grace," Sam spoke then teleported away.

Alexa turned her attention to Logan and Dorian. "What can I do for you Maester Logan?"

"Well, your coronation is tomorrow and so is your birthday. Dorian has made you a outfit for tomorrow and we are having your celebration in the kingdom gardens. Dorian will help you tomorrow morning," Logan spoke.

"Fantastic. Thank you both." Alexa smiled.

"You're welcome, your grace. We are glad you are home. Good day," Logan spoke and both of the men left the room.

***

Alexa walked out of her room and down the corridor to the dragon cave door. She smiled at the guard as he unlocked the door allowing her to walk through.

As she got to the bottom, she saw her dragons flying back in from getting their food. Spitze was first with fifty fish in his mouth, Zepter next with sixty fish in his mouth then Draco last. When he landed, he opened his mouth and let one-hundred fish drop out. Alexa laughed and sat down next to her boys.

Alexa smiled as she watched her boys burn the fish and eat them and then her stomach rumbled. Draco noticed and burnt a fish for her. He nudged it over to Alexa and then moved closer to her with his fish.

"Thank you, Draco." Alexa hugged him then ate the fish.

As the dragons ate, Draco shared his with his Dragon Lord. After they had finished, Alexa looked at Draco and idea popped into her head.

"Do you want to go for a ride?"

All three dragons screeched at the same time. Spitze and Zepter went to the opening to the cave and flew off. Draco lowered slightly so Alexa could climb onto his back. Alexa climbed on and Draco walked over to the edge of the cave. Draco looked up at Alexa and she smiled down at him.

"Eitilt." And Draco swooped down until they were close to the sea, then pulled himself up so they were gliding through the sky. He caught up to the other two dragons and screeched in happiness.

Alexa didn't realise how amazing the view was from such a height. The clouds were shaped as dragons and wolves, the sky was becoming dark blue, the sea was clear with the sun sparkling down on it as it started to set. The castle seemed so small from up in the sky. From the sky, the village looked small too. Alexa saw all the people rushing around trying to get home before it got late.

She didn't realise how much she was missing out on.

"Téigh abhaile." Alexa commanded and Draco and the two dragons flew home.

When they got back into the cave, Draco lowered himself so Alexa could climb off of him. Alexa gave all of them a hug good night. She watched they all went to sleep then she quietly walked back up the steps to the castle.

***

That night, Alexa and Shinara laid in bed, cuddled up.

"Are you looking forward to tomorrow?" Shinara questioned, smiling up at her girlfriend.

"Yes, I am." Alexa smiled, kissing her girlfriends head. When she looked down, Shinara was asleep.

Alexa played with her necklace as she was deep in thought. Knowing that her best friend was dead and couldn't be with her on this special day was heart breaking. Alexa missed Lena more than anything in the world and she would do anything and everything she could to have her here with her sharing all these magical memories.

Alexa closed her eyes as she let the darkness take over and her mind flow into the dream world.

***

The next morning, Shinara was nowhere to be seen, Alexa got up and walked over to the door. As she opened the door, Dorian standing there with her coronation outfit.

"Good morning, come in." Alexa smiled as Dorian walked in.

"I-I-I didn't mean to wake you, your grace," Dorian stuttered.

"Dorian, you didn't wake me. There is no need to be nervous, the name is Alexa. Just don't tell Logan that." Alexa winked.

"I have always been nervous around people." He lowered his head.

Alexa walked up to him and held his head up. "I won't judge you. You don't have to be of me though." They smiled at each other then Alexa started to get changed.

She put on a two-piece black smart but casual suit with an electric blue shirt that she left undone so the laces hung over her chest accompanied by a black jacket, black skinny jeans with smart black boots. Dorian brushed Alexa's hair and made two plaits, one either side of her hair and tied them in the middle with dragon beads. He then made a braid that hung behind her ear and put dragon beads decorating it.

Alexa then looked in the mirror and smiled while holding her best friend's necklace. "Wow Dorian, you did a great job. I just wish that my best friend was here to join me."

Dorian noticed the change in behaviour and placed a kind hand on Alexa's shoulder.

"Your friend will always be with you Alexa."

Alexa smiled at his kind words and turned on her heal to face him.

"Time to go for my coronation." Alexa smiled as both her and the boy walked out of her room and down to the throne room.

The doors were closed when they got there and there were two guards either side of the door. Alexa smiled at Dorian and the guards.

"Are you nervous, your grace?" Dorian asked.

"A bit but I can't wait."

The doors opened and the sight was amazing. Everyone from the kingdom was standing at both sides of the room. Alexa walked down the middle and everyone cheered. She walked up the steps and was met by Logan. They both smiled at each other then the crowed went silent.

"Elves, witches, wizards, animagis, we are here today to witness the crowning of our new queen, Alexa Snow. Now may I have the crown," Logan began.

He was then handed a crown made of gold and in the shape of a dragon by Leonard. And on the other side, Jasper handed Logan a golden ring in the shape of a dragon. Alexa knelt down onto one knee as Logan began. "Repeat after me, I Alexa Snow, first of my name, queen of Brunuhville and the dragon lord."

But what came next, he didn't expect. "I Alexa Snow, an chéad cheann de mo ainm, Banríon Brunuhville agus an Dragon Lord."

Logan was shocked but he carried on. "Vow to protect this kingdom and the kingdom's people until my last breath."

"Dearbhaíonn sé an ríocht seo agus muintir na ríochta a chosaint go dtí an anáil dheireanach."

Alexa stood to her feet as Logan placed the crown on her head and the ring on her finger.

"I hereby pronounce you Alexa, queen of Brunuhville."

The people of Brunuhville cheered as Alexa smiled at everyone.

Alexa walked out of the castle and into the gardens for her birthday celebration and everyone else followed.

The garden was beautiful. There were water fountains scattered here and there, rich green bushes with colourful flowers on them and there were a few benches for people to sit on scattered around the gardens. Alexa was standing by one of the fountains drinking her wine when she felt arms snake around her waist.

"Happy birthday your grace."

Alexa recognised the voice and turned around.

"Thank you Shinara," Alexa said as she kissed her girlfriend.

Shinara took Alexa's hand and walked her over to a bench.

"How does it feel to be queen?" Shinara questioned.

"Normal. I don't feel any different apart from wearing a crown, sitting on a throne and living in a castle," Alexa laughed.

Just then Logan and Dorian walked over with Leonard and Aria.

"Where did you learn to speak the native tongue?" Logan questioned.

"Sam taught me. I knew some words but I asked him to teach me. I'm a little rusty still but I'm working on it," Alexa smiled.

***

Link and Shadow had heard about the coronation and were angry. They still couldn't find Jasper and Elsie anywhere but what Link didn't know was that they were in the kingdom grounds.

Link looked around for some clothes and put them on. Shadow rushed into his room and told him that Elsie and Jasper were in the kingdom.

"WHAT!! I'm going to kill all of them," Link spat.

Link and Shadow ran out of the caves leaving everyone look at them confused.

"Where are they going?"

"I don't know but I know Link knows about his sister being queen now."

They ran through the forest and came upon the pebble path.

"Here's my chance to kill this stupid little girl."

Link and Shadow put their hoods up so no one could recognise them. They walked around the village looking for Elsie and Jasper but they weren't anywhere to be found.

Link looked up at the castle doors and got extremely angry, until he heard a dragon screech. He and Shadow covered their ears as the sound rattled through them.

"Bloody dragon!" Shadow spat.

They walked off through the village a bit longer until they saw Elsie talking to Alexa. He noticed that Alexa was wearing the crown.

"That's meant to be my crown!"

Link and Shadow walked over to Elsie and tapped her shoulder. She turned around and was instantly pulled behind Alexa.

"What are you doing in my kingdom?" Alexa shouted making everyone go silent.

"Don't you mean MY kingdom? This was meant for ME not YOU!" Link spat.

"Mother and father left it for me. You don't deserve it after murdering them."

At this point the guards had surrounded Link and Shadow. Link started to make a fire ball and he hit one of the guards.

"Draco I need you and your brothers," Alexa thought to herself.

All of a sudden, large wings were heard across the kingdom. Everyone looked around themselves, up at the sky, trying to find the source of the sound. Then at that moment, the three dragons screeched as they landed. Draco landed by Alexa and the other two either side of them. Link looked at them and smirked.

"What's three dragons going to do to me? Burn me? Well, that worked out great last time, didn't it?" Link laughed.

Draco snarled at Link and screeched. Link started to make an energy ball. Alexa started to get worried. Link flung the ball at Alexa but Draco blocked it. The ball rebounded and hit Shadow, making her go flying.

"You ungrateful beast. You'll pay for that," Link spat as he started to make another energy ball.

This time he aimed it at Draco but Spitze and Zepter blocked him and it flew back at Link making him fall to the ground.

Link got back up and clenched his fists along with Shadow.

"This isn't the end of this. Mark my words Snow," he shouted as both him and Shadow turned on their heels to teleport out of the kingdom.

But before doing so, Alexa called out to them. "Don't you mean queen Snow?"

The kingdom people laughed at their queen's comment as the two dark elves grunted and teleported out of the castle grounds.

Shinara and Jasper came running over to see if Alexa and Elsie were alright. Elsie was shaken up but Alexa was angry. She wanted her brother dead.

Alexa turned to the people who were still silent. "Is mise an dragan Tiarna. Geallaim duit tú a chosaint, agus ní ligfidh mé do dhochar teacht gar duitse, mo dhaoine."

The kingdom people cheered and went back to having a good time.

"Alexa are you okay?" Shinara asked.

"Yeah, I'm fine. But I want him dead." Alexa and Shinara walked over to Elsie and Jasper.

"Elsie are you okay? I'm sorry he came here and did that," Alexa said apologetically.

"Yeah, I'm okay and don't be sorry, you didn't know that he was going to do this." Elsie smiled.

"I'm going to make sure you and Jasper have extra guards until this all goes away. I wouldn't run it past him to come here at night," Alexa stated.

Alexa walked over to Sam and told him that Elsie and Jasper need extra guards. Sam walked off and arranged the command that his queen had given him.

"Sam is getting you extra guards. I'm just glad you are okay." Alexa smiled, putting a hand on her arm.

"I'm just glad that the dragons saved you both," Shinara said hugging her girlfriend.

"Me too, me too," Alexa said as she looked at her dragons that were enjoying the fuss from the kingdom people.

"Let's get back to having a good time. Wine anyone?" Alexa said as everyone laughed and continued to party.

***

The day went by quick. Alexa enjoyed her birthday and coronation and she enjoyed the people of Brunuhville's company.

Alexa and Shinara were in their room laying on the bed. Shinara was already asleep. Alexa couldn't help but think of Lena. All she wanted was her friend. She hated these sleepless nights. Every passing moment, she thought of Lena just running through the castle gates. Everyone who knew about Lena, never really knew how much it broke Alexa.

"Thinking about Lena?" Shinara questioned, pulling her queen out of her thoughts.

"Yeah, I'm sorry." Alexa smiled at her girlfriend.

"Don't be. I know what it feels like to lose someone you love so dearly. Never be sorry for thinking about her."

Alexa couldn't believe how amazing her life was turning out. She was queen of a kingdom, she had three dragons, she had an amazing girlfriend and she had an amazing support network of friends. But the one thing she was missing was her best friend.

Alexa fell asleep, wishing that Lena was still alive.

***

The next morning, Alexa felt something odd going on with her stomach. Shinara noticed that Alexa was in pain but as soon as she tried to move, she felt the same pain in her stomach.

Alexa called for Sam and he teleported in.

"Girls what's wrong?" Sam questioned with worry.

"Get Logan and Dorian," Alexa winced.

Sam did as he was commanded and teleported to get the two men.

A few minutes later, Logan and Dorian entered the room and saw what was going on.

"Your grace, you need to lay still, same with you my lady. This is so we can see what is going on," Logan said.

The women did as they were told as Logan and Dorian looked at the girls stomachs. Alexa's stomach was glowing blue and Shinara's red.

"This is odd," Dorian spoke. "This could only mean one thing and they would have to wait it out for an hour."

Just then, Leonard, Elsie, Aria and Jasper came rushing into the room but all fell on top of each other as they hit the floor. They all laughed and stood back up.

"Oh my god, are you okay?" they all said in unison.

They all laughed at each other. Shinara and Alexa tried to laugh but it hurt too much for them to try.

As Logan and Dorian examined the girls a bit longer, Logan had figured out what was going wrong.

"Right Alexa, I am going to transfer the pain from Shinara into you. You have to bear with the pain for a while while I examine what is happening."

Alexa nodded. Logan transferred the pain into Alexa and Alexa screamed. The pain was antagonising. Alexa's stomach started to glow both red and blue but then it started to change.

"What's happening? Is she going to be okay?" Shinara questioned, worried about her girlfriend.

"Yes, she will be fine," Logan spoke

Alexa's stomach stopped changing colour and began to glow blue.

"What does that mean?" everyone said in unison.

Logan and Dorian walked to the window and started talking.

"She is pregnant with a boy. But she is going to have to have it magically removed. This boy is fifteen years old. This happened to her mother," Logan began.

"This is because, here in Brunuhville, when a woman falls pregnant, the child is often much older than we realise," Dorian stated.

"Yes, that's why."

They turned back to Alexa and began.

"Alexa you are pregnant with a boy. Your mother had this happen too when she was pregnant with Your brother. We are going to have to magically take it out of you but the one thing that is different between you and your mother is that you have having a fifteen-year-old boy, not a ten-year-old."

"Can you just get him out of me please?" Alexa screamed.

The men nodded and started. Magical sparks come out of their hands as they placed them on top of Alexa's stomach and their magic turned red. They started to make circular movements over her while muttering an incantation.

"Shinara can you give her that potion please?" Logan pointed to the bed where there was a vile lying there. Shinara opened it up and poured it down Alexa's mouth.

"What does it do?

"Helps you give birth your grace."

Dorian stepped back and started to mutter something but no one could work out what he was saying. Suddenly Logan started to lift his hands up as a figure started to appear. Alexa started to scream as the body then came out of her stomach completely.

Logan stepped away and placed the body on the floor. He then clicked his fingers and the body stood to its feet and looked at the men.

The boy had blonde hair and ice blue eyes. He was and elf like Shinara and had the same abilities as Alexa. Logan gave the boy some clothes when suddenly and shock wave crossed the room, knocking everyone onto their backs.

***

After a while everyone stood to their feet.

"What was that?" Leonard questioned.

"That was a memory wave. We all have memories of each other with Alexa and Shinara's son," Logan stated.

"His name is Lee Snow," Alexa said smiling as her and Lee shared a look.

"We will leave you guys alone. Welcome to the family, my lord," Logan said as everyone left the room apart from Shinara.

Shinara sat on the bed and looked at Lee.

"Lee come and join us."

Lee walked over to his mothers and smiled.

"I finally get to meet you guys. Why did that man call me his lord?" the boy questioned.

"You are my son Lee. I am the queen of Brunuhville. You are the prince," Alexa stated.

Lee smiled and all three of them walked out of the room.

Shinara left the two to get to know each other.

Alexa took her son into the throne room and showed him the throne.

"Wow that's amazing," he said running to the throne and sitting down on it.

"It suits you, my boy." Alexa smiled as Sam walked into the room.

"My lord, your grace," Sam spoke.

"Sam I would like a crown made for my son and my girlfriend. My son will have a dragon one like mine and Shinara will have the same but made from the ice mountains."

"Of course, your grace."

Sam clicked his fingers and two crowns appeared in his hands. He walked up to Lee and placed the crown on his head.

"My lord, your grace." He bowed slightly then left to find Shinara.

Alexa looked at Lee and smiled. "Have you ever wanted to fly on a dragon?"

"Oh my god yes mum," Lee said excitedly.

"Then follow me."

Alexa led Lee through the castle and to the dragon cave door. The guards opened the door allowing the mother and her son to walk down the steps so Lee could meet the dragons.

When they got down to the caves, the dragons looked up. They ran to their dragon lord and got a hug then they looked at Lee.

Draco started to snarl.

"Lee, hold your hand out and let Draco come to you. If he says he likes you then Spitze and Zepter will too."

Lee did as he was told and held his hand out. Draco walked closer to Lee and sniffed his hand. After a while of trying to suss the boy out, Draco let him stroke him.

Lee smiled as the other two came over for some fuss. Draco lowered slightly allowing Alexa to get onto his back. Lee looked at his mother and smiled.

"Choose a dragon Lee." Alexa smiled.

Lee looked at the two dragons and walked over to Spitze. The dragon lowered himself, allowing Lee to get onto his back. All three dragons went to the edge of the cave then stopped.

"Just say Eitilt and he will take off," Alexa said as Draco and Zepter swooped down.

Lee looked at Spitze and smiled.

"Eitilt." And Spitze swooped down until they reached the sea then he pulled up, gliding through the sky.

Spitze caught up to Draco and both Lee and Alexa sat up straight. Lee looked around to see how beautiful the kingdom was. He had the same look on his face that his mother had the first time she went out with Draco.

***

After a long ride, the dragons landed back in the cave, with Draco and Spitze letting Lee and Alexa off of them. Alexa and Lee said good night to the dragons and walked back up to the castle.

"That was awesome mum. Can we do that again some time?" Lee questioned.

"Of course, son, whenever you like." Alexa smiled.

"Can we go again now?" Lee asked with a cheeky smile.

"Okay mister, time for bed. We can go out tomorrow. The dragons need their sleep and so do you," Alexa said as she showed her son to his room.

Alexa and Lee walked into his room. Lee got into bed as Alexa sat on the edge.

"That was fun mother." Lee smiled.

"I love you, Lee. Sleep well," Alexa said as she kissed the top of his head.

"I love you too mum." Lee smiled.

Just then Shinara came in and smiled.

"Bed time already? You were gone long." Shinara laughed as she walked over to her son.

"Good night Snow. Sleep well."

"I love you mother. Good night," Lee said as he fell asleep.

Alexa and Shinara left his room and walked to their room.

"Did he have fun?" Shinara questioned.

"He loved it. That much he wanted to go out again tonight." Alexa laughed as she snuggled up in bed with her girlfriend.

"I got that crown you made for me. Thank you. It was very sweet," Shinara said as she kissed her girlfriend on the lips.

"You're welcome. Now get some sleep," Alexa said.

Both of the girls closed their eyes and fell asleep straight away, dreaming of what tomorrow will bring.

4
The Engagement

Lee woke the next morning, overwhelmed still by last nights' adventure with his mother. Lee got changed in the same way that his mother did and placed his crown on top of his blonde hair as he walked out of his room, down to the throne room, where he met his mother there.

"Good morning son, did you sleep well?" Alexa smiled as her son sat next to her at a table.

"I did thank you. Would there be a chance we could go for a ride later? I'd love to bond with Spitze more," Lee asked politely.

Alexa smiled at Lee and nodded her head. "Of course, Lee, But first, I need you to meet the kingdom army."

"Sure. Anyway, where's mother?" Lee questioned as he scoffed some food into his mouth.

"She is out in the village with Aria and Elsie. She's having some girly time with them while me and you have some fun." Alexa winked at her son causing him to laugh.

After breakfast, Alexa and Lee walked out into the courtyard to find the army training. Lee looked around and smiled. "Wow mum, they are amazing. Maybe one day I could be like them."

"Maybe son, maybe." Alexa felt sadness when her son spoke those words. This was her boy, she never wanted to let go of him, especially if he went into the army. What if there was a battle and he never comes home? She couldn't lose him the way she lost her best friend.

Lee put his hand on his mother's shoulder, pulling her out of her thoughts. "Are you okay mother?"

"Yeah, I'm fine." Alexa smiled and turned her attention to the soldiers.

She walked over to Sam, who was in charge of the training. As she approached, Sam had noticed and called the training for a break.

"Your grace, My lord. What do I owe this pleasure for?" Sam smiled.

"I wanted Lee to meet the army, as of course, these are the men protecting him." Alexa smiled back.

"Of course, your grace. My lord, follow me." Lee followed Sam over to the soldiers as Alexa stayed back and watched.

"He will be sixteen soon," Leonard spoke, making Alexa jump.

"Ah yeah, don't remind me," Alexa sighed. Even though she has known her son for less than a week, she still has the feelings and memories of when he was born to now. Even if those memos aren't real, they are in Brunuhville.

Lee returned to his mother after he finished meeting the soldiers.

"Well? What do you think of them?" Alexa questioned.

"They seem awesome. I like them." Lee smiled.

"Well, I think it's time to stretch the dragon's wings today, don't you think?" Alexa smiled.

"Definitely!" Lee exclaimed. Both mother and son walked back into the castle and down to the dragon caves.

When they reached the bottom, Draco, Spitze and Zepter were just finishing up their breakfast. All three looked at Alexa and Lee and walked over to them, with Draco and Spitze allowing them to climb onto their backs. All three dragons walked to the edge of the cave waiting for their command.

"Eitilt," Alexa and Lee spoke in unison. The dragon's swooped down and took off into the morning sky.

***

Durning the morning walk through the village, Shinara, Elsie and Aria had bought a lot of goodies. Elsie has decided to buy a few things for Jasper, Aria bought some clothes and Shinara bought Lee a few things.

They walked in and out of the village shops until they came upon a jewellery shop. Shinara stood out the front, admiring a beautiful gold dragon ring with Ruby's as eyes.

"Wow that's beautiful." Shinara smiled. Her eyes sparkled.

Elsie and Aria walked to Shinara's side and followed her gaze to the ring.

"Wow that is nice," Elsie said.

"Yeah, I'll second that," Aria chuckled.

Shinara walked into the store with the two girls behind her and picked up the ring. A young boy walked up to the girls and smiled.

"Hey, I'm Ray, do you need any help my lady?" the boy spoke.

Shinara looked at the boy. He had neck length, brown hair with a tinge of red in it, brown eyes and he wore a white and black checked shirt, grey jeans and smart black shoes.

Shinara smiled and then looked back at the ring. "How much would this be?"

"Usually it's nine-hundred gold but for you it is four-hundred and fifty gold." Ray smiled.

Shinara smiled and pulled out nine-hundred gold from her purse. "Don't question how much I gave you. Keep the rest." Shinara winked.

Ray smiled as the three girls walked out of the shop.

"My lady."

Shinara heard Ray call back. "Yes, Ray?"

"Your son is Lee Snow, am I right?"

"Yes it is. Why may I ask?" Shinara questioned.

Ray walked closer to the three girls and smiled. "I was wondering if I could meet him?"

"Of course. Come by the castle when you have finished with work and I'll let you meet my son."

Ray smiled and walked back to his shop. The three girls carried on walking through the village.

"Why did you buy that ring, Shinara?" Elsie questioned.

"I'm going to propose to Alexa."

"You're what?" Aria smiled.

"Yeah. I've been thinking about it for a while and I want to marry her. We are home now, we have our son, she has her dragons and we are happy." Shinara blushed.

"Well let's get you back to your soon to be fiancé," Aria and Elsie squealed as they hurried Shinara off to the castle.

***

Link and Shadow were walking through the forest listening to the kingdom villagers, who were out in the forest, talk about the prince.

"So Alexa and Shinara have a son? When did this happen?" Link spat.

"A few days ago. They say he is a fifteen-year-old."

"Fifteen hm, magic would of caused this. I bet they are loving it. Well, if I can't kill the queens, I'll kill their stupid little son instead."

"You'd kill a young boy?" Shadow questioned.

"Not going soft on me now, are you?" Link spat at Shadow.

Shadow shook her head and Link smiled.

"Good. I just need to find out what he looks like and when his birthday is."

"Why his birthday?"

"Because I am going to kill him," Link smirked.

They carried on walking through the forest until they came to their home.

They walked into the cave and Link walked up to one of the dark elves.

"Spark, I need you," Link said as a young boy with black hair and eyes walked up to him.

"What's up Link?" Spark questioned.

"I need you to find out everything you can about the Prince," Link commanded.

"Sure. I'll head off now." And Spark left.

***

Shinara, Elsie and Aria walked into the castle to see that Lee and Alexa were nowhere to be seen.

"Where are they?" Aria questioned.

"Probably on their morning ride with the dragons." Shinara smiled.

They walked into the throne room and decided to wait in there. Just then the throne room doors opened and Lee and Alexa came in laughing and Alexa's hair was wet.

"What happened to you guys?" Shinara questioned.

"Draco thought it would be a great idea to dive bomb into the sea for some fish while I was still on his back." Alexa laughed. "I got changed though when we came back."

Lee was on the floor crying with laughter. Alexa just rolled her eyes at her son and walked over to her girlfriend. Alexa cupped Shinara's face and kissed her lightly on the lips.

"Alexa, I need to ask you something," Shinara nervously spoke.

At that point, Lee had stopped laughing and was standing by his mother's friends as everything turned serious.

"What is it my love?" Alexa questioned.

Suddenly Shinara got down on one knee and held out the dragon ring that she bought earlier in her hand.

"I've been thinking about this for a while now and today just feels right," Shinara began. "Since the day I met you, things have been different. There have been girls before you that I never clicked with and they never lasted long and then there's you. You make me laugh, smile, feel alive. You are my home Alexa and I want nothing more than me, you and Lee to be happy. So what I'm asking is, will you marry me?"

Lee gasped as the two girls next to him smiled. Alexa looked at Shinara and smiled as a tear rolled down her face.

"Yes, I will marry you." Alexa jumped into Shinara arms and squeezed her tight. After she let go, Shinara put the ring on Alexa's finger and smiled. Alexa kissed her fiancé's lips then looked at her ring.

Shinara followed her gaze and smiled. "I can't wait to be Mrs Snow."

The girls smiled as Lee, Elsie and Aria cheered.

***

News went around fast in the kingdom about Alexa and Shinara getting married and everyone was going crazy.

Spark was walking through the village, listening to what the people were saying. He looked around trying to see if the prince was about but he was nowhere to be seen until he saw two guards with a young boy in between them walking in his direction.

Spark quickly walked over to a nearby shop and started to look through things as the boy walked past. Spark watched as people were bowing slightly as the boy walked past.

"That must be the prince," he said to himself.

He followed behind the prince, not letting any attention get drawn to him until the prince stopped outside a shop.

The Dark elf walked up to the window as the prince walked in. The boy smiled at another boy and handed him something wrapped up.

Spark hid as both the boys walked out of the shop and up to the guards.

"Ray will be coming to the castle with me. Mum said he could," the Prince spoke.

The guards nodded and they walked off in the direction of the castle.

"Thank you, prince Lee," Ray spoke.

"Please just call me Lee."

Spark followed them again but this time listening to their conversation.

"I can't believe your mother's are getting married," Ray spoke.

"Me neither. I can't wait." Lee smiled and they carried on walking.

Spark stopped in his tracks and smirked. "I can't wait for Link to find out all this information." And then fled back to the caves to tell Link what he had found out.

***

"YOU WHAT!?" Link shouted causing everyone in the cave to look at him. "What are you all looking at? Mind your own business."

Everyone went back to what they were doing and Link turned his attention back to Spark. When Spark came back, he had told Link and Shadow everything he found out today about the prince.

"So, you're telling me, Lee is the prince and has a friend called Ray but also Alexa and Shinara are getting MARRIED?"

"Y-Yes, Link." Spark stuttered.

"Leave me be. I need time to think," Link spat as Spark left him and Shadow alone but stood outside of the door and around the corner so he could listen to what's being said.

"My sister is getting married."

"What do you want to do about it?" Shadow questioned.

"I need to get to know this Ray boy better. He would help a lot with finding out everything we need to know about the prince. Maybe if I pay him, he would help me? I mean help us get into the castle without being spotted so I can kill them all and take the throne," Link spoke.

"How are you going to do that?"

"Spark, I need you."

"Yes, Link?" Spark questioned as he walked back into the room.

"I need you to become friends with this Ray and get him to tell you everything about Lee and all the secret ways into the castle."

"Of course. I'll leave now." Just as Spark was about to leave, Link called him back.

"And Spark." Link threw ten small bags of gold at Spark. "Pay him one of these every time he helps us out." And with that, Spark left for the castle to befriend Ray.

***

Lee and Ray were down in the dragon caves watching the three brothers fight over some fish that they had caught earlier that day. All of a sudden, a black and electric blue dragon flew in and landed in the cave.

Draco, Spitze and Zepter all moved out of the way and bowed their heads as Smok looked at them.

"All grown up now and still fighting over fish? Your Dragon Lord won't be happy." the dragon spoke within his mind.

"W-Who are you?" Lee spoke.

The dragon looked at Lee and smiled. "Ah you must be Prince Lee, Alexa and Shinara's son. I am Smok, Alexa's guardian," Smok spoke making the two boys jump.

"You can talk?" Lee questioned.

"Yes my lord. I can. Could you go and tell your mother I am here?" Smok asked.

Lee nodded his head and went to walk up the steps to the castle when Alexa stood face to face to him.

"What's all that noise?" Alexa questioned as she walked down into the caves and saw Smok standing there.

"Smok. It's so good to see you," Alexa spoke as she walked up to the dragon and hugged him.

"Likewise, your grace. Your son is handsome," Smok said as both him and Alexa looked at Lee.

"I heard you and young Shinara are getting married. Congratulations."

"Thank you. May I ask why you are back from your travels?" Alexa questioned.

"Well, I had finished my journey for a gift for you, your soon to be queen and your son and I also had a feeling that your dragons would be needing a little help growing up."

"Ah yeah well Draco is a little bugger and does what he wants, Spitze and Zepter are both good but they all fight over their food," Alexa laughed.

"Well, why don't you and the boys go to the throne room and see the gifts I have bought you and I'll stay down here and talk to the dragon's," Smok suggested.

"Of course." The boys and Alexa went to walk up to the castle when Smok called Alexa back.

"Alexa come here for a second."

Alexa walked over to Smok and Smok blew two rings into Alexa's face.

"What did you just do," Alexa spoke.

"I can now communicate with you through your thoughts. Say something in your head," Smok spoke.

"It's great to have you back," Alexa's said in her head.

Smok smiled letting Alexa know that he heard what she said. Alexa walked back up to the castle and to the throne room to see her fiancé and son standing in front of the throne. Beside the throne there were three big objects, the size of her throne, covered by a red cover.

"Take them off," Alexa spoke to the guards.

The guards walked over to the objects and pulled at the covers, revealing three beautiful thrones. The guards moved Alexa's old throne and moved her new one to the space.

Alexa's, Lee's and Shinara's thrones were made out of dragon glass and sculptured into dragons. Alexa's had three dragons and each dragon had Ruby's as their eyes, Shinara's had two dragons with ice jewels as their eyes and Lee's had one dragon with sapphires as its eyes.

"Wow they are beautiful," Shinara spoke as her and Lee walked up to the steps and sat on their thrones.

"Wow Smok. Thank you so much. They are amazing."

"You're welcome your grace."

Alexa walked up the steps to her throne and sat down. She looked at either side to her to see her fiancé and son smiling at her. Leonard, Elsie, Aria and Jasper walked into the throne room and smiled.

"Smok is back, I see?" Leonard spoke.

"Wow those are beautiful," Aria and Elsie said in unison, making everyone laugh.

"Who brought them in here? Smok couldn't possibly of done it himself," Jasper said.

Just then Dorian walked in and smiled. "Smok asked me to help him so I brought them in for him, your grace."

"Thank you, Dorian. That is much appreciated." Alexa smiled.

Everyone smiled at the sight of the queen, soon to be queen and prince.

"You really do look like a great family," Leonard spoke.

Everyone started to leave, leaving the two girls and their boy alone until Shinara called Leonard back.

"Leonard, I need to ask you something," Shinara spoke.

"Of course."

"As my dad is dead and me and Alexa are getting married, will you give me away?" the young elf questioned.

"Of course. I'd be honoured."

Shinara and Leonard smiled and hugged each other.

Alexa looked at Lee and knelt down to his level as he was still sat on his throne. "Will you be my best man?"

"Definitely mother. I'd love to be," Lee spoke with excitement and kissed his mother's cheek.

***

Later that day, the castle gardens were decorated in beautiful engagement decorations and everyone from the kingdom was there to celebrate their queen and soon to be queen's engagement.

Alexa's pack along with Elsie and Jasper were all in the gardens, drinking, eating and laughing while Alexa was in her room talking to Maester Logan.

"How did I get pregnant?" Alexa asked.

"This time it is hard to say. Did you think about having a child with Shinara?" Logan questioned.

"Of course. But what does that mean?"

"In Brunuhville, if a couple talk or think about wanting a child, the ancient warlock will grant you that wish of having a child. But he makes the child older so there would be a shock wave, where we all remember everything about the child," Logan replied.

"So, say if me and Shinara spoke about having another child, I would become pregnant again?" Alexa questioned.

"Yes, your grace. Now go and enjoy your party. It's not every day you get engaged," Logan laughed.

Alexa walked out of her room and out into the castle gardens to join everyone. As she got out into the gardens, she was greeted by her son and fiancé.

"Mother, what were you doing?" Lee questioned.

"Yeah, what took you so long?" Shinara asked.

"I was talking to Master Logan about how I got pregnant and he told me," Alexa replied.

Alexa put an arm around her son's shoulders and smiled. Dorian then walked down into the gardens and approached Alexa.

"Your grace, a letter from Stone Grave," he spoke, handing the letter to the queen.

"Stone Grave?" Alexa questioned.

"Yeah, there are three kingdoms around this part of the world. Brunuhville, Stone Grave and Smoke Tower. Stone Grave is Queen Caity and King Ripp Lotz's castle and home to the wizarding community and Smoke Tower is King Jofree and Queen Dany Clarke's castle and home to the pixies and fairy community. This letter is from King and Queen Lotz," Dorian stated.

Alexa looked at the letter then opened it to read what it said.

Queen Alexa,

It's so nice to hear that you are on your mother and father's throne after everything that has happened. I am dreadfully sorry to hear that your brother killed them, but I am glad you are here to make Brunuhville strong again.

As I know that you are new to the kingdom and don't really know much about it, I am queen Caity Lotz of Stone Grave. My husband is King Ripp and we have our daughter, Princess Alana.

On the north side, Smoke Tower is home to Queen Dany and King Jofree Clarke along with their daughter, princess Gwen.

In your absence, we held Brunuhville as your mother and father commanded. We hope that you will still hold us as allies.

I also heard you are engaged to Shinara Ondovir and we are happy to hear that you are happy and have your son Lee by your side.

Would love to hear back from you and meet you all.

Queen Catiy of Stone Grave.

Alexa smiled as she finished reading the letter and looked up at Dorian. "Put this in my room and I will answer it when the party is over."

Dorian bowed slightly and did as commanded. Alexa turned her attention back to her son and fiancé as music started to play. Elsie and Jasper were dancing along with Leonard and Aria.

"Lee, why don't you go and find Ray, me and your mum need to talk," Alexa smiled at her son.

Lee smiled the walked off to find Ray. Alexa turned her attention to Shinara and smiled. "What would you say about having another child?"

"I'd love to. Maybe another boy?" Shinara winked.

"Hmm that sounds great. After the party, I'll tell Logan and hopefully, if Logan told me the truth, we will go through what we went through last time with Lee." Alexa smiled.

Just then, the music stopped and Lee and Leonard were standing on a table shouting "SPEECH! SPEECH!"

Alexa laughed and with the help of her son and best friend, her and Shinara stood up on a table.

"I'm useless at speeches but here goes nothing. I'm glad I met this most beautiful person. I never knew what love was until I met Shinara. I never knew the love for a child that my parents had until I had Lee. I'm glad that I can share this with everyone here." Alexa kissed Shinara on the lips and hugged her son.

Everyone cheered and went back to partying.

***

The sky started getting dark and the party was at an end. The guards were taking the decorations down and the people of the kingdom were heading back to their homes.

Shinara and Alexa walked up to Lee's room with him by their side.

"Good night, Lee."

"Good night mother, good night, mum." Lee kissed his mother's cheeks then went to bed.

The girls walked back down the corridor until they came to Logan's room. The girls walked in to see him reading a book.

"Logan me and Shinara have spoken and we want another child. Another boy," Alexa spoke.

"Well then. Take this and it will help. I'll follow you to your room and I'll be there to help. Dorian, come on." Logan handed the girls a potion and with Dorian at their heal, all four headed to the queen's room, ready for another royal child.

***

Three hours had gone by and everyone including Lee, were standing in the queen's room, watching the figure being pulled out from Alexa's stomach.

"I hope it's a boy," Lee whispered to Leonard.

Logan moved the figure to the floor as Dorian stopped his incantation. Everyone watched as the figure stood to their feet. Logan gave the figure some clothes for it to change into.

As the figure turned around, they noticed it was a boy, about the same age as Lee. The boy smiled and looked at his parents and brother.

"Mum, mother, yo bro," the boy said.

Just then a memory wave spread across the whole kingdom making everyone fall onto the ground. But this time it wasn't as bad as the first.

"I bloody hate those things," Jasper said as everyone laughed.

"Felix, Lee, come here," Alexa said as the boys came over to her and Shinara and they group hugged.

Everyone smiled at the sight of the happy family. Everyone went to bed as Alexa smiled knowing exactly what she wanted to do with Felix and Lee tomorrow morning.

***

The next morning, Shinara, Alexa, Lee and Felix were in the throne room having breakfast. Alexa was writing back to Queen Caity.

After she had finished the letter, she handed it to Dorian. Dorian clicked his fingers and the letter was gone.

"She should receive the letter soon your grace," Dorian spoke and then left the room. Alexa turned her attention to her sons.

"Hey boys, want to go for a dragon ride?"

"Hell yeah!" Lee grinned.

"It will be my first time but sure let's go," Felix spoke.

Alexa kissed Shinara lightly on the lips then walked out of the room and to the dragon caves with her two sons behind her.

Once they got down to the bottom, Draco, Spitze and Zepter were just finishing up their breakfast. After they were finished, Draco and Spitze lowered themselves so Alexa and Lee could climb on top of them.

Felix looked at Zepter and smiled.

"Just hold out your hand and let him come to you," Alexa spoke.

Felix held his hand out and Zepter sniffed it. He then lowered himself, allowing him to climb onto his back. All three dragons walked to the edge of the cave.

"To make him fly, say Eitilt." Alexa smiled at her son.

Both Alexa and Lee spoke the word and Draco and Spitze swooped down. Zepter looked at Felix as he spoke. "Eitilt." And Zepter swooped down until he reached the sea and flew off, catching up with his brothers.

***

At Stone Grave, Caity was sat in her throne room while her husband and daughter were out in the gardens. Master Aslan walked into the room holding an envelope.

"Your grace, a reply from Brunuhville," Aslan spoke as he handed her the letter.

Caity opened the letter up and read what it said.

> *Queen Caity,*
>
> *It was nice hearing from you. Yes I am engaged and not only do I have my son prince Lee but also my son Prince Felix. And also as you have heard, I have my three dragons as well.*

> *I will be getting married in a few days' time and I would love for you to attend. I would love your daughter to meet my son Lee.*
>
> *I have sent a letter to Smoke Tower as well inviting them to the wedding.*
>
> *Look forward to seeing you.*
>
> *Queen Alexa.*

Just as Caity finished reading the letter, Ripp and Alana walked into the room.

"What's that?" Ripp questioned.

"A reply from Queen Alexa. She has invited all of us to her wedding and she wants her son Lee to meet you, Alana." Caity smiled at her daughter who was now sat at the table.

"Well then, I will go and pack," Alana spoke.

"We will leave tomorrow," Ripp smiled.

And with that, they all went to their rooms and started to pack for tomorrow's journey.

But what Caity didn't tell Alexa, was that the Lotz family were in fact brother and sisters. Caity planned on breaking this wedding up. Since she found out that Alexa was back home, all her old feelings came back, remembering how much she had loved Alexa's mother and how much Alexa looked like her.

***

At Smoke Tower, Queen Dany and her daughter Gwen were in their rooms packing. King Jofree walked into his and the queen's room to see what she was doing.

"Why are you packing my love?" he questioned.

Dany handed him the letter and he read what it said.

> *Queen Dany,*
>
> *As you may know I am getting married in a few days. I would love if you could join. I want to meet my parents' friends.*
>
> *Queen Caity and her family will be joining too. I would love for your daughter to meet my son Felix.*
>
> *Hope to see you.*
>
> *Queen Alexa.*

Jofree put the letter on the side and smiled. "Looks like we are going to a wedding."

And with that they all started packing.

***

Alexa and her boys arrived back at the dragon caves. As the three dragons landed, they knelt down to let Alexa, Lee and Felix jump off them.

"Well, how did you find that?" Alexa asked Felix.

"That was awesome." Felix smiled as he fist bumped his brother.

"Good I'm pleased. Now you two head up and change and I'll meet you in the throne room."

The two boys ran off up the steps and to their rooms to change while Alexa left her dragons to rest.

As she got up to the castle and to the throne room, Sam and her boys were waiting for her.

"Felix, I would like you to meet the kingdom army and both you and Lee will be doing some training with Sam," Alexa spoke.

Sam bowed slightly and left with the two boys at his side and two other guards behind them.

Shinara walked into the throne room and walked up to her fiancé.

"Did you invite the two families?" Shinara questioned.

"Yes, they should be arriving tomorrow hopefully. Then our wedding is the day after," Alexa spoke as she kissed Shinara.

Alexa walked up to one of the guards and handed him some letters. "Could you make sure everyone in the kingdom gets one of these?"

The guard nodded and walked off.

Alexa and Shinara walked out into the castle gardens and saw people putting decorations up for the wedding, even though it was getting dark. They walked over to the training yard to see that their sons were just finishing up there training. Sam noticed that the boys' parents were watching them and hinted for the boys to go over to them. The boys ran over to their parents and smiled.

"Hey boys, how was training?" Alexa spoke.

"It was fun!" Lee spoke.

"I enjoyed it!" Felix smiled.

They all walked back into the castle and went to their own rooms, readying for tomorrow's visitors.

***

The next day, Alexa and Shinara were in the throne room, waiting for their boys to join them. It was only midday, but the boys were with the dragons, having some bonding time.

A few days ago, Alexa had a fourth throne made for Felix, the same as Lee's but he had all the jewels on the dragon.

Lee and Felix finally joined Alexa and Shinara and sat down on their thrones, just in time. The throne room doors opened and Alexa stood. She watched as her visitors walked in and stood before her and her family.

"Alexa Snow, wow how you have grown to be such a beautiful woman," Caity spoke as she walked up to Alexa and hugged her.

"It's so good to see you, Alexa," Ripp spoke and shook Alexa's hand.

"This is our daughter, Alana," Caity spoke as Alana walked up to Alexa.

"It's nice to finally meet you," The girl spoke as she bowed slightly.

"No need to bow, Alana. You're a friend," Alexa spoke.

The Lotz moved aside so the Clarke's could see Alexa.

"Alexa, it's so good to see you again," Dany spoke.

"Likewise, you are still beautiful as ever, like your mother," Jofree said smiling. "This is our daughters, Gwen and Navona."

Gwen and Navona walked forward and just smiled.

"It's so nice for you to be here. This is my soon to be wife, Shinara," Alexa began. Shinara walked forward and smiled. "And these are my two sons, Lee and Felix," Alexa said as the two boys walked up to their parents.

"It's nice to meet you. It's nice to meet you Alana, Gwen, Navona," Lee spoke as he kissed each of the girl's hands, making them blush.

"It's great to meet you too," Felix spoke, mirroring his brother's actions.

"Right, you must be tired after your journey. Sam and his guards will show you to your rooms so you can unpack. I'll meet you guys here when you are finished. I have some best man and ring bearing talking to do with my sons," Alexa spoke.

Sam and three of his guards led the Lotz and Clarke's to their rooms.

Shinara kissed Alexa on the cheek and smiled. "I'm going to see Leonard and the girls. I want to make sure everything is perfect."

"Okay, my love."

And Shinara left to see how her side of the wedding was doing. Alexa turned her attention to the boys.

"Right. Time to talk about the wedding."

***

Shinara was sat with Leonard, Aria and Elsie in the gardens, discussing the wedding.

"So when Leo walks you down the middle of the throne room, we follow behind until we get to the steps then we stand aside?" Elsie questioned.

"Yes. Then Aria, you will hold my flowers."

"Of course. I give them back to you when you have kissed your bride," Aria smirked making everyone laugh.

"Yes, that's it."

***

Spark was walking around the village when he saw Ray in his shop. He walked into the shop and smiled.

"Ray, isn't it?"

"Yes, who's asking?" Ray questioned.

"My name is Spark. I'm new around here. What's with all the decorations?" Spark began.

"The Queen is getting married tomorrow. We have visitors here as well, so if you don't mind, I need you to leave as I am quite busy," Ray spat as he carried on making the rings for tomorrow's big day.

Spark looked around the shop and found a notebook. He looked around to see if the boy was looking then opened it up. He flicked through the pages, trying to find something useful when he came across a page that had all the secret entrances to the castle. He smirked. Taking a plain sheet of paper and placing it to the side of the notebook, he placed his hand over the top of the notebook page and muttered an incantation. Just as he finished the incantation, the secret passageways appeared on the plain sheet of paper. He closed the book, placing it back in the spot where he found it and walked out of the shop smirking. As he exited out into the kingdom village, he clicked his fingers and the paper was gone.

"There won't be a wedding when Link is done here," he said to himself and walked off to check out the secret passageways.

But what he didn't realise was that Ray had heard everything he had just said.

***

Link walked into his room to see a piece of paper on his bed. He picked it up and smirked.

"What is it?" Shadow questioned.

"It's all the secret passageways to get into the castle. I will stop this wedding and that throne will be mine," Link smirked.

***

Ray ran to the castle and looked for Lee. He ran into the throne room to see Lee with his mother and brother.

"Your grace. This is urgent."

"What is it, Ray?" Alexa questioned.

"Someone named Spark is here in the kingdom. He's working for Link. They are going to kill you tomorrow."

"SAM," Alexa shouted.

Sam teleported into the throne room.

"Yes, your grace?"

"Look for someone named Spark. He's working with my brother. Make sure you capture him and bring him to me."

And with that, Sam teleported out of the castle. He gathered his army in hope to find Spark.

"Thank you for telling me, Ray. You are definitely amazing. How are you doing with the rings?" Alexa spoke.

"All finished. I also did something a bit extra for you. No need for money, this was just from the kindness of my heart." Ray handed the rings over and then showed Felix a golden dragon crown.

"It's the same as your mother's and brother's. This is what I've been working on Felix."

Ray handed Felix the crown and Felix placed it on his head. "Thank you, Ray. It means a lot." The boys fist bumped and Ray walked out with Lee and Felix at his side, followed by three guards.

***

Later that day, everyone was in the Throne room, talking and drinking. That was until Sam and his army came walking in with Spark, his wrists in chains.

"Your grace, we found him," Sam spoke as he threw the boy forward, causing the chains to rattle.

Alexa walked up to him and Smirked. "So you're the one helping my brother out? Well unfortunately for you, that will be no more. What did he have with him?"

"Just this gold. He says Link asked him to pay Ray to help him out. Ray never did," Sam spoke.

"I'm glad. You really are a true friend Ray. Sam, give Ray the bags of gold. I will pay him for being so loyal. And for you Spark. I think I have the right thing in mind for you," Alexa smirked.

Alexa walked out of the throne room and out to the courtyard with everyone following behind her. Sam and his guards placed Spark in the centre of the yard.

"Boys I need you," Alexa spoke in her mind and suddenly the sound of screeching was heard across the whole kingdom.

Draco, Spitze and Zepter landed next to Alexa and screeched.

"Spark, for being on my brother's side and for trying to make a loyal friend betray me, I sentence you to death," Alexa spoke.

The dragons were ready, they just waited for their dragon lord to give the command. Everything went silent for a while until *"Brennen."*

As Alexa gave the command, all three dragons burned Spark. Caity walked up to Alexa and placed a hand on her shoulder.

"It's nice to see you do that. Your parents would be proud."

The dragons stopped their fire after a while and everyone watched in silence.

"Make sure every secret passageway around the castle and the kingdom is completely blocked off from him and have guards there twenty-four seven. I'm not having this day ruined for us," Alexa commanded Sam.

Sam went off and did as he was commanded. All the guards and the army blocked off all the passageways and had twenty guards guarding them.

After Spark was burnt to a crisp, the dragon's went back to the cave and everyone went back into the castle.

Once they were back in the throne room and sat down, Caity lifted her glass up and dinged it with her ring.

"Can I have everyone's attention please," Caity began and the whole room went silent. She looked at Alexa and continued with her speech. "If it wasn't for Alexa being like her parents, none of us would be safe. She has an amazing family and three fantastic dragons. All I want to say is Chun lá bainise Dragon Lord agus Snow!"

Everyone raised their glasses and in unison, spoke "Chun lá bainise Dragon Lord agus Snow!"

Alexa and Caity looked at each other and slightly nodded their heads. Everyone drank their wine and started to talk again. Alexa and Shinara watched as Lee was getting along with Alana and Felix with Gwen.

"One day, they will be just like us," Shinara spoke as she placed a hand on her fiancé's hand.

"That they will, that they will." Alexa smiled and kissed Shinara tenderly on the lips.

As she pulled away, she raised her glass slightly. "To our wedding day."

"To our wedding day."

And they tapped their glasses together and drank their wine.

Alexa and Shinara sat back down, watching as everyone enjoyed themselves. Alexa thought of her dragons and decided to talk to Smok through her thoughts.

"You know what's going on, right Smok?"

"I do. I'll do everything I can to protect you and this kingdom."

"Thank you. I know my dragons can look after themselves but protect them please. They are my babies."

"With all my life Alexa Snow."

Alexa came back into the real world and sighed. *"I hope nothing ruins my perfect day."*

5

The Royal Wedding

After the long evening of everyone talking and getting drunk, everyone started to head to their rooms as they had to be up early for the royal wedding tomorrow.

Alexa and Shinara put their boys to bed while Ripp, Dany and Jofree put their daughters to bed and followed behind them. Shinara and Alexa were just about to head to bed as well until someone tapped Alexa on the shoulder. She spun around to see that it was Caity.

"Sorry Alexa, I didn't mean to make you jump, I just needed to talk to you for a second."

"Of course. Love I will be back shortly." Alexa kissed Shinara then walked off with Caity.

They sat down by the dragon cave door, knowing they won't get disturbed.

"What's wrong, Caity?" Alexa questioned.

"I should have written it in the letter but I wanted you to hear it. Have you noticed why your boys won't take an interested in Alana?"

"They have been playing games with her but they don't act the way they do with the other girls, why?"

Caity hesitated then replied. "Your mother had a sister. She was there when you were born."

There was a silence. Until Caity started to talk again. "I'm your aunt, Alexa. Why do you think I have been eager to meet you?"

"After all this time, I finally get to meet someone who is connected to me. That would explain my boys and your daughter."

Alexa smiled at the thought of having someone who was family.

"But then you deserve this crown, not me," Alexa stated.

"No alexa, you're the queen. I married into the Lotz family, I am a Lotz now. You are still a Snow."

Alexa took the time to take all of this in.

After a while she smiled then looked at Caity.

"It's nice to have more family." Alexa hugged Caity and they stood up.

"We better head to bed. It's your big day tomorrow," Caity spoke as she rested a hand on her shoulder.

Both the women stood up and walked back to their rooms. Before they could bid each other good night, Caity stopped Alexa in her tracks.

"I am also very sorry to hear about your friend you lost. I know how hard that must be to still live with that in your mind."

"Thank you."

They bid their good nights and closed their doors behind them.

"What did she want to tell you?" Shinara questioned, making Alexa jump.

Alexa walked over to the bed and snuggled up to Shinara.

"Caity is my mum's sister. She's my aunt."

"That's amazing. But why do you look so glum?" Shinara questioned.

"Yeah. It's just, I don't remember my mother telling me she had a sister, and how would she know about Lena? She couldn't possibly know," Alexa spoke as she held onto her necklace.

"I'm not sure. It doesn't makc sense."

Both of the girls cuddled up in bed and drifted off to sleep, Shinara thinking about tomorrow and Alexa thinking about who this woman must be and getting married.

***

The next morning, everyone was up early. Shinara was rushed off to get changed with Logan and Alexa was changing with Dorian.

Alexa put on an electric blue two piece female suit with a black shirt that she always wore in the same style but with the sleeves covering her hands, enough to show just her fingers, that was accompanied with a belt around her waist tight enough that the shirt hung slightly baggy and black skinny jeans that were accompanied by a pair of black smart shoes and Dorian put her hair the way she had it for her coronation. Two plaits from both sides of her hair that were joined in the middle by dragon beads and a braid hanging behind her ear, decorated in dragon beads. She placed her crown on top of her head and smiled.

There was a knock at the door and Dorian walked over to it, opening it to reveal Caity in a short black dress with an electric blue pattern over it and black heels.

"You look stunning, Alexa," she smiled.

"Thank you, so do you," Alexa spoke as she hugged her so-called aunt. "I can't wait to see what Shinara looks like."

Suddenly Lee and Felix walked in with Gwen and Navona attached to their arms.

Both the boys were wearing electric blue tuxedos with black ties and shoes, both wearing their crowns.

The girls were wearing red dresses with black dragons over them and black heels.

"Wow mother you look beautiful," Lee spoke.

"I'll second that," Felix said.

Alana walked in behind the boys and looked at Alexa.

Alana was wearing the same dress and shoes as her mother and had her hair the same as Alexa's.

"Wow Alexa, you look stunning."

"You got that right." Alexa smirked, acting slightly big headed.

The boys looked at Alexa and smirked. "Are you ready?"

"Yeah. Let's get married."

***

Shinara had just finished getting changed and Logan was just finishing off her hair. She was wearing a short, strapless electric blue dress with black frills at the bottom of it and black heels. Logan had put her hair half up half down and the half up was put into a plait decorated in Elven beads.

Shinara got up and looked at herself. "Wow, thank you Logan."

Logan smiled. Elsie and Aria rushed through the door and stood there in awe.

Both the girls were wearing black dresses with electric blue dragons over them with black heels.

"You're stunning, Shinara," they both said in unison.

"Thank you, girls," Shinara laughed.

Leonard walked through the door and smiled.

He was wearing a two-piece black suit with a electric blue shirt and blue shoes.

"Your parents would be proud of you," he said and hugged Shinara.

"Are you ready?"

"Yeah."

***

Link and Shadow had made it to the kingdom walls. The gates were closed, locked and guarded. They both split up to look for the secret passageways and see if they could get into the castle and stop the wedding.

Shinara went to the right of the walls and with every passageway she found, they were blocked with enchantments.

Link went to the left and found the same issue as Shadow. They met back up and thought of another way into the kingdom.

"Why not teleport in? Surly we can do that?" Shadow said.

"You might be on to something."

Link and Shadow readied themselves and Link clicked his fingers hoping they would have teleported into the kingdom but failed. They were still standing on the opposite side of the wall. They tried again but again failing in getting into the kingdom.

"How is this possible?" Link spat.

"Climb the wall. We should be able to get over," Shadow replied.

"You better be right."

Link and Shadow started to climb the wall, feeling hopeful that they will get into the kingdom. They got halfway up the wall and smiled at each other.

"Not much further," Link spoke.

They carried on climbing until an energy wave hit them, making them let go of the wall and be flung backwards, hitting their backs against a tree and falling to the ground.

Link and Shadow struggled to stand to their feet but when they did, Link grabbed Shadow by her throat and pinned her against a tree.

"WHAT THE HELL WAS THAT?!" he shouted in Shadow's face, spitting slightly.

"I-don't-know. I-can't-breathe," Shadow spoke, trying to catch her breath.

Link removed his hand, making Shadow fall to the ground with a thump. Link and Shadow saw two guards coming and made a run for it.

"I will get my chance. Even if it's without you," Link shot at

Shadow.

They carried on running until they returned to the cave.

"Link where are you going?" Shadow questioned as Link walked away from her.

"Leave me be."

***

Alexa was standing by her throne with Logan in front of her, Lee holding the rings and Felix holding Alexa's vows. Caity, Ripp and Alana were standing behind the boys along with Dorian.

The throne room looked amazing with all the wedding decorations. There were red, black and electric blue roses dotted around the walls along with wedding banners in the same colours. The thrones had black, electric blue and red cloths hanging over them and the throne room doors had black, red and electric blue ribbons on them.

Everyone in the kingdom was sat and standing in the throne room, talking to one another, waiting for Shinara to come in.

Everyone went silent as music started to play as the throne room doors opened, revealing Shinara attached to Leonard's arm.

Shinara and Leonard started to walk down the middle of everyone with Elsie and Aria at their heal. Everyone smiled and words of "she's beautiful" and "Alexa is so lucky" filled the room. Alexa watched as her soon to be wife walked towards her smiling.

Shinara finally reached Alexa and she smiled. Shinara and Leonard exchanged a smile and a kiss on the cheek before he and the two girls stood at Shinara's side as she handed Aria her flowers.

"Wow you look beautiful," Alexa grinned.

"As do you."

Alexa and Shinara held each other's hands as Logan began the ceremony.

"Ladies and gentlemen, we are gathered here today to witness the marriage of Queen Alexa Snow, The Dragon Lord and Shinara Ondovir, The Ice Elf. Now before these two women exchanged their vows, if anyone wishes that these two women do not get married, speak now or forever hold your peace," Logan spoke.

"Well, are you going to say anything?" Rip muttered to Caity.

"Huh? What did you say?" Caity questioned.

Rip rolled his eyes and looked back up to watch the ceremony.

The whole room was silent so Logan carried on.

"Alexa, your vows."

Alexa went to take her vows from Felix but then took her hand away and looked at Shinara.

"Shinara, words can't even explain my love for you. Before I met you, I never knew how to love, man I didn't even know what love was. Then you walked into my life and everything changed. You made me feel love again and I'm happy I fell in love with you. You took down my walls, which is hard to do, trust me, after losing Lena, Leonard knows how hard it's been for me. We have two handsome boys and three amazing dragons. I'm just happy to finally call you my wife." Alexa smiled as she saw a tear roll down Shinara's cheek.

"Shinara, your vows."

Shinara looked at Alexa and smiled. "When I first met you I was in a dark place, I was struggling with my life and everything was hard then I finally got to know you a bit more, I fell in love with you, the good side and the bad. There have been girls before you and nothing made me feel happy and then you came around, made me fall in love, brought dragons into my life and two beautiful boys. I can't wait to be Mrs Snow."

They both looked at Logan and smiled.

"Do you have the rings?" Logan spoke to Lee.

Lee walked up and gave Alexa Shinara's ring and Shinara Alexa's ring.

"Alexa Repeat after me, I Alexa Snow, the dragon lord, swear to protect and love you for the rest of my life."

"I Alexa Snow, a tiarna Dragon, swear chun tú a chosaint agus grá duit don chuid eile de mo shaol," Alexa spoke as she placed the ring on Shinara's ring finger.

"And Shinara, repeat after me, I Shinara Ondovir, swear to protect and love you for the rest of my life and sit by your side to protect this kingdom."

"I Shinara Ondovir, mhionnaím tú a chosaint agus grá duit don chuid eile de mo shaol agus suí le do thaobh chun an ríocht seo a chosaint," Shinara spoke as she placed the ring on Alexa's ring finger.

"Now I pronounce you wife and wife, you may kiss your bride," Logan spoke.

Alexa and Shinara shared a passionate kiss as everyone cheered.

"The Queens of Brunuhville, Queen Alexa Snow and Queen Shinara Snow. Long live the queen's," Logan spoke and everyone in the room began to chant "long live the queens."

The queen's walked hand in hand down the middle of the room while everyone cheered. They got to the throne room doors and Alexa tilted Shinara back and kissed her, making everyone cheer louder.

***

The wedding after party was going amazingly. The music was great, everyone was drinking, eating, having a laugh. Everyone was having a good time. There were a lot of "congratulations" and "I'm so happy for you" being said to the newly wedded couple.

The castle gardens looked beautiful with all the wedding decorations. There were black, red and electric blue canopies dotted here and there, some with food under them, some with drinks under them, some with people under them talking and having fun and there was one empty one which was left for the wedding cake.

Alexa and Shinara were talking to their group of friends that they call "family" when they heard the music stop and someone tapping their glass.

Everyone turned around to see Caity, Aria and Elsie standing on a table smiling.

"FIRST DANCE! FIRST DANCE! FIRST DANCE!" they chanted in unison.

Alexa and Shinara laughed and walked over to the centre of the castle gardens where everyone left a space for anyone to dance in. Shinara put her arms around Alexa's neck and Alexa put her hands on Shinara's hips. The music played and the women swayed along.

Everyone was watching. People smiling, people looking at them in awe. Everyone was happy that the Snow's daughter is home and is finally happy.

Shinara and Alexa both looked into each other's blue eyes deeply.

"So, what's it like to be Mrs Snow?" Alexa smiled.

"Amazing. I'm just so happy that I'm with you." Shinara kissed Alexa and they smiled into the kiss.

Alexa pulled away and looked down with a tear in her eye.

"She's looking down on you love. She would never miss this for anything," Shinara spoke as if she could read Alexa's mind.

It felt like they were dancing forever. Neither one of them wanted this moment to end. They were both happy finally.

The music stopped, making both girls come back to the real world. The turned to face where their family was to see Lee, Felix, Logan and Dorian bringing the wedding cake out.

They placed it down on one of the tables and stood either side of it. Alexa and Shinara walked up to the cake and smiled.

The cake had five layers. Three electric blue, one red and one black. Around the cake, on the electric blue layers, there were red dragon decorations glued on with icing, on the black layer, there were electric blue dragon decorations glued on and on the red layer, there were black dragon decorations glued on. On top of the cake there were two cake ornaments standing together. There was a Dragon Lord Queen in the same outfit as Alexa standing with its arm around an Elven Queen that was wearing the same outfit as Shinara.

The women smiled at each other and walked up to Logan. At this point, everyone in the kingdom was standing or sitting around the canopy, waiting for the queens to cut their cake.

Logan handed Alexa a cake knife that had "die Drachen Lord und der Elfenkönigin" written on it. The women smiled and turned towards the cake. Alexa stood behind Shinara with her arms around her waist holding the knife and resting her head on her wife's shoulder while Shinara held her arms out, holding Alexa's hands around the knife.

They both lowered the knife, smiling at each other as they cut into the cake. Everyone cheered and Logan and Dorian handed everyone a slice.

The music started playing again and loads of people went into the centre of the gardens to dance. The queen's watched as Lee was dancing with Navona, Felix with Gwen, Caity with Ripp and Dany with Jofree. Everyone looked happy.

Alexa noticed Alana sat watching everyone looking lost and sad. Alexa walked over to Ray and placed a hand on his arm.

"Would you be okay to dance with Alana? She looks a little down," Alexa stated.

Ray smiled and walked over to Alana. He held out his hand and Alana took it with a smile as the boy led them both to the dance area.

"That was sweet of you," Shinara said as she walked up to her wife and hugged her.

"Not really. I just gave Ray a nudge in the right direction."

"What do you mean?"

Alexa looked at Shinara and smiled. "Ray hasn't been able to keep his eyes off of Alana. He likes her but too nervous to make the first move, so I helped."

Both women smiled as they watched everyone have a good time while they drank wine and cuddled.

***

The party was coming to an end. Most people had already gone back to their homes and gone to bed after getting wasted from all of the alcohol. The people that were left in the gardens were everyone who lived and were staying in the castle.

Everyone that was left was laying down on the floor, looking up at the beautiful night sky as the stars shimmered and the moon glistened. Alexa and Shinara didn't want this day to end. Nothing was ever going to come between these two.

Caity, Alana and Ripp stood to their feet and walked over to Alexa.

"We are going to head to bed. Congratulations to you both. I'm happy for you," Caity said as she hugged Shinara and then Alexa.

"Your parents and Lena would be so happy of you."

"Yeah, I know. I just wish they were here," Alexa said as she pulled away.

Caity saw the sadness fill Alexa's eyes and felt bad for her. She knew how much the girl she knew, loved her parents and best friend, but she won't ever see them again.

Caity kissed Alexa's cheek and then walked into the castle and straight to bed. Shortly after, Dany, Jofree, Navona and Gwen bid their good nights and went to bed as well.

Leonard walked up to Alexa and sat down next to her.

"Where has Aria and Elsie gone?" Shinara questioned.

"To bed. They had too much to drink," Leonard laughed.

There was a comfortable silence that filled the air as everyone that was still out, watched the stars.

After a while, they all stood to their feet and walked into the castle and to their rooms. The women bid their sons and friend good night and they all entered their rooms.

Alexa and Shinara snuggled down in bed and relaxed.

"I love you Mrs Snow," Alexa muttered.

"I love you too. I could get used to this," Shinara spoke.

"What? Mrs Snow," Alexa whispered the last part into Shinara's ear.

"Hmm," was all Shinara could manage as she found herself consumed by sleep. It wasn't soon after that Alexa followed the same path.

***

The next morning, Lee, Felix and Alexa were out with the dragons after saying their goodbyes and thank yous to the Clarke family. Smok had joined them as Alexa had told him about what Draco has been doing.

Lee and Felix were up front with Spitze and Zepter while Alexa, Draco and Smok hung back to talk.

"Your boys are extremely gifted, like you Alexa," Smok spoke.

"What do you mean?" Alexa questioned.

"Dragon riders. Just like you, when they are crowned princes of Brunuhville, they will be gifted three dragons."

Alexa smiled as she remembered the words Smok spoke and she looked at her boys.

"Come on boys, time to head back," Alexa shouted.

The boys turned around and smirked at their mother.

"Race you home!" the boys shouted in unison.

Suddenly Alexa was whipped by wind as her two boys flew past her. Draco and Smok flew after them as fast as they could. The boys were laughing until Alexa flew past them.

"Come on, slow coaches," Alexa shouted back as the three dragons and her boys started to fly faster.

They got back to the cave and the dragons landed. Draco, Spitze and Zepter lowered themselves so Alexa, Lee and Felix could climb down. As they got off of the dragon's, they flew back out for their breakfast.

"Good morning beautiful."

Alexa turned around and saw Shinara smiling at her.

"Good morning." Alexa walked up to her wife and kissed her.

"Ewe, get a room," Lee spoke.

The women pulled away from each other and smiled.

"Go upstairs and find Alana, I'm sure she'd want to spend time with her family," Alexa spoke, making the boys run up the steps to the castle.

"You haven't told them that she might be lying to you guys?" Shinara questioned.

"No, I know our boys will find a way of figuring this all out. But for now, where were we?" Alexa smirked as she turned to Shinara and kissed her again.

***

As the boys got up to the castle, they walked into Alana's room but she was nowhere to be seen.

"Where is she?" Lee spoke.

"I don't know. Maybe if we split up, we can look for her," Felix spoke.

They boys existed the room and split up to go and find Alana.

Lee went out into the kingdom gardens while Felix looked around the castle.

Felix looked in every room within the castle and found no trace of Alana. He walked into the throne room to see Shinara and Leonard talking.

"Mum, uncle Leo, have you seen Alana?"

"The last I saw her she was in the gardens. Have you tried there?" Leonard spoke.

"No but Lee is out there. I'll go and find him and give him a hand. Thank you, guys," Felix spoke as he ran off out into the gardens to find his brother.

When he got out into the gardens, he saw Lee talking to Caity. He walked over to his brother and great aunt and smiled.

"Hey, have you found Alana?" Lee questioned.

"No, have you?"

"No but I was just asking aunt Caity if she knew," Lee smiled between his great aunt and brother.

Felix glanced at Caity, noticing a 'what have I done look' plastered on her face. Caity noticed Felix looking and changed her expression. She smiled at Felix as he returned it with a sarcastic smile.

"Alana is by the water fountain over there." Caity pointed in the direction and the boys saw Alana sat on the edge of the fountain.

The boys walked off in the direction of Alana.

"There's something off with Caity," Felix announced.

"What do you mean?" Lee questioned.

"Mother never told us her mum had a sister and then suddenly out of the blue, Caity walks in saying she's family."

"Yeah, that doesn't seem right. Let's ask Alana," Lee spoke.

"Yeah, if she tells us the truth," Felix muttered to himself as they approached the girl.

"Hey boys, how are you both?" Alana spoke as she smiled at the boys.

"Fine, how are you?" Lee asked.

Felix elbowed his brother in the side, causing him to get a 'ouch' and 'sorry look'.

Alana noticed this and looked confused.

"We need to ask you something and you have to tell us the truth," Felix spoke.

Alana nodded her head and Felix questioned her.

"You aren't our cousin, are you? Caity isn't mother's aunt, is she?"

Alana swallowed hard. She hesitated at first but then answered.

"No, she isn't and I'm not your cousin."

"They why lie to us?" Lee spat, angry at finding out the truth.

"It was Caity's idea. I just went along with it. Ripp and Caity are my brother and sister."

The boys gasped at what was just said.

"Then why did you come here?" Felix shot as he clenched his fists.

"Caity likes your mum. Like a lot and she wanted to meet her and get close." Alana lowered her head, feeling ashamed of what her older siblings have done.

"This is sick," Lee spat.

"All this time mother was thinking she had a long-lost aunt and the thing that made me question that was she had never even mentioned her mum having a sister," Felix said.

"I know and I'm sorry."

"Forget the apology. Mother is happy and she is married to our mum," Felix spat.

The boys started to walk away when they heard Alana call out.

"Tell me one thing, why did you lie to mother?" Lee spoke.

"I don't know. Don't tell your mum, please."

"No promises." And the boys carried on walking leaving Alana destroyed by what she had made this family feel.

***

Alexa and Aria were in the throne room, talking about how amazing it is that Alexa finally has some family left that connects her to her mum.

"But I don't even remember having an aunt," Alexa spoke.

"Yeah, but you were young don't forget, so you may not have even met her." Aria smiled.

"Aria, she said I had met her. If I had, why would I have forgotten her?" Alexa questioned. Aria shrugged her shoulders, not knowing what to say.

Just then, Lee and Felix walked into the throne room to see Alexa talking to Aria.

"Mother could we talk to you please?" Felix questioned, bringing his mother's attention to him and his brother.

"Of course." Alexa walked over to her boys and smiled. "What is it?"

Lee hesitated at first but then began. "Caity isn't your aunt. We just found out."

"What do you mean?" Alexa's smile faded.

"When they came for the wedding, I had my suspicions as you had never mentioned having an aunt or your parents having any siblings. When we found Alana, I questioned her about this," Felix began. He stayed quiet for a little bit trying to figure out how to break the news to his mum.

"Well, Caity isn't your aunt. Alana said that Caity wanted to get close to you as she has strong feelings for you. And the three of them are brother and sisters."

Alexa was in shock but anger grew in her eyes. "Where is Caity right now?"

"The last we saw her she was heading back into the castle, to her room," Lee spoke.

Alexa walked out of the throne room leaving her boys alone. She made her way down the hallway until she stopped in front of Caity's door. Alexa knocked and after a few short seconds, the door opened, revealing Caity's figure.

"Alexa, What's Wrong?" Caity questioned, seeing the anger in the woman's eyes.

Alexa barged into the room and turned around to face Caity.

"You lied to me! Here I am, thinking my mum had a sister but she never did!" Alexa spat.

"Alexa, calm down, it's not like that."

"What is it like? You lied to me and my family! And my boys found out from your sister!"

Caity lowered her head, tears threatening her eyes.

"And you know I am happy! Why come here just for me to find out that you have feelings for me?"

"I'm sorry Alexa. I…"

"Don't even finish that sentence. I want you and your family gone by tonight." And with that, Alexa walked out of the room, leaving Caity crying and packing her family's belongings.

Alexa walked back down the hallway to the throne room and saw her two boys on their thrones. Alexa walked up the steps to her throne and smiled at the boys.

"Thank you for letting me know about Caity. I don't know what would of happened if you didn't."

"Well let's just say you and mum wouldn't be happy." Lee smiled, giving his mother's hand a squeeze.

"What did I do to deserve such amazing sons?"

"I know, we are awesome," Felix smirked, making his brother and mother laugh.

***

Alexa and her boys spent the last few hours joking and laughing, which was great in Alexa's mind as it was taking her thoughts away from the truth that she had been told.

Shinara walked into the throne room, seeing her wife and sons having fun.

"Hey love, Caity said she is leaving."

And there it was, the thoughts falling back to the front of Alexa's mind. Alexa sighed and her and the boys got up and walked towards Shinara.

"Better say goodbye then." And with that, the four of them walked out of the castle to bid their farewells to their guests.

As they got to the castle gates, Caity, Ripp and Alana were standing there looking upset and disappointed in themselves.

Alexa walked up to Caity and smiled.

"Thank you for coming but next time tell me the truth."

Alexa hugged Caity and she smiled.

"Does that mean you forgive me?" Caity questioned.

"Not in the slightest." Alexa pulled away and continued. "Stay in touch."

Everyone said their goodbyes and the Lotz siblings clicked their fingers and they were gone.

***

When Caity and her siblings got back to their castle, Caity went straight to her room and cried. Ripp walked in seeing his sister curled up in a ball on her bed, crying her eyes out.

"What's wrong?" Ripp spoke as he walked over to the bed and sat down.

Caity sat up and looked at her brother. "Alana told Alexa's boys about us and Alexa doesn't even want to know me."

"Well, she is married and you wanted to break that up."

"You agreed on this!" Caity spat.

"Actually, I recall myself saying "do what you want."

Ripp moved slightly so Caity could cry into his lap.

"You do realise YOU brought this on yourself, right?" Ripp asked.

"Yeah, I know."

***

Link and Shadow were sat in the forest, looking through books about the mortal world. For the last couple of days, both the dark elves had been reading books and looking at visions of what the mortal world looked like and been wondering what it would be like to live there.

Link turned over the page of the book he was reading and saw a picture of Buckingham Palace.

"Wow I like the look of this place," Link announced.

"Damn it is nice," Shadow spoke as she leaned over to look at the picture.

"The queen of the mortal world lives in that place." Link's eyes sparkled and he noticed the same look in his friend's eyes. "Are you thinking what I'm thinking?"

"Take over the mortal world."

"Yes, but we need a plan."

"What do you mean a plan?" Shadow asked.

"We can't just go to the mortal world. We need to figure out how to."

***

A few hours had passed and Link and Shadow had finally come up with a plan.

"So what we are going to do is teleport to the mortal world. We will then get a place together so we can get ourselves on our way and we will get jobs for the money. Once we have settled in and everyone thinks we are normal, we will take over by kidnapping the queen and her guards, lock her up and the throne will be ours," Link stated their plan.

Shadow smiled at the plan.

"I just need to do one more thing," Link spoke as he started to write a letter.

"Who is that to?"

"There is someone I know who lives in the mortal world that is like us. I'm going to ask him for help."

Link carried on writing the letter then once he was finished, he read it over to make sure it was right.

> *Brook Lincoln,*
>
> *It's been a while. Me and my companion as wanting to come to the mortal world and we are planning on teleporting.*
>
> *I have been thinking about time travel but I am consulting in you so we can meet at the right place and time.*
>
> *Talk soon. Link.*

After he had read the letter and was happy with it, he clicked his fingers and the letter was gone.

"What do we do now?" Shadow questioned.

"We sit and wait for the reply."

***

1869 - Victorian London

Victorian London, not the best place to live within but neither was the rest of the world. Victoria crowned queen, the streets were full of homeless people, men were out working, women were at home looking after the kids and working at home. Some places were richer than others, some were poorer. But there was no sign of magic anywhere. All the magical folk acted like normal mortals and kept their magic to themselves.

Down a dark, winding, creepy street, there was a little, tilted, brick shack right at the end and in the middle of the dead end. There was two huge gaps between the shack and the other houses. It was like the mortals knew what was lying inside the creepy building.

Inside the shack was a different story. From the outside it looked like it had been there for centuries. Like it had been burned and rebuilt. But the inside, in the living room there was a lovely fireplace with a fire burning, a coffee table in front of it with a sofa, a chair and a rocking chair.

There were three rooms that led off from the living room. To the right there was a bedroom and a bathroom. The bedroom was big. It had a king size bed with two pillows and a cotton cover along with a wardrobe, chest of draws that were both made out of wood and two oil lamps either side of the bed.

The bathroom was standard. There was a white bathtub, sink and toilet in there.

On the left of the living room there was the kitchen. There was a sink, fridge and a stove.

Everything in the shack looked from the future apart from the oil lamps.

All of a sudden, a folded sheet of paper appeared out of nowhere and floated down onto the coffee table with the name 'Brook Lincoln' written on the front of it.

The door to the shack opened and a tall, masculine figure walked through.

As the figure walked in, he closed the door behind him and as he walked through the room, he clicked his fingers and the oil lamps began to burn.

"Ah, that is better. A bit of light after the dark, rainy day I have had."

The man was wearing a white shirt with a red tie and a brown over coat on top along with black, skinny work trousers with black smart boots.

He walked over to the coffee table and noticed the sheet of paper. He picked it up, unfolded it, sat down on the sofa and began to read.

***

Brook Lincoln had short, spiked, blonde hair with blue eyes. He was the world's greatest and most well-known warlock, in the mortal world and in the magical world.

Brook is from Brunuhville but five years ago he had time travelled to 1869 Victorian London to start a new life. He wanted to understand the mortals and how their world works. He kept his powers to himself so war didn't break loose within the mortal world as the mortals are afraid of magic. The mortal world was known for executing magical types as they are scared of what they didn't know.

When Brook was twenty-one, he was turned into an immortal warlock by a blood curse that was caused by the blood moon. Brook was the one that told Link that he was a dark elf and the one that told Alexa that she was a witch.

But Brook wasn't the only magical being in 1869.

***

After reading the letter, he decided to write one back.

> *Link,*
>
> *It has been a while. I'm glad you got in contact with me.*
>
> *As you know, time travel comes with a price. When you come to the mortal world, you can not use your magic. The mortals are scared and they have a history of murdering us magical types if they see us use magic.*
>
> *I have also sent you the incantation for you and your friend to time travel.*
>
> *You will be travelling to 1869, Victorian London. I will have a place set up for you two and will have a job for you both.*
>
> *My partner Constantine will be with me when you arrive.*
>
> *Look forward to seeing you.*
>
> *Brook.*

Brook folded up the incantation along with the letter, clicked his fingers and the letter was gone.

Just then, Constantine walked into the shack and closed the door behind him. He noticed the books on the coffee table and smirked at Brook as the blonde turned around and smiled at him.

"Let me guess, one of your friends is going to be time travelling her and we have work to do?" the man spoke.

"Yes, we do."

The men walked out of the shack and headed out for work as they knew it would be at least a few days to a week until Link and Shadow arrived, so they didn't have to start on any work for their friends anytime soon.

Constantine was born in 1839 in Victorian London. When he

reached twenty-one, he also was turned into an immortal warlock. Unlike Brook, he was born into a world that every mortal feared magic. When he turned sixteen, he was told that he had magic but he had to keep it under control.

In Victorian London, there was a building that looked abandoned by the mortals but to the magical types, it was a school for magic.

There were a lot of buildings within London that look like this but were clocked with magic so the mortals didn't figure out that there were magical types living among them.

Constantine also wore the same outfit as Brook but had jet black, spiked hair with red eyes. Unlike the other warlocks that could change their eyes when they did an incantation, Constantine could change his eyes whenever he wanted to. He mostly did that when he was around the mortals.

Brook and Constantine worked at a magical police department close to where they lived. A lot of magical folks liked to show their powers off and scare the mortals so the two men would jump in, erase the memories from the mortals and take the magical folk into custody.

***

A couple of days later, Link had received the letter and incantation from Brook.

Him and Shadow were sat in his room drawing out the symbols they needed to make this incantation work.

Link tossed the letter aside and finished the drawing. He looked at the incantation and then handed it to Shadow.

"Are you sure we can do this?" Shadow questioned.

"Of course. All we have to do is stand in the centre of the drawing and I will speak the incantation."

Shadow smiled and both of them walked to the middle of the drawing and Link began the incantation.

"Praeteriti vel futuri temporis nostri. Restitui nos vita nostra."

The symbols on the floor started to glow electric orange.

"1869 Victorian London. Et tunc apertum in nobis."

All of a sudden there was a blue flash of light and Link and Shadow were gone.

6

Victorian London

Constantine and Brook had just finished magically making a house next to theirs for Link and Shadow when a blue flash of light appeared behind them. Two figures walked out from the light and smiled.

"Brook, long time no see," Link spoke as he walked up to his friend and gave him a bro hug.

"Link this is Constantine." The blonde pointed to the black-haired guy behind him.

"Hi, how's it going?" Constantine and Link shook hands.

"This is Shadow." Link pointed to Shadow as her and the two men exchanged a kind-hearted smile.

Brook and Constantine walked towards a shack that looked the same as theirs, with Link and Shadow at their heels. The blonde opened the door, allowing his friends to walk into their new home.

"Wow it's amazing," Shadow spoke as she looked around the shack.

It was exactly the same as Brook's but there was an extra bedroom and bathroom for them.

"Well, we will let you get settled in and tomorrow, we will get you guys to work." Brook smiled at him and his black-haired friend left them alone.

When they got back to their shack, they sat down in front of the fire.

"There's something off about them two," Constantine said.

"I know. We just need to keep an eye on them." And with that, they both picked up a book each and began to read.

***

Link and Shadow were sat down in the living room playing a game of cards. Shadow placed down three matching cards and smiled.

"Damn that's the third time you have won against me. How did you get so good?" Link questioned as he picked up all the cards and started to shuffle them for another game.

"My father taught me mostly, the rest I figured out by playing against others." Shadow smiled.

Link handed the cards out and placed the rest on the coffee table. They both rearranged their cards and looked into each other's eyes, smirking. Link placed his cards down first, being all smug that he knew he was going to win but that soon changed when Shadow placed her cards down and she had won, yet again.

"I bet you're cheating," Link stated.

"I would never cheat against you," Shadow mocked.

Link packed away the cards and looked at the time.

"We best head to bed as we will be starting work tomorrow," Link spoke and shadow nodded her head.

They bid their good nights and both went straight to bed.

***

The next morning, Brook was up and waiting outside his shack for his partner and two friends.

He waited for another ten minutes when all three of them came walking out of the shacks, dressed and ready for work.

"About time. Don't want to be late for your first day and Constantine, you should know better," Brook spoke.

"Sorry I wanted a lay in." Constantine winked as he sorted his collar and tie out.

"Sorry, I am a woman. I take pride in what I look like for work," Shadow smirked.

"Okay fair enough. Link, what's your excuse?" Brook questioned, knowing exactly what the answer would be.

"I'm not used to working. Other people do my work."

Everyone rolled their eyes at Link and they all walked off to work.

***

The walk to work was peaceful. Constantine lit a cigarette and smoked on the way to work. Brook and Shadow talked about 1869 Victorian London and Link took in the sight and thought of ways to take over this place.

When they got to the magical police centre, Shadow and Link looked up in amazement. They both stood there taking in the sight while the two partners walked in front of them.

"Welcome to the magical police centre," Brook spoke and they all walked in.

From the outside, it looked like an abandoned building but the inside was quite a sight. On the ground floor there were offices scattered around, the second floor, there were more offices, the third floor, there were conference rooms and the fourth floor was where all the prisoners were in their cells.

As they walked in, Shadow and Link took in the sight. Neither one of them had seen magic just like this before.

Constantine walked off to his office to start on some paperwork while Brook took his friends to their offices.

"Right, these will be your stations. You'll be working as partners," Brook spoke as the dark elves took their seats.

As Brook walked away, Link scooted over to Shadow.

"Hey, Buckingham Palace isn't far from here. We can totally take it when the chance is right."

"That sounds like a good idea." Shadow half-heartedly smiled then got back to doing some work.

Shadow was having second thoughts about Link's plan. She was given a chance to make a new start in life where she can learn to keep her magic under control and become a better person. After meeting Brook and Constantine, she really thought she had a chance at changing her life around.

Link went back to his desk and looked through all of his paperwork, seeing all of the convicts that had been taken in and the ones that were still at large.

***

After looking through some of the paperwork, he came across a convict named Jackson Lawson, who was known for his numerous attempts at breaking into Buckingham Palace. Link smiled to himself as he thought of finding this man and teaming up with him.

An alarm was heard all the way around the building.

"What's that noise?" Link questioned as he held his hands over his ears.

"That is a bell to let us know that it is time for us to go on lunch," Brook spoke as he walked up to Link's desk.

Shadow walked away from her desk and walked towards the exit. When she walked out of the building, she noticed Constantine smoking.

"Do you mind if I could try?" Shadow asked.

"Sure, but they are strong," Constantine spoke as he handed the woman the cigarette.

Shadow took a drag and straight after, she started coughing. She handed Constantine his cigarette back as he laughed.

"I told you they were strong."

"I know. I just wanted to try. I need something to drown out these thoughts," Shadow sighed as she slid her back down the wall until she was sat on the floor.

Constantine followed her actions and smiled. He pulled out another pack of cigarettes and handed the woman one.

"Here these are weaker."

"Thank you," Shadow said as she lit the cigarette and started to smoke it.

***

"What's going on?" Brook spoke as he walked outside and sat with his friends.

"Nothing really, Shadow is just having some hard thoughts," Constantine spoke.

"What about? You can tell us."

Shadow sighed and began to tell them what was on her mind.

"Link wants to take over London. He wants to kidnap the queen and take her throne. He wants me to do it with him, but I am sick of being in his shadow. I never thought I would say this but I actually miss my sister. I miss being good."

"You are still good. Right now you have done a GOOD thing by telling us this," Brook spoke as he put his hand on Shadows.

"That's not the only thing. He was looking through his paperwork when he came across someone called Jackson Lawson. He wants to find him so they can help each other out," Shadow continued.

"We will all keep an eye on him," Constantine smiled.

"I will let the rest of the police know so we can all watch him," Brook spoke.

"Thank you. Just don't let him know about it."

"Of course."

The sound of the alarm went off again to indicate that lunch was over. The three of them walked in and decided to tell everyone what Link was up to.

***

Back in the magical world, Caity and her siblings were plotting against Alexa.

"But how are we even going to get back into the kingdom? Alexa won't see you again." Ripp spoke.

"There is one way but I don't know if you would do it Caity," Alana spoke with hesitation.

"Are you trying to tell me to contact Link?" Caity questioned.

Her brother and sister nodded their heads and Caity smirked.

"Get me my quill and something to write on. Link will enjoy having new companions."

Alana ran off to get her sister's quill and Ripp, something to write on. They hurried back and handed their sister the stuff. Caity picked up her quill and began to write a letter to Link.

Ever since Caity told Alexa the truth and got rejected, she had been planning on breaking the queens of Brunuhville and taking the kingdom as her own.

***

Link didn't care about the job, he was more interested about finding Lawson. The Dark Elf decided to go out through London to find this criminal. It was time for a new ruler.

As he was walking through London, Link spotted a piece of paper floating down from the sky. Link stopped in his tracks and took the paper into his hand. He noticed on the front of it, it had his name on it. He looked puzzled but opened it up and started to read it.

Link,

I know you don't know me personally but I know you have heard of my family. The Lotz family of Stone Grave.

I know how you and your sister are at war and I would be delighted to join you against her. She rejected me and I want to avenge her.

Let me know what you think.

Queen Caity of Stone Grave.

Link smirked at this letter and thought to himself. *"This would be brilliant. I can build an army."*

He continued walking the streets of London when he came face to face to an abandoned house.

The house had an old, rusty, metal fence around the outside of it with an overgrown, dead garden. It also had broken, brick walls, with smashed windows while the broken glass was on the ground. Link walked up to the door and noticed how rotten the wood was. He knocked on the door but there was no answer. He knocked once more but this time the door creaked slightly open. He walked in, slightly pushing the door open. He looked around but something was off. Unlike the rest of the magical folk, where their houses were cloaked in magic, this one wasn't. This house was abandoned in and out. It was like no one had ever lived there.

Link walked around for a while, looking for a sign of any life, but not finding anything.

"Lawson! Jackson! Anyone home?" Link called around the house but gaining no answer.

Link looked everywhere around the ruin but to his luck, there was no Jackson Lawson anywhere to be found. All there was to be seen was everything in the house broken.

Just then the door creaked open and a tall, black-haired man walked in.

"Who are you?" the man spoke.

Link span around and smiled as he noticed that the man in front of him was, in fact, Jackson Lawson.

"Ah Jackson, my name is Link Snow. I am a dark elf," Link smirked.

"And I should care because?" Jackson questioned as he walked off, away from Link.

"Because I want to help you break into the palace."

Jackson looked back at Link and smiled.

"You're going to help me? What do you get out of this?"

"A new partner in crime."

Both of the men smirked at each other and began to come up with a plan to get into the palace.

But what Jackson didn't know was that Link would help him get in but he would take the palace as his own.

***

After telling everyone, the three magical folks noticed Link was gone. The three of them split up and looked all over the building but Link was nowhere to be found. They checked outside and even that was a bust.

"Where the hell has he gone?" Constantine grunted.

"I don't know but when we find him, he has a lot of talking to do," Brook spoke.

They went to walk back inside as they had no luck when their chief walked up to them.

"Just the three I was looking for."

"What's up chief?" Constantine spoke.

"I need you to go to Buckingham Palace. Jackson is trying to break in again but this time he has the help from another dark elf. He goes by the name Link? Surely it's not the one that works here."

"On it, chief."

The chief walked back in and Brook looked at Shadow.

"Are you ready for your first task?"

"Yes! Let's go!"

"I am going to kill that creature," Constantine spoke with anger in his voice.

And with that, the three of them went off through London to catch Jackson in the act and find out what Link was trying to do.

***

As Link and Jackson made their way into the palace underground, Link thought about the magical world, about Caity, the words she had written to him and what she wanted to do to avenge his sister.

Suddenly the two men came to a halt. There in front of them was a rather heavy looking, brown, wooden door with a silver lock keeping it shut.

"Where are we?" Link questioned.

"This is where I got to last time before the cops came. This is the entrance to the queen jewels," Jackson answered.

Jackson looked at the lock and sighed with anger.

"But the only problem is, I don't have the sort of magic to break this lock."

Link pushed his friend aside and began to mutter words while swirling his fingers just under the lock. The lock suddenly clicked and fell to the gravelly ground underneath the men. The door creaked opened slightly to Jackson's surprise.

"Were in."

Jackson walked up to the door with a smiled on his face,

impressed by Link's talents. He leaned against the heavy door and Peered through the crack to see if any of the guards were walking around. And just to his glee, there was no one in sight.

Jackson pushed open the door as slowly as he could, making sure that there was no sound, until there was enough room for the two men to get through into the other room.

Once the men were in and the door was shut and locked, both men stood in awe of the view. Neither one of them had seen anything quite like this.

The men stood in a room that was decorated in red and gold walls and marble flooring. There, in front of the men, stood about one hundred, maybe more, glass casings full of jewels.

"Wow this is heaven," Jackson exclaimed as he walked around the room, admiring all the shining jewels.

Link didn't pay much attention to the younger magical man. He was more interested in finding where the queen's throne room was located and where the queen was. While Jackson was preoccupied, Link decided to cast a spell to help him locate the queen and her throne room.

Link started to mutter an incantation with his eyes closed, while swirling his fingers, letting purple sparks emerge.

A dark purple pentagram with other strange symbols appeared underneath where Link was standing and began to glow, then suddenly a map of Buckingham Palace appeared in front of Link's eyes. All of the underground passageways began to show up and Link looked over the map to find the throne room.

Just then, the queen's crown showed up on the map and began to move towards the throne room.

"Ah, there you are. This will be like killing two birds with one stone," Link muttered to himself with an evil smirk plastered across his pale lips.

Link looked over the map one last time to make sure he knew exactly which passageways he had to take to get to the queen.

He clicked his fingers and the pentagram was gone. He looked around the room to find a door that led him to the right passageway.

After a while of looking, he came across the right door. He watched Jackson out of the corner of his eye, making sure he didn't notice that he was off on his own adventure.

As he got to the door, he noticed it was the same as the door he unlocked and walked through but the only difference was that there was no lock. Link took hold of the mental handle and pulled the door opened as quietly as he could.

As he walked into the passageway, he closed the door slowly and quietly so Jackson wouldn't notice. Once the door was closed, Link looked down the dark, winding passageway.

"Can't wait to get what is finally mine."

And with that, Link was gone.

***

Back in the mortal world in 3019, where there was no magic to be seen or heard throughout the dimension, something magical was definitely going on.

With all the new technology and more countryside, London looked amazing.

Throughout London, there were people driving their hover cars or riding their hover boards, there were roads that hovered twenty feet off of the ground and some old buildings that had been knocked down so there was room for the green land. London looked beautiful. But something was different and everyone felt it.

***

Everywhere was peaceful far out in the rich part of London. Magic filled the country air. Stone tombs, some new, some old, surrounded parts of the country fields that was home to one of the biggest, most beautiful mansions in all of the dimensions.

Surrounding the mansion, there were 4 magical villages, that were protected by four guardians, Air, Fire, Earth and Water, which also held a magical barrier so no mortal could see in or enter this misplaced piece of magic. Families lived among these villages and they all had incredible gifts and spirit animals.

When the children were born, they were born with magic but it was not determined which power they would portray until they became five years old. When they became five years old, the children had a mark appear on the palms of their hands. This mark was linked to their power and which village they would fall into. The children would take classes on how to understand their power, where it came from and how to use it. When they became eighteen, they would finally leave the village and go on a quest that would help them find out their spirit animal and understand what their magic could do, but unfortunately, one child was not able to do this.

The tombs that were around the country were guarded by sacred people that wore red hooded robes. The sacred people that would guard these stone tombs were possessed by dark magic. They would conjure up bad spirits and could manipulate the dimensions magic for their own uses. Some say that the family that live in the mansion controlled these sacred people.

***

A couple, Samantha and Thomas Corp owned this beautiful mansion and this land. They lived here along with their son, Andrew Corp, their adoptive daughter, Lena Corp and Lena's best friend, Bear, the wolf but was also an animagus. No one in the Corp family knew about Rascal except for Lena.

The Corp family, before they adopted Lena, were ten centuries old. Samantha and Thomas had been together since the dawn of time, as they put it and had always lived a happy life, controlling this land until Lena came along.

Lena was eight when she was adopted. Her mother and father died in a horrible incident to protect the Snow family. The Corp family were nice enough to bring her into their family but the nice front didn't last long, so she brought Bear along with her.

Bear was the most beautiful white wolf with a light brown eye that looked like it had tiny dark brown worms wiggling through it. Whenever Lena needed her best friend, Bear transformed himself into a charming young man, with one light brown eye, platinum blonde, emo like hair that covered where his other eye used to be that was now nothing but scars.

The story of Bear losing his eye isn't a very long one. Being the best friend he was, he protected Lena when Andrew wanted to cause his adoptive sister some pain by making her feel alone. He tried taking Lena down to the mansion basement where he would lock her down there making her feel alone and claustrophobic. Bear had stopped him by biting his arm but what he didn't know was that the spoilt brat had a pocketknife on him, which was the cause of Bear losing his eye. The ungrateful boy sunk the knife into the wolf's eye and pealed it out of the socket making Bear scream out in pain. Lena kicked her brother in the shin, picked up her wolf and ran to her room. Luckily, Lena's magic was strong enough to heal her best friend.

Lena was the black sheep of the family. Andrew was always number one, but she couldn't blame him, he was Samantha and Thomas 's son. Lena was a burden to everyone, except for Bear. No matter how hard she tried her best to do everything right, she was always wrong in the Corp family's eyes.

Lena always questioned the Corp family's judgement and actions. As an outsider, Lena saw the world from a different perspective. She saw the pain and fear her family would spread across this land and would stand up for the people. Lena always fought against Samantha and Thomas. She hated what they were doing to the people. Lena knew that the people of this land hated her family but she also knew that they loved Lena. She would always question people, asking why they loved her and they would always give her the same answers.

"You are nothing like your parents."

"You have a kind heart and would never let any of us suffer."

"We would be better off with you leading us."

Lena knew that she was nothing like her adoptive family. She hated what her parents had done and were still doing to these people. If it were up to her, these people would be free and wouldn't have to take orders from no one but themselves.

***

Lena had beautiful, long, raven hair with Emerald, green eyes. Lena was twenty-two in a months' time and she knew for a fact that the Corp family wouldn't remember. But she knew that once she was twenty-two, she was able to leave this horrible life behind and start a new one.

Lena was the only child when she became eighteen that couldn't go on her quest. She wasn't "Of this world" as her parents put it. She was an outsider. Lena was happy that she didn't have to do a stupid quest. But she knew that the rules were different for her. As she couldn't go on this quest, she had to wait until she was twenty-two to leave her family home. She had the choice to stay but she knew that her brother would be taking his parent's place and she didn't want anything to do with that.

***

It was midnight and Lena and Bear were both laid down on the roof, looking up at the stars.

"Aren't they beautiful?" Bear asked.

"Aren't they always Bear?" Lena chuckled.

Lena's smile soon faded as she remembered that her birthday was coming up. She remembered the last time she had a party while she held onto the necklace that she was given by her best friend, Alexa. She was only eight.

***

FLASHBACK

Brunuhville

Lena ran down the hallway of her family hut and into the living room, where her parents were sitting, screaming in excitement.

"Mummy! Daddy! I'm eight today!" Lena screamed.

Her parents laughed.

"That you are beautiful. How about you go upstairs and change and me and mummy will go and get your presents? How does that sound?" the father spoke.

"Okay daddy!" Lena ran back to her room to change.

Her mother and father invited all of her friends over for the party and prepared all the food, drinks, entertainment and presents.

***

A few moments passed and Lena and her friends were enjoying the party. Lena's parents laughed and smiled at the sight of their daughter playing with her friends.

Just then, there was a knock at the door. Lena's mother made her way over to the door and opened it to reveal Leonard and Alexa standing there.

"Alexa, Lena is in the back garden, go and head out there."

Alexa skipped happily out to the garden to find Lena sat with the rest of her friends laughing.

Lena turned her head slightly and a massive grin spread from ear to ear on her face.

"Alexa!" Lena screamed as she jumped up and hugged her best friend.

"Happy birthday Lena." Alexa smiled into the hug.

The girls pulled away and Alexa pulled out a small, black box with a red ribbon over it from her jacket pocket.

"I hope you like it. Leonard helped me pick it out."

Lena looked at the box then back to her father. Her father gave a slight nod and Lena opened the box, stunned by what she saw inside.

Inside the box there was two necklaces that formed into one. Together they made the ring of eternity.

Alexa took one half of the necklace and put it around her raven-haired friend's neck and the other, she placed around her own.

"We will be best friends forever and ever!" Alexa exclaimed.

The two girls hugged and promised that no matter what happens, they would always be best friends.

FLASHBACK ENDS

***

Just in the split of the moment, Lena jumped to her feet.

"Lena what's wrong?" Bear questioned, concerned about his friend's actions.

"Nothing. I just need to write to someone really important."

Both Lena and Bear jumped down from the roof, onto Lena's bedroom balcony and ran into her room. Lena sat down at her desk and pulled some paper, ink, wax and her quill out from a draw. Lena began to write when she felt a hand place down on to her shoulder.

"Who are you writing to?"

"Someone that I haven't seen in a very long time. And now that I'm turning twenty-two and I'm ready to start my own life, I think it's time I reach out," Lena replied to Bear and carried on writing.

***

Back in Brunuhville, Alexa and Shinara were sat in the garden talking while their two boys were out riding the dragons.

"So, Lee and Felix have their coronation in a couple of days,"

Alexa spoke.

Shinara looked at her wife and smiled.

"We should invite the kingdom to celebrate with us."

"I think that's a great idea. Well, I could always get Sam to gather the guards to decorate the gardens and me, Elsie and Aria can send the invitations to everyone," Shinara suggested.

"I think that is a splendid idea, your grace. I will get right on it," Sam spoke as he appeared in front of the queens.

The two women jumped but laughed as they realised who it was.

"Sam, you gave me quite a fright," Alexa stated.

"I'm sorry, your grace. I'll be on my way now to prepare for tomorrow." And just when he was about to leave, he turned back around to face his queen. "Oh, and this came for you today." And he was gone, leaving a letter sealed in gold wax on Alexa's lap. Alexa looked at the seal. Her heart fell to her stomach and the colour drained from her once so tanned skin.

"Who is that from my love?" Shinara questioned with concern.

"I'm not sure." She lied. "I'll go and read this inside. Could you check on the boys?" Alexa kissed her wife on the cheek and walked back into the castle and to a little room hidden within the walls.

Alexa sat down at the old, wooden desk in front of her as she carefully opened the letter, making sure to keep the seal intact and began to read.

> *My dearest Alexa,*
>
> *Not a day has gone by that I haven't thought about you. My only best friend in the entire world.*
>
> *I know I haven't written to you and this is why I have written this letter. I want to explain.*
>
> *I know you don't remember this as Leonard took you away for your own safety, but my parents helped your parents in that*

horrible incident when I was eight and you were seven. When they died I was put into care. I got adopted by this family that seemed nice but it was all an act. I was never allowed to write to anyone, not even you. I have letters that I have secretly written that I was never allowed to send. There is so much that I want to tell you but I don't know how much time I have until the parents wake up.

I'm turning twenty-two next month which means I am finally free from this hell hole. I wrote this letter at night so no one knew about it.

I know this may hit a soft spot deep within, as it did I but Alexa, I truly miss you and I am coming back to Brunuhville.

I have heard so much about your family and the dragons. News still travels to my neck of the woods. I miss you, I miss our friendship. I still wear that necklace every day.

I hope you write back. If you do, make sure it goes to my room and under my pillow. I'll check every day.

Lena.

By the end of the letter, Alexa was crying and holding onto her half of the necklace. She didn't notice until a tear splashed down onto the desk and she saw her hand squeezing the necklace tight.

"Oh, how I miss you, Lena."

Alexa pulled some paper, her quill, ink and her wax out of a draw and began to write a letter back to Lena.

My long-lost Lena,

You have no idea how much I have missed you. With everything that had happened, I thought you had died.

I'm so sorry to hear about the family you are with. It must be terrible. I wish I was there for you throughout this struggle.

I would love you to come home. I really have missed you. I want you to meet my wife and boys. I know my boys would love to meet their auntie Lena.

Reading your letter made me cry. I want you to come home. I will make a room up for you so you can stay here within the castle.

I miss you, Lena. I have always worn my half of the necklace. I have never taken it off, not once. I'll make sure this goes under your pillow.

Alexa.

Alexa sealed the letter and with a click of her fingers it was gone.

***

Back in Victorian London, Shadow, Brook and Constantine made it to Buckingham Palace. They had split up and made their way through the building to find Link and Jackson.

Shadow went through the underground passageway and come out into the queen's jewels room. She looked around the room and noticed Jackson drawling over the jewels.

"Jackson, you're coming with me."

Jackson froze but obliged to the woman. Shadow walked through the rest of the building to find the two other men standing in front of the throne room.

"Guys what are you doing?" Shadow questioned.

"Can't you hear that?" Brook asked.

"Hear what? I don't hear anything."

"Exactly. This place is never quiet."

The two men kicked down the doors and saw Link with the queen's neck in his hands.

"Link what the hell dude? You said you'd help with the jewels!" Jackson spat.

"Oh, I forgot to say, I never had the intention of helping you, I'm here to take over London," Link sniggered.

"You'll ruin London!" Brook stated.

"You're dead, mate," Constantine spat.

Constantine lunged himself at Link but Link pushed the queen towards him, making him fall to the floor.

Brook tried the same as his partner, but failed also as Link flung a energy ball at him, causing him crash to the floor also.

Link took one look at Shadow and smirked.

"May we meet again." And with a click of his fingers, he was gone.

***

Lena was on her way up to her room from dinner with her "parents" when she was called by Andrew.

"Hey twerp," he called.

Lena stood there waiting for him to finish the rest of his statement as whenever he called Lens names, he wanted to start trouble.

"Who was you talking to this morning?"

"No one, why?" Lena asked, confused as to why he even cared.

"It sounded like you had a boy in your room."

"Ah me have a boy in my room? You're having a laugh," Lena chuckled, realising that was the wrong move to make when she noticed her brother's face change as he began to walk closer to her.

"Are you calling me a liar?" he spat.

"N-n-no. I-i wouldn't." Lena lowered her head, not wanting to meet his gaze.

"Good because I wouldn't want to tell mummy that you are. She wouldn't be happy with the way you treat your poor brother now, would she?" he smirked.

Andrew backed away and walked back to where he had come from, leaving Lena alone. She shook the feeling of her brother being so close to her and began to walk back to her room.

When she entered her room, she noticed Bear with a letter in his mouth.

"Oh, who's a good boy," she mocked as she walked up to the wolf and took the letter.

"You better not do that again. Next time I will bite your hand off," Bear smirked as he changed into his human form.

Lena couldn't help but laugh at Bear's insecurities. She opened the letter and began to read it.

***

After reading the letter, Lena flopped down onto her bed and smiled.

"Was that from Alexa?" Bear questioned, causing Lena to look at him funny.

"Don't give me that look. I know you were or still are best friends to the queen of Brunuhville," he scoffed.

Lena smiled at the thought of her best friend being jealous of her childhood best friend.

"Aw Bear, are you jealous?" Lena laughed.

"Ah me jealous? Not a chance," he frowned, not looking at Lena.

"Hey, no need to be." Lena hugged her best friend. "Nothing could ever come between us. You will like her. I can't wait for you to meet her."

Bear smiled.

Just then, Lena heard footsteps coming towards her door and panicked.

"Bear, change back qui…"

But before Lena could finish her sentence and Bear change back, Samantha bursted through the door. As she noticed Lena and Bear sitting there on her bed, a look of pure disappointment and hatred appeared on her face.

"WHAT IS A BOY DOING IN YOUR ROOM?" Samantha shouted making the boy and girl jump.

"I… I… Can expla… explain," Lena stuttered, lowering her head in shame.

"No, you can't. No wonder why your parents didn't want you."

"MY PARENTS ARE DEAD YOU OLD CROW! HOW DARE YOU BE SO CLOSED MINDED! ALL YOU EVER THINK ABOUT IS YOURSELF AND YOUR COLD-HEARTED FAMILY!" Lena screamed, letting all of the feelings that she had felt towards this woman and family for fourteen years out of her mouth.

Samantha looked at Lena with anger spread across her now bright red, wrinkled face, but also gob smacked at what her adoptive daughter had just screamed.

"I have had it up to here with you," the old crow began as she pointed a finger above her head. "I want you out of this house in the next hour and YOU ARE NEVER COMING BACK."

"GLADLY!" Lena shouted as the old crow slammed her bedroom door closed behind her, leaving Lena and Bear to pack all of their belongings up.

Lena and bear magically packed all their belongings, not because they were lazy but because it was easier and faster.

They decided to change before leaving so they could fit in. Lena dressed herself in a black, oversized shirt, that she left slightly undone so her laces hung over her chest, black, skinny jeans, accompanied by black boots and a purple, hooded cloak.

Bear dressed in a similar way but his shirt was white and was tied up to the top with a belt tied around his waist, that was accompanied by a brown jacket.

"Are you ready to meet the queen?" Lena questioned.

"Yeah, let's do this."

And with a click of the fingers, they were gone.

Meanwhile in Brunuhville, Alexa was out flying on her dragons with her boys while Shinara, Leonard, Elsie, aria and jasper were talking in the throne room.

***

In the kingdom village, black and white mist appeared letting two silhouettes emerge. As the two figures walked out from within the mist, Ray was standing there, eyes wide open, watching what was happening before his eyes. As Lena and Bear walked out, revealing all of their features, Lena noticed Ray standing there.

"Excuse me?" she called out to Ray.

"Y… yes?"

"Would there be a chance you could take me to the queen please? She would be expecting us. I'm Lena…" but before she could finish, Ray interrupted her.

"Lena Corp?! Oh my, yes of course. Please follow me," Ray spoke, shocked at what he was hearing.

"I thought she was dead?" he thought to himself.

Ray allowed the two visitors to follow him up to the castle gate. Sam being on gate duty, noticed Ray with Lena and Bear and opened the gate, got smacked at what he had just seen.

As they approached the throne room doors, they heard people talking. Suddenly the doors opened, allowing the three of them to walk in. As they walked in, the five members of the dragon lord's pack stopped what they were doing and watch Ray, Lena and Bear walk up to them in the centre of the room.

"L... Lena is th... that y... you? Leonard stuttered, looking at the raven-haired woman.

"Hey Leo. Yeah, it's me." Lena smiled and before she knew it, she was wrapped in a teddy bear hug.

"Struggling to breathe." Lena managed to just get out.

"I'm sorry. It's been so long," he spoke as he released the young woman.

Just then, the throne room doors flung open, revealing Alexa and her two boys.

"What's the emergency? Sam said there was an emer..." Alexa trailed off as she saw her long-lost childhood best friend.

"Hey Lex, it's been a while," Lena spoke.

Alexa didn't answer, she just ran full speed up to Lena, tackling her to the floor into a bone crushing hug.

"Merlin, how I've missed you," Alexa spoke into her friend's ear as tears fell down her cheeks.

"I've missed you too."

***

After an hour, everyone was still standing around, watching as the two best friends cried in each other's arms.

"She's meant to cry in my arms," Shinara spoke.

"Shinara, these two haven't seen each other in fourteen years, I'm sure Alexa is entitled to hug her," Leonard spat, causing the young elf to stiffen.

"After all, Lena was meant to be dead," Aria spoke, causing Shinara to storm out of the room.

"Was that really necessary?" Leonard spoke.

Bear walked over to Leonard and stuck his hand out.

"Hi, I'm Bear. I am Lena's w..."

"Wolf, yes, I thought I could smell a familiar scent on you." Leonard took Bear's hand and shook it gladly.

"Maybe we should leave these two to catch up. I know they have a lot to talk about."

Leonard and the rest of the pack agreed and quietly walked out of the throne room, leaving the two women alone to catch up or well cry.

After a while, Lena and Alexa broke away from their long, wet hug and stayed seated on the throne room floor.

"Wow, you look…"

"Amazing. Ah, yeah, so do you. Your wife back there didn't seem so happy to see me." Lena's smile faded.

"Ignore her. I knew she would get like this whenever you would have turned up," Alexa stated, knowing that the gut feeling she was having, was true.

***

A few hours went by after the girls had caught up everything that had happened in the last fourteen years and now, Lena and Alexa were walking through the gardens, enjoying each other's company when Alexa's sons and wife came walking towards them. When the boys noticed their mother, they ran up to her and hugged her.

"Lee, Felix, this is your auntie Lena, the one I told you about."

Lee walked up to Lena and hugged her.

"Hi Lena, I'm Lee."

The raven-haired woman smiled into the hug and looked up at Felix.

"And you must be Felix. It's really nice to meet you both finally," Lena spoke as she stuck her hand out for Felix to shake and he did so.

Shinara walked over and gave her wife a tender kiss on the lips.

"Lena this is Shinara, my wife."

Lena walked up to Shinara and hugged her, taking the young elf by surprise.

"It's nice to finally meet you as well."

"You too. I have heard so much about you." Shinara smiled.

For the rest of the evening, the Snow's and Lena took the time to get to know each other over dinner, with the rest of Alexa's pack.

After everyone had finished their food, they all decided to part their ways and head to their rooms for an early night. After Shinara and Alexa put their sons to bed, they parted their ways so Alexa could show Lena and Bear to Lena's room, leaving Shinara to wait for her wife in their room.

As the two women and Bear got to Lena's room, Alexa opened the door and allowed her best friend and wolf to walk in.

"I got my head of guards, Sam to bring you things up earlier so you needn't worry about it all," Alexa stated.

"Thank you so much. Are you sure you don't mind me staying here in your castle?"

"Of course. Now get some sleep. I want you to meet my dragons tomorrow. Good night." Alexa and Lena hugged good night and Alexa left to meet her wife in their room.

As Alexa walked into her room, she felt eyes burning into the back of her head.

"My love, what's wrong?" Alexa questioned as she walked over to the bed that she shared with her wife.

Shinara sighed and moved over slightly so her queen could sit.

"Nothing darling." She lied.

"Shinara, please tell me. You haven't been yourself since Lena has arrived. Has she offended you in some way?"

"No, no, not at all. I guess I just got a little bit jealous," the young elf confessed.

Alexa placed a hand over Shinara's and squeezed it gently.

"Why my love? There is nothing to be jealous over."

Shinara sighed again, but this time, getting up off of the bed and she began to pace the room.

"Alexa, she's gorgeous. Do you not remember what happened the last time with Caity?" Shinara raised her voice slightly, making Alexa's eyes grow wide in shock.

Alexa stood up from the bed and walked over to her wife, taking Shinara's hands in her own and bringing them up to her lips, lightly feather kissing them.

"Shinara, my love, there is nothing to worry about. Lena has been the only best friend that I could have ever asked for in life. When my brother did what he did, I really and truly thought that my best friend was gone forever. I never thought that I would see her again," Alexa began, letting a few stray tears fall from her eyes. "But then the letter Sam gave me that day changed everything. It was like my w… world had st… stopped. I thought it was a c… cruel j… joke someone was p… p… playing on m… me but it wasn't. L… L… Lena really was a… alive." Alexa fell to her knees and covered her face with her hands but no matter how hard she tried to stop the tears, they just kept coming.

Shinara went down onto her knees so she was level with her wife. she tilted Alexa's chin up with one finger and noticed the sadness and sorrow in her eyes. All of the colour and the spark that was always in her wife's eyes was now gone. Alexa was truly broken. Shinara pulled Alexa closer to her, letting the broken dragon lord cry into her chest. This was a side of Alexa that she had never seen before and it broke her. Alexa was always the strong one and knowing that she had all of this holding on to her chest, tightly, made the young elf wonder how long her queen had been keeping this inside of her.

***

The next morning, Lee and Felix were waiting in the dragon cave for their mother to join them for their morning ride but she was late. Draco walked up to Lee and nudged him.

"I know mate, she's never late," Lee spoke as he stroked Draco's snout.

"I hope she's okay," Felix stated, feeling a little hurt.

But little did the young princes know, their mother was going through the hardest time of her life and just wanted to be left alone.

Smok flew in and landed within the cave and noticed the two boys looking a little glum. He walked over to the boys and smiled.

"You are worried about your mother?" he questioned.

"She's usually here by now," Felix spoke.

"Yeah, where is she?" Lee questioned, his voiced filled with worry.

Smok sighed. "She is dealing with a lot right now and sh wishes to be left alone. You can see her after your boring ride, but for now, she needs to be alone."

The boys sighed but obliged by what their dragon guardian had said.

***

After a while of waiting, the two boys went out with the dragons, without their mother for their morning ride. They were a little disappointed but after Smok explaining to them what was going on, they decided to head out for their morning ride and worry about their mother when they came back.

***

Alexa was still on the floor curled up to Shinara, not wanting to move. They were both up all night, Shinara letting her wife cry everything out as she could see that these feelings were a burden to her.

There was a knock at their bedroom door and Shinara beckoned for whoever it was to come in. The door opened slowly, revealing Lena's slim figure. Lena closed the door and noticed her best friend and her wife huddled up on the floor.

"Oh, I'm sorry, am I interrupting something?" Lena questioned.

"Not at all," Alexa sniffed.

Lena noticed her best friend's voice and crouched beside her.

"Alexa, what's wrong?"

Alexa didn't answer. She didn't trust her voice enough. Shinara slowly moved Alexa over to her best friend to cuddle up to and Alexa began to sob again.

"She needs you right now Lena. Please, help her," Shinara spoke as she got up and left the room in search of her sons.

Lena looked down at the queen. Never has she ever seen her best friend this broken. As Alexa cried, Lena stroked her hair trying to calm the queen down.

"Shh Shh Shh, it's okay, I'm here," Lena cooed in hope that it would calm her friend down.

Alexa finally looked up into the green orbs and a small smile appeared on her lips.

"I'm sorry, I never wanted you to see me like this. I have never let Shinara see me this broken but I couldn't hold these feelings in much longer, Alexa stated, finally trusting her voice.

Lena sat down, cross legged on the floor, making it more comfortable for her friend and herself.

"Don't ever apologise for being like this. I would never judge you. You know this." Lena's voice was softly heard.

Alexa relaxed slightly, moving away from her friend so she could sit up straight.

"What's wrong?" Lena questioned, taking her chance as she didn't know if her friend was ready to talk yet.

"For so long I thought you were dead. After seeing what my brother had done, I never thought I would see you again, but then I get your letter," Alexa began. "I thought someone was playing a cruel joke on me but it was real. You really wrote to me. Every day I wore my half of the necklace, hoping that you could somehow still be here with me. But then the letter came and it was like everything had stopped. As I read your letter, my heart shattered. I knew you were still alive and I just wanted to see you so bad. When you told me how that horrible family treated you, it broke me. Having everyone feel sorry for me and telling me that you will always be with me was so hard. I understand why you couldn't write to me. but Merlin, how I missed you. I am so happy that you are here with me," Alexa rambled on.

Lena listened to every word that came out of her best friend's mouth and silent tears began to fall down her cheeks. Alexa noticed her friend crying and moved a hand to her face and wiped them away.

"I'm sorry, I didn't mean to make you cry," Alexa spoke.

"What did I say about apologising? Stop doing it. I'm not crying because of what you said, I am crying because you have been through so much and I wasn't here with you to walk alongside you," Lena stated.

Both of the girls hugged each other, feeling safe and happy in each other's arms.

"I'm so glad that you are alive. I 've missed you so much." Alexa smiled.

"I've missed you too. I have Bear to thank for keeping me alive." Lena smiled back.

Both of the girls pulled away and stood to their feet. Alexa and Lena could both smell breakfast being cooked and smiled.

"Fancy some breakfast?" Alexa asked.

"I'd love some." Lena smiled.

"I'll race you. The last one there has to go shopping with the girls," Alexa shouted as she shot out of the room and ran down the hallway, dodging all of the guards that were carrying the decorations for her boys' coronation today.

"You haven't changed one bit," Lena shouted back as she shot down the hallway after her best friend and avoiding the guards as her friend did.

"Lena Corp and Alexa Snow finally reunited after fourteen years," Alexa thought to herself.

***

After the long run through the hallways of the beautiful castle, Alexa and Lena were standing, hunched over, in front of the dining hall doors.

"You certainly haven't changed, your grace." Lena spoke between breaths.

"Really? You are going to pull *your grace* crap on me now? After all this time?" Alexa joked.

"Oh, shut up." Lena shoved her best friend. "Come on, let's get something to eat." And with that, both of the girls walked into the dining hall and joined the rest of Alexa's pack and the castle staff.

***

As the girls sat down with their friends, Alexa noticed that her boys and wife weren't anywhere in the room.

"Leonard, where is Shinara and my boys?" Alexa questioned.

"They came in here earlier for some food but shortly left after eating so the boys could get ready for their coronation, that will be happening in a matter of hours," Leonard explained.

Just then, Measter Logan and Dorian walked in and approached the table where Alexa was sat.

"Ah Logan, Dorian, it's so nice to see you. I hope the

preparations for Lee and Felix's coronation is going well." Alexa smiled at the two men. "Please, sit, I would like you to meet Lena."

The two men sat down and looked across the table and smiled at Lena.

"Lena, it is a pleasure to see you again after so long, I am Measter Logan and this is my apprentice, Dorian," Logan spoke and Dorian shyly smiled at the raven-haired woman.

"It is a pleasure to see you again." Lena smiled, the turned her attention to the young man. "And it is very nice to meet you, Dorian." Lena winked, making the young man go bright red in the face.

Logan, Alexa and Leo noticed this action and smiled. Logan looked at Alexa and began.

"Alexa, we will leave you to feast and we will be ready for the coronation in two hours." Logan and Dorian stood from their seats, bowed slightly and left the queen to eat with her family.

After they had left, Alexa turned her attention to Lena.

"What was that all about?" Alexa questioned with a smirk.

"What? He's a good-looking lad. I can appreciate that can't I?" Lena argued as a blush rose to the surface of her cheeks.

"Just be careful with him. He seems to have been through a lot and struggles to talk to people," Alexa stated, filling her voice with concern for the boy.

"I understand Alexa. I promise to take it easy with him. Maybe I just want to play with him a bit," Lena smirked causing Alexa to give her a death glare. "Alexa, I'm messing."

Alexa's face relaxed and she decided to stand from her seat. "I am going to prepare for the coronation. I will see you both later." And with that, Alexa left to go to her room to get ready for her son's big days.

***

Lena and Bear met Alexa in her room to help her prepare for today when Alexa remembered what she wanted to do with her best.

"Lena, bear, before I forget, I want you to meet my dragons," Alexa chimed.

"Of course. Lead the way Dragon Lord," Lena laughed.

Alexa punched Lena's arm and they walked out of Alexa's room and down the hallway to the dragon caves.

As they got to the cave door, the guards opened it, allowing the two women and the animagus to walk down the stone steps to see the dragons.

When they got down to the bottom, Draco, Spitze, Zepter and Smok were sat eating their breakfast. Smok noticed the young Dragon Lord and stood to his feet.

"Ah, your grace, I have finally got the boys to eat without fighting over their fish," Smok laughed.

"That's great Smok. Err this is…" But before Alexa could finish, Smok interrupted. "Bear and Lena Zor-El, or should I say Corp now."

"I don't go by my adoptive parents name no more, they were nothing but hateful towards me and my friend," Lena stated, losing her smile.

"My lady, forgive me, there was no offence that was intended, and Bear," Smok began as he looked at the one-eyed man. "It has been a while to say the least."

"It has, it is good to see you, old friend," Bear spoke as he placed a hand on Smok.

As bear turned around, Alexa and Lena gave him a *what the hell* look and Bear began to explain. "Before you met me as a pup, I was tossed aside by my own father. I wasn't good enough. One of the other pack members used to pick fights with me and it was always me that ended up in the worst punishment," Bear began as he looked Lena in the eyes. "When my father tossed me aside, I found myself lost and looking for shelter and food. I was close to death until Smok came along and helped me become the man, well wolf I am today."

Lena and Alexa walked up to Bear and hugged him.

"I'm glad you are alive," Lena spoke.

"I'm glad you kept my best friend alive," Alexa spoke then turned to Smok. "And I am glad that you helped Bear become the animagus he is today. If it wasn't for you helping him and for Bear saving Lena, I don't think I would be standing here with them today."

As they pulled away from the hug, Lena looked behind Smok and smiled.

"Are these the dragons?"

"Yes. Draco, Spitze, Zepter Teacht," Alexa commanded and the tree dragons left their breakfast and walked over to their Dragon Lord.

"Bear, Lena, just hold your hands out and let the dragons come to you."

Lena and Bear did as they were and held their hands out. Draco walked up to Lena an Bear and sniffed their hands. He walked around the two of them until he came face to face with them. After a little while, Draco let them stroke him, making Spitze and Zepter know that Lena and Bear were their new friends.

***

After giving the dragons a bit of a fuss, Alexa, Bear and Lena left the dragons to finish off their breakfast. As they walked back up to the castle, Alexa told Lena to do something special for her sons but she couldn't tell no one, it had to be a surprise.

***

Two hours had passed and the castle looked beautiful. There were gold and black banners hung on all of the castle room ceilings and blue ribbons on every door. The castle staff were dressed colour coordinated with the decorations as they hurried around to make sure that the feast was perfect for Lee and Felix, even the guards had dressed colour coordinated to the decorations thanks to Ray being a very skilful young man.

As the kingdom people filled into the castle, readying for the big day, Shinara was helping her boys change for their coronation, while Alexa was preparing with Logan and Dorian.

"Where's mother?" Lee questioned.

"Well, being the queen, she has to prepare a speech and she also not allowed to see you two until you enter the throne room, its kingdom rules," Shinara stated as she tied Lee's shirt up.

"Well, I think you two are ready. Let me have a look at you both," Shinara spoke as her two boys stood side by side.

"Wow," Shinara exclaimed.

Lee was dressed in a black shirt that was done up to the top accompanied by a gold belt and a black jacket, black skinny jeans accompanied by a pair of black, smart shoes. Thanks to Lee not wanting a haircut for a few months, he had his hair brushed so it wasn't such a blonde mess and his fringe swooped over his forehead, just covering the end of his eyebrow and showing his ice blue eyes.

Felix was dressed in a white shirt that was half tied up accompanied by a gold belt and a black jacket, black skinny jeans accompanied by a pair of black, smart shoes. Felix had his black hair brushed and gelled back slightly, enough to give it some volume.

Shinara looked at her boys and smiled. "I can't believe you two will be sixteen soon. You are both so handsome, but Lee, you really need a haircut."

Lee looked at his mum and laughed. "You would have to catch

me first. I will get it cut when I feel that it is too long."

The two brothers and their mum laughed and left the room, walking down the hallway to the throne room.

***

Alexa was standing in front of the thrones with Bear, Logan and Dorian to the right of her and Lena, Leonard, Elsie, Jasper and Aria to her left. Alexa looked around the room, seeing the last of the kingdom people walk to their places. All of a sudden, music began to play and the throne room doors opened, revealing Lee and Felix along with Shinara behind them.

The two boys walked down the middle of the room until they got to the steps before the thrones. Shinara kissed both of her son's cheeks and walked to the left of her wife. The boys went down onto one knee and looked up at their mother.

The music stopped, the room went silent and Alexa began. "Witches, wizards, elves and animaguses, we are gathered here today to witness the coronation of Lee and Felix Snow and welcome them to their lives of becoming a prince. Now Logan, Dorian, could you please be ready with the crowns."

Logan and Dorian stepped forward, Logan in front of Lee and Dorian in front of Felix, with the crowns in their hands. Logan stepped lightly forward and began. "Lee, repeat after me, I Lee Snow, vow to protect this kingdom with all my power until my last drawing breath."

"I Lee Snow, a dheimhníonn go gcosnóidh mé an ríocht seo le mo chumhacht go léir go dtí go dtarraingeoidh mé anáil anuas," Lee repeated in the naive language as Logan placed the crown on top of Lee's blonde mop of hair.

Dorian then stepped slightly forward and began. "Felix, repeat after me, I Felix Snow, vow to protect this kingdom with all my power until my last drawing breath."

"I Felix Snow, a dheimhníonn go gcosnóidh mé an ríocht seo le mo chumhacht go léir go dtí go dtarraingeoidh mé anáil anuas,"

Felix repeated in the native language as Dorian placed the crown on top of Felix's head.

The two men stepped back and allowed Alexa to finish the coronation. "Arise prince Lee of Brunuhville, arise prince Felix of Brunuhville."

Both Lee and Felix stood from their spots and turned to the crowed.

"Long live the princes," Alexa began and the rest of the room chorused after her.

7

The New Age

The rest of the day went down with a blast. The feast the cooks had prepared was amazing, Lee and Felix had an amazing time talking and dancing with the kingdom people in the castle gardens and Shinara and Alexa enjoyed watching their boys enjoying their special day.

Lee and Felix were talking to Leonard, Elsie, Jasper and Aria when a glass being chimed was heard. Everyone went silent and looked around to see that Lena was standing on her seat.

"Sorry to everyone that was enjoying the party, I just wanted to make an announcement. I know I haven't been around to see Lee and Felix grow up but I have heard how amazing the boys are and I know for a fact that their mothers are proud of the young men they are becoming. And well, all I want to say is fada beo na prionsaí."

Everyone cheered and chorused after Lena, but before everyone could go back to what they were doing, Lena began again.

"Sorry again, but my lords, this is also a surprise for your coronation. *Ad opprimendum iuvenem et draconem vocat duces prodeunt,"* Lena spoke and at that split second there were dragon screeches to be heard overhead.

Everyone looked around up at the sky when they all saw three dragons flying over the castle and down towards the gardens. As the dragons landed, Lena began to speak again.

"Lee, Felix, this is for you guys. Happy coronation boys. Enjoy your dragon ride." And with that, the boys climbed onto their dragons and they flew off into the distance.

As everyone watched as the dragons flew off, the guards began to clear up all of the decorations and the kingdom people began to make their way back to their homes.

"Before everyone heads off," Alexa began, making all of the kingdom people stop in their tracks and look to their queen. "I will be heading out within the night so I would like everyone to make themselves scares within the early hours of the morning until just after mid day."

The whole of the kingdom obeyed their queen and set off, back on their tracks, back to their homes.

Lena went to walk into the castle when Alexa called her back.

"Lena, I need you to come with me tomorrow."

"Where are you going?" Lena questioned.

"Follow me and I will tell you."

***

After all of the decorations were down and all of the people were back in their homes, everyone who lived in the castle, went back to their rooms, all but Lena, Shinara and Alexa. They two queens made their way down the dragon caves to meet with their boys with Lena.

"Where will you be going?" Shinara questioned.

"I will be traveling to Sky-guard with Lena," Alexa replied, looking at her best friend.

"What for though? You never told me," the raven-haired woman stated.

"I will tell you when we get going."

"My love, please be careful on your travels," Shinara spoke. "You son's don't need their mother and auntie to never come back."

As they got down there, the dragons were just coming with the boys. Alexa looked at her wife and smiled.

"Don't worry, I will be with Smok," Alexa spoke as the two women looked at Smok.

"Don't you worry, your grace, I will look after them, as I have always done," Smok spoke, bowing his head slightly.

As the dragons landed, the boys climbed off and walked up to their parents.

"Thank you so much for today. It was the best day ever," the boys said in unison.

"You're welcome, now it is time for bed," Shinara spoke.

The five of them walked back up to the castle, bid their good nights and went to their rooms to bed.

After an eventful day, everyone was exhausted.

***

During that night, in one of the alternative dimensions, there was a black, purple and orange mass of smoke that appeared in the middle of a green meadow. Once the smoke had cleared, three hooded figures appeared. The figures pulled their hoods down to revealed that they were Brook, Constantine and Shadow.

They began to walk through the meadow when they came face to face with a temple.

"What is this place?" Shadow questioned.

"You will find out soon," Brook spoke as the door to opened to the temple.

"Ah we have been expecting you," a hooded figure spoke, allowing the three magical folk step into the temple, closing the doors behind them.

***

Lee and Felix were up extremely early the next morning, already dressed and making their way down to the dragon caves. As they approached the door, they noticed that there were no guards.

"That's odd, where are the guards?" Lee spoke.

"In fact, where is everyone? I know it is early but there are usually people still up and about around the castle," Felix spoke as he knew what the castle was like early hours of the morning.

Not thinking about it too much, the boys walked down the steps until they reached the bottom. Draco, Spitze and Zepter were there, ready to go out with the boys. The boys climbed on and commanded their dragons, letting them take off into the icy air, inhaling the cold wind as it hits them in the face.

***

Later that morning, the sky looking as if it was still night as it was still early hours of the morning, Lena, Alexa and Smok arrived at the old kingdom of Sky-guard. Only the royal families of every kingdom knew about the other kingdoms as they were in a different dimension. This was to hold the safety of their people and the other dimension's people as if this information was to be said to the wrong person, who knows what could happen. The royal families thought about this and thought it best to keep it between the royals as the dimensions could end up broken if war were to break out.

Vanaheim was once a beautiful and peaceful kingdom. That was until war had broken out between this kingdom and the kingdom of Avalon. Avalon was also one of the most peaceful and beautiful kingdoms known around these lands in this dimension.

Before Vanaheim was destroyed, it was magical. The castle stood tall with the tips of the pillars surrounded by the clouds, The castle staff were always busy, hustling around making sure that the royal family that once lived there were happy, the village was busy with the kingdom people, working, shopping while the children would play and run around. The forest was full of magical creatures that would make themselves known, the streams and sea flowed freely and at night the water would change colour to a beautiful electric pink. But now it was a burial ground around a ruin, with dragon skeletons laying here and there, elves, wizards, mortals and horses skeleton scattered around. The buildings that once stood tall were now blown apart around the once so magical kingdom. The forest, was burnt down to the ground, the streams and sea that once flowed freely were now dried up. Everything that was once the beautiful Vanaheim was now sad, sorrowful wasteland.

Avalon was just the same sight as Vanaheim. The once so magical kingdom was now a deserted wasteland. Skeletons from dragons and horses to the people of the kingdom were scattered anywhere possible, the forest was burt to a crisp, the streams and sea were no more and the castle was no more than a few pillars, the rest of the once so stunning building, was now demolished. The sky that hung above these two kingdoms was once a bright blue blanket but now, it was just a dark, brown dust cloud that hung over the deserted kingdoms.

These two kingdoms were at peace with each other, that was until the day it all changed. King and queen Vancore of Vanaheim were very protective of their daughter. She was their only heir, that was until the day the princess made a huge mistake. King and queen Vance had a son, their only successor as well. After the meeting of the two royal families, the prince and princess fell deeply for each other but the Vancore's forbid the two to ever see each other again or there would be a price to pay. But of course, the prince disobeyed the king's orders and carried on seeing the princess in secret. That all changed when the princess did not come home from her morning ride. The king sent out a patrol to see if they could find the princess but when they did, it was a sight that the king could not bear. The princess was found in a small shack, just on the border between Vanaheim and Sky-guard, along with the prince. The patrol took them back and after hearing what had happened, he commenced war against Avalon. Neither side had one, which ended up leading to the two kingdoms becoming a wasteland.

But there were two more kingdoms in this dimension that were still at peace with each other. The kingdom of Acheron and Sky-guard.

Acheron was just as big and as beautiful as Brunuhville. The forest went on for miles, the castle was on top of a hill that overlooked the sea and the kingdom village, the streams flowed freely throughout the forest and ran down through the middle of the kingdom itself. The village people were always busy making time to shop or do work while the children were out playing or splashing around in the stream.

Sky-guard on the other hand was not much of a kingdom but more of Temple of Magicka. In the old religion, magic was known as Magicka. The Temple of Magicka stood on the edge of a grass mounded cliff that hung over the sea. Looking at the temple, you wouldn't think that it was anything special. The temple was built from the finest stone, tall enough so the clouds covered most of the top. The temple was surrounded by beautiful, rich green meadows that went on for miles, that were decorated in multicoloured flowers along with a stunning stream that ran through the meadows and down, off the cliff, into a waterfall that fell to the sea beneath it. The inside of the temple was something spectacular. The interior was made completely out of the finest stone but the walls also had the old religion symbols of Magicka legends and stories that to this day, are still told to the children of the old religion. To the left of the entrance there was a staircase that spiralled up to what looked like nothing but in fact, at the top, there was a portal that sent you up into the clouds to were other parts of the temple, that stood above the clouds and the same to the right of the entrances.

Within the clouds, the different parts of the temple were used for different things. Some rooms were used to practice magic, others for learning the old religion, most were used to bring in the needy and ill so they had somewhere to keep warm and be given food and water. The people of the old religion took in anyone that was in need of help but they didn't take too kindly to the none-believers. If anyone were to wrong or cross the wrong path with the old religion, they would be in a world of pain. The people of the old religion were more powerful than any other magical being within the dimensions and it would be wise to stay kind to them.

***

Smok had landed in one of the gorgeous meadows, allowing Alexa and Lena to climb down from his back. Alexa looked around, amazed by the beauty of what was in front of her. After the tiring journey the dragon and dragon lord had just been on, they walked over to the beautiful stream to gather a drink and refresh themselves before carrying on with their journey.

As they began their journey again, the two best friends took in the view around them. Magical creatures flew freely around, showing off their multicoloured sparks as the sun began to rise. Lena noticed a temple made out of the finest stone, that stood on the edge of a cliff.

"What is this place?" the woman questioned.

"This is Sky-guard, the Temple of Mgaicka. One of the oldest temples that still stand tall. This is where the old religion is home to. This Zor-El is where your magic comes from," Smok replied.

Lena stood there, her green, emerald eyes open wide at what she had just heard. Alexa looked a little confused at what the dragon was going on about.

"We both know that Lena has magic, but does her magic really come from the old religion?" the dragon lord questioned.

"All magic comes from the old religion but Lena's has never progressed into the new religion, which is the magic you possess, your grace. The powers you both posses are just as strong as the other but yours has kept up with time, whereas Lena's hasn't," the dragon answered.

Both of the girls' faces relaxed after Smok's explanation. They carried on walking until they reached the large, wooden doors of the temple. Both of the girls looked nervous. Being in such a highly respected kingdom was something new to them. Being in charge of one was different to traveling through to a different dimension to another one. Especially one that was home to the old religion.

Just as Alexa was about to push open the door, the door swung open, revealing a figure dressed in a blue, hooded robe with gold linen decorating around the outline of the robe, black skinny jeans accompanied by a pair of black boots.

"Queen Alexa Snow, Dragon Lord of Brunuhville, Lena Zor-El, I am glad to finally meet you. Smok, I am glad to see you after so long," the hooded figure spoke.

The girls looked at Smok and he explained. "As you should know, I am from the old religion. All magical creatures are from then."

The hooded figure looked at the girls and stepped aside, allowing them to walk through, into the temple.

"Smok, you know your entrance. Oh, and just last night, we had three others come here. They are inside, Alexa, you may know two of them," the figure spoke as the girls walked in and Smok found his entrance.

***

As the girls walked in, they noticed magical folk walking around in their hooded robes when suddenly there was a flash of light. Lena and Alexa looked in the direction of where the light came from, seeing three figures walk down the staircase. As the figures got to the bottom of the stairs, they stopped, noticing the two girls looking at them. One of the figures walked towards the girls and took down their hood as they came to a halt.

"Oh, my, Merlin! Brook! It has been so long!" Alexa spoke as she hugged her old master.

"I am so sorry to hear about your brother. We almost had him back in 1869 Victorian London," Brook spoke, leaving a confused look on Alexa's face. "I'll explain everything later. Anyway, this is Constantine and Shadow, as I am sure you know about," he continued as the other two figures came forward, removing their hoods.

As Shadow removed her hood, Alexa's features turned cold. "You," she growled as she stepped forward. Brook and

Constantine stepped in-between the two girls, holding them back.

"Please, she is a changed elf now," Constantine spoke, laying a protective hand on Shadow's arm. "She helped us try and catch Link, she was the one that told us what he was really up to, That is why we are here. We know that he will be coming back for you at some point so we wanted to help you. It was Shadow's idea," he continued.

"Well, I would like to see the changed you but I am not sure how your sister is going to react," Alexa spoke.

Everyone gave a small smile until Brook noticed Lena.

"Oh, I'm so sorry, this is Lena Zor-El. My childhood best friend.

"Hi," Lena spoke as she stuck her hand out for every to shake and they gladly did.

The hooded figure, that still hadn't revealed his identity, lead the magical folk, apart from Alexa and Lena, up to the top of the staircase to one of the portals. When they went through all the portals, the reached a wooden door that appeared to be locked. The hooded figure waved his hand over the door's key holes and the sound of a soft clicking noise from the metal tumblers inside resinated as the door unlocked, creaking open slightly, allowing the hooded figure to telepathically open it, stepping aside as the three magical folk walked into the room. As Constantine walked through last, the hooded figure closed the door with his mind and waved his hand over the key holes so no one would disturb them.

The room wasn't like the other rooms around the temple. This room was as empty as a dragon skull that had begun to gather dust from many years of being forgotten. There was nothing but a couple of rotten wooden tables that were covered in spider webs that were accompanied by wooded chairs that were in the same state as the tables.

The hooded figure walked up to the front of the room while everyone was magically cleaning the tables and chairs. After doing so, they all sat down and looked at the unknown hooded figure.

"I am sorry for being so secretive. My name is Scar Mon-El." The figure took his hood down, revealing a young male face, with a scar starting from the top of his right eye, going over his eye lid and finishing just under his bottom eye lid. His eyes were as red as a rose but his right eye was slightly darker from the scaring. He had short, spiked hair that went from being blue at the roots then ending in yellow at the tips of his hair, as if it was a flame.

Everyone looked at Scar not knowing what to say or do so they waited for him to continue. Scar smiled and began to talk again.

***

Down in the main part of the temple, Lena and Alexa stood, waiting for the others to finish when Smok walked up to them with a hooded figure beside him. The figure took down their hood, revealing a young girl with blonde, long hair with piercing blue eyes.

"I am Scarlett Dark, your grace," the girl spoke through her thoughts, as she bowed slightly to the queen, but when she looked at Lena, her smiled grew making the raven-haired girl seem uncomfortable.

Alexa bowed her head slightly and smiled. "It is nice to meet you, Scarlett. This is Lena Zor-El. As you may know of the Zor-El family, I am in need of your help. Lena's magic is from the old religion but she has no understanding."

Lena stood, awkwardly looking at Smok as she knew that he could hear what they were taking about. Lena gave the dragon a look and he understood. They both walked away, leaving the two women alone to talk. As they walked out into a beautiful courtyard, Lena stopped in her tracks and turned to look at Smok.

"Why can't I talk through my thoughts?" she questioned.

"As you may know, you are a telekinetic. You manage so much through your mind that having another power like telepathy would instantly drain you, may even kill you," Smok stated, knowing Lena understood him. "Maybe one day things will be different, but for now, it is safer that you don't have that power."

Lena and Smok walked around the courtyard until the came to a grassy patch, where Lena sat down, allowing the old dragon lay next to her. She looked around them, taking in the sight of the courtyard. Trees stood tall above the clouds, there was a fountain made from the the finest stone in the sculpture of Merlin himself, that stood in the centre of the courtyard with water that fell gracefully out of the staff that was sculpted into Merlin's hand. Suddenly, an envelope floated down from the clouds and landed in Lena's lap, pulling her out of her thoughts. She looked down at the wax mark on the back and sighed in confusion.

"No one has ever written to me from 3019 London. No one cares enough," Lena muttered as she opened the letter.

> *Lena,*
>
> *I know you may not know me personally but my name is Scarlett Dark. I lived in one of the villages that Mr and Mrs Corp was in charge of. I have run away, they were trying to find out where you and Bear had gone, I couldn't stay there with everything they were doing. I ran before they had got to me. I am only sixteen, I have nowhere to go. I am in Sky-Guard and I am really hoping to see you again.*
>
> *You were never like that dreadful family, you always helped us and saw things in a better light than them.*
>
> *I am sorry for the sudden letter but I had to get a hold of you.*
>
> *I hope we meet soon.*
>
> *Scarlett Dark.*

Just as Lena had finished reading the letter, she jumped to her feet, ready to run to this girl when Alexa and Scarlett stood eye to eye with her.

"I am so sorry, I have only just got your letter," Lena explained.

"No need Lena. It is nice to meet you again. Now I know you need help with your magic. Alexa has asked me to come back to

Brunuhville to help you, if you are willing?" Alex spoke.

Lena nodded and the rest of the magical folk joined them. Constantine, Brook, Shadow and Scar sat around on the grassy patch by the fountain with Lena, Alexa, Scarlett and Smok, talking and laughing, everyone forgetting that Alexa was a queen.

The night came around quickly. Sky-Guard looked beautiful at night. Magical creatures flew around so freely, showing off their beautiful colours. All of the magical folk and Smok decided to head to bed knowing that they will be traveling back to their dimension the next day.

The morning came around fast and Alexa's pack was getting ready to leave. They were all standing out in the beautiful meadow that laid out just in front of the Temple of Magika. Alexa and Shadow climbed onto Smok's back while Constantine and Brook opened a portal to Brunuhville. Scarlett looked at Lena confused.

"Lena, you should go, I will follow you soon," Scarlett spoke.

"No, I want to stay for a while. If I am here then I will be able to learn more about what my magic can do and how to understand it," Lena confessed as she looked at her best friend.

"Of course, you need to do whatever you need to do. Stay in contact please. I can't lose you again," Alexa spoke.

Lena and Scarlett bowed their head slightly and the four magical folk and Smok disappeared through the portal leaving Lena, Scarlett and Scar standing in the meadow.

Scar lead the two women back into the temple and to a room far up in the sky. Scar unlocked the door and allowed the two women to walk in. As they entered the room, Scar closed the door and left them alone.

Lena sat down at one of the tables and looked around the room. It was like an old classroom. There were tables laid out in six rows of three with two chairs at each table. At the front of the classroom, there was a big blackboard with chalk and a rubber along the bottom of it. At one side of the room, there were three double windows that looked out into the cloud filled sky.

Lena looked to the front of her to see that Scarlett had pulled a chair from the table in front of her. She had placed it and sat on the other side of Lena.

Scarlett looked to Lena. "Now, are you ready to learn about your magic?"

***

As the dark clouds hung over the ruins of Vanaheim, there was patches of colourful smoke appearing out of nowhere. For a place that was completely abandoned, this was certainly unusual. Out of the smoke, hooded figures began to walk out into the ruined kingdom. The hooded figures met around a broken part of a tower that was once apart of the once so beautiful castle.

"Why have we met here?" one of the figures spoke.

"He told us too," another said.

"Well, if he doesn't turn up soon, I'm leaving," the last one spoke.

"By all means, leave." Just then the three hooded figures jumped, spinning around at the male voice they had just heard.

A hooded figure emerged from a patch of red smoke. As the figure walked towards the three other figures, he took his hood down.

"Link?" the three figures questioned as they lowered their own hoods, revealing Spike, Sparrow and Angel.

"It's nice to see my three men still alive. Where did you head off to after that stupid battle?" Link questioned.

The three men huddled together and hung their heads. "We thought you were dead," Sparrow answered.

"Aha, me dead. You underestimate me. And I thought you were smart," Link spoke, finding the lame excuse highly hilarious.

The four men gathered around the broken part of the tower and began to think of ways to take down Link's sister.

After a couple of hours going through different plans, they finally came up with one.

"I think I have the right plan," Angel spoke.

"Go for it. I would like to hear what idea you have," Link replied.

"Well on our search to try and find Elsie when we got word that her and this elf went missing, we found that she was in Brunuhville, we also found out that Alexa had changed her wolf into an animagus."

"Yeah, yeah, get on with it," Link spoke getting highly annoyed at the amount of babbling that his follower was doing.

"Sorry, well maybe we could cast a spell over the kingdom, making Elsie and Kohana stay in the wolven form," Spike announced.

Link's mouth curved into a mischievous grin. "Do you know of such spell?"

Spike nodded to which was to Link's delight.

"I will teleport us to Brunuhville and then you can cast the spell. We have to make sure that the two animaguses are in their wolven form to do this spell," Link spoke.

Link began to create their portal as the three men waited.

As they arrived on the outskirts on Brunuhville castle, just on the other side of the wall, they watched over the kingdom with their x-ray vision in sight of the two wolves.

After a while of looking, Angel had spotted the two wolves walking around with the young elf that took Elsie away from Link.

"There," Angel spoke.

Link looked in the direction of where Angel was pointing and smiled.

"Spike, you know what to do."

Spike nodded and began to say the incantation to make the two animaguses wolves forever.

***

As Elsie and Kohana were strolling through the kingdom village with Jasper when green sparks started to emerge around them. Jasper looked in shock, not knowing what to do so he called on Sam.

"Sam!" he shouted as Alexa's guard teleported next to him.

"What is the matter young elf?" he questioned.

"What's happening?" he questioned as Sam looked down at the two wolves.

"Take them to the castle straight away. Leonard will know what to do." And with that, Sam teleported the two wolves, Jasper ad himself into the throne room where Leonard was standing.

The green sparks were still emerging from the two wolves and Leonard looked scared.

"How did this happen?" the man questioned.

"I don't know. We were just walking through the village when this started to happen," Jasper replied.

Leonard waved one of his hands over the two girls then clicked his fingers. An image appeared of four hooded figures smirking under their hoods.

"This can mean only one thing," Leonard began.

***

Alexa arrived back in Brunuhville along with the rest of the magical folk. It was a beautiful morning in the kingdom of Brunuhville and it was also a month before Christmas, but also the day of Lee's sixteenth birthday. As the queen and Shadow climbed off of Smok, Alexa had her guards show Shadow, Constantine and Brook to their new shacks.

"Alexa, they will love their presents. Now go and be with your family," Smok spoke as he handed Alexa a bag.

Alexa walked through the kingdom village dressed in her robe, getting bows by the people. As she reached the castle gates, she noticed Sam up on the wall on patrol. She stood there for a while waiting for Sam to notice, but he never did, so she decided to do the only thing that would get his attention.

"Sam," Alexa spoke telepathically, making Sam jump.

Sam looked around trying to find the source of the voice until he noticed that the queen was standing in front of the gate.

"OPEN THE GATE!" Sam shouted, making the other guards open the gate that allowed Alexa to walk through up to her home.

As the other guards closed the gate, Sam teleported down to Alexa's side and walked her up to her home. As she walked through the doors, she was welcomed by her beautiful wife and Bear.

"Alexa, you are home," Shinara spoke as she hugged her wife.

Bear walked forward, noticing that Lena wasn't with the queen.

"Where is Lena?" he questioned.

"She is back in Sky-Guard. She is learning about her magic." Alexa saw the panic on Bear's face. "I promise, she is safe. She will be home before Christmas."

Bear dismissed himself allowing the two women to make their way to the throne room. Just as they reached the doors they heard screeching. Alexa looked to the floor and smiled.

"I think the boys know I am back."

"I think so. Do you want to go and see them?" Shinara offered.

"No no, it's okay. They must have Smok down there by now. I will see them soon but first, I need you and the boys," Alexa stated as her and her wife opened the throne room doors.

As they walked in, they saw Lee and Felix sat on their thrones talking to Leonard. There were two wolves running around playing with Jasper. The two princes noticed their mother, got up from their thrones and ran to Alexa, smothering her in a teddy bear hug.

"Mother we've missed you so much," the boys said in unison.

"I have missed you too. I have something for you two and your mum," Alexa spoke as the two boys pulled away from the hug.

Leonard walked up to Alexa and smiled. "It's great to see you safe." He pulled away from the hug and his smile faded. "But there is something I have to tell you."

"What is it Leo? You are scaring me," Alexa spoke, worry filling her voice.

"A lot has happened in the day you have been gone."

***

Leonard explained everything to Alexa and her face looked red with anger.

"There is only one person I know who would do this," Alexa began as Leonard looked at her to continue. "This is the work of Link," she finished with anger in her voice.

"I thought that would be the case," Leonard answered.

Alexa walked over to Kohana and Elsie and knelt down to their level.

"How could he do this to you guys. Oh, and Jasper." Alexa turned to Jasper, who was standing near the wolves looking to get a telling off. "Don't worry, okay? I will sort this out and don't look so upset, there was nothing you could have done to stop this from happening."

Jasper looked at Alexa and smiled knowing that his queen was right. Alexa stood to her feet, allowing Jasper and the two wolves to carrying on playing. Alexa began to walk out of the throne room when Leonard called back.

"Where are you going?" he questioned.

"Lena needs to hear about this. She may know how to help."

"Take someone with you please," he spoke.

"Don't worry, Sam is outside waiting." And with that, Alexa turned on her heels and walked out of the hall, walking side by side with Sam.

"Where are we heading to, your grace?"

"To my secret room. I need to write to Lena."

Sam nodded and carried on walking with his queen until they were met with the said room door that was enchanted to look like the wall.

"Stand outside please Sam. I need you to keep watch for me. No one can know that this room even exists," Alexa spoke as she walked into the room.

Sam bowed his head slightly and disguised himself as the wall, allowing Alexa to close the door. Alexa walked to the table and sat down, opening a draw and grabbing paper, her quill and ink, her wax and stamp. She picked up her quill, dipped the end into the ink and began her letter to her best friend.

> *Lena,*
>
> *I have just arrived back at Brunuhville and found that Link has done some dirty work. He has cast a spell over Elsie and Kohana, making them stay in their wolven form.*
>
> *This is magic that I am not strong enough to yield. I am hoping you can help me with this.*
>
> *I know it hasn't been long but I miss you like crazy. I don't want to lose you again.*
>
> *I hope things are going well and I hope you come home soon.*
>
> *Alexa.*

Alexa folded up the letter and put her stamp on it. With a click of her fingers, the letter was gone. She put everything away and walked out of the room.

"Thank you, Sam," Alexa spoke as she looked both ways of the hallway to make sure that it was clear.

Sam emerged from the wall and smiled. "Is everything done?"

Alexa nodded and they began to walk back to the throne room while Alexa hoped that Lena would get the letter soon and be able to help.

***

Lena and Scarlett were sat in one of the meadows in Sky-guard, not too far from the temple, on a break. All morning Lena has been studying her magic and where it comes from and for anyone that knew Lena, would know she is not much of a book worm. But she had learnt much more than just what was told in the books.

"In a matter of hours, you have been able to cast most of the extremely powerful spells known to the old religion, Such as;

Summon:
- A Spirit
- A Dragon
- The Dead
-A Portal
Command:
- A Wish
- A Luck

A Sleep spell along with:
-Fire
-Earth
-Air
-Water

Call Upon:
- Animals
- Guardians

Can move:
-Rocks
-Water
-Earth
-Fire
-Air
-buildings

With her mind, along with:
-Throwing objects across a room
- Freezing objects and time," Scarlett spoke with such excitement.

Lena just smiled. After a few hours of learning her powers, it has drained her. She looked over at Scarlett seeing that her new friend had a look of glee and pleading in her eyes. Lena knew exactly what her friend was after. After learning how to call upon guardians, Scarlett had found that by the way Lena kept herself so calm and level-headed, by the way she kept her head clear and up in the clouds and the way she channeled her energy from the earth itself, was something to be admired.

After a few short moments of Scarlett staring at Lena, the raven-haired women gave in. Lena crossed her legs and closed her eyes, clearing her mind and letting the energy from the earth travel through her. She lifted a hand up level with her eyes and opened her eyes. As she concentrated on her hand, she twisted it slightly then as her eyes changed to an electric green, she spoke,

"Es Ther Ra…" Then she clicked her fingers, allowing a silver lining to flow from her hand.

The blonde hair woman watched in awe as the light from her friend's hand turned into a silhouette of an eagle. The two women watched as the eagle soared through the air and as it landed on top of Lena's shoulder, it faded into a mist.

"Wow, this will never get old," Scarlett spoke.

"Well, I should hope not. I'm not getting old too fast aha," Lena laughed.

Just then something had crossed Scarlett's mind. "Lena, how old are you?"

"Twenty-one. Why do you ask?" Lena asked, slightly more abrupt than she was intending.

Scarlett hesitated at first but then answered the question. "There is something that I haven't told you get about the old religion and it is only written in one book."

"I thought I had read all the books I need to?" the raven-haired woman questioned in confusion.

"You have but this one is meant to be read just before the person's twenty-second birthday."

A heavy silence fell over the two women. The only noise that could be heard was the sound of nature. It was comfortable but also suffocating.

"So where is this so-called book you are talking about?" Lena spoke, breaking the silence.

"It's not quite a book," Scarlett began. "Follow me." And with that, the two women walked in tow with each other back through the meadow and to the temple.

As they walked through the temple doors, Lena followed the young witch down a corridor to the left of the ground floor. There were so many doors, some open, some closed down this straight and long corridor. The doors that were left open, Lena took a quick glance in them, noticing that they were all very different. some were classrooms, some were conference rooms and others were for where the children of the old religion would spend their time if they did not want to venture outside.

They soon arrived at two large, wooden doors at the end of the corridor, that appeared to be locked. Scarlett waved her hand over the door key holds and then moved to the side, allowing the doors to magically open.

"Welcome to the Temple of Magicka library," the blonde woman spoke then walked onwards into the room.

Lena looked around in amazement. Never in her life has she ever seen so many books and scrolls. Scarlett walked through the library with Lena at her heal, guiding her up to the third floor, where every shelf was crammed with at least ten scrolls in one cubby hole. Lena sat down at one of the tables in a area that wasn't full of other magical folk talking, while Scarlett was rummaging through the shelves in search 0f the scroll she was after.

After a while of looking, Scarlett had found the scroll and began to walk to where Lena was sat. When she reached the table, she placed the scroll down and sat at the opposite side of the table.

"There are two entries on this scroll," Scarlett spoke.

The scroll looked like it had been untouched. The off-white paper was rolled up neatly with a blue ribbon tied around it, keeping it together so it wouldn't roll undone.

Lena carefully took one end of the ribbon and pulled at it, allowing the ribbon to fall gracefully off of the scroll. She unrolled the paper and began to read it.

> *394AD*
>
> *Entry no.1 written at the Temple of Magicka…*
>
> *My name is Alice Zor-El. I was just getting ready to celebrate my twenty-second birthday when my body went limb. I had no clue what was going on so I called for my mother Angelica Zor-El. When she came in, my body felt stone cold, as if I was going to die. And then I passed out. I don't remember anything after feeling cold and everything had gone black.*
>
> *I woke in the presence of my mother who had explained to me that every woman that possesses magicka, on her twenty-second birthday will turn immortal. The process is scary as I have witnessed but with becoming immortal, the power you hold will make you feel like you have only just awoken from being reborn.*
>
> *End of entry.*

Entry no.2 written in the Temple of Magicka…

Mother of Alice Zor-El.

I was so happy to had witnessed my daughters immortality change. It was such a beautiful sight. She was on her knees in her room and everything around her and her body had gone stone cold. a purple and green mist had emerged from around her body and a blue light began to shoot into my daughter's body and then she had passed out.

I had explained what had happened, but it was such a beautiful sight to see. To see your only daughter become immortal is something every m0ther wants to see.

End of entry.

Lena looked up from the scroll, tears building up in her eyes as the memory of her mother loomed in her mind. Scarlett didn't know what to do except take the scroll away and roll it back up, tying the blue ribbon around it again.

Scarlett led Lena out of the library and temple and back to the meadow they were sat in a little while ago. As they reached the spot they were sat at earlier, Lena screamed at the top of her lungs, causing trees to tumble down to the ground, rocks from mountains to crumble down and the wildlife to scatter, fly and scurry away. Lena was beyond upset, she was broken. After fourteen years, she had finally released all of her broken emotions that were held onto her mother, the women she missed so dearly.

After the raven-haired woman had calmed down, Scarlett approached her and placed a hand on her shoulder.

"I know how you must feel, having your parents taken away from you. And if you don't feel up to it, that's okay, but there is one more thing you need to learn before we can head to Brunuhville," Scarlett spoke.

"I'm ready for anything, what do I need to learn?" Lena questioned.

"To summon the dead."

Lena nodded her head and Scarlett lead her friend to and graveyard that wasn't too far from the temple.

The graveyard was small but beautiful. There were hundreds of rows of gravestones that had flowers and other decorations that were neatly placed in front of the stones. At the very back of the graveyard there were tombs that held the corps of the highest priests and priestess of the old religion.

Scarlett lead Lena to the middle row of the graveyard and to a small stone that sat alone at the end of the row. Lena crouched down and looked over the stone. There were more flowers, teenage magic books and candles around this stone that the others. Lena looked at the stone and read the name.

"Tommy Mon-El. That's Scar's brother, right?" Lena spoke as she stood to her feet.

"Yeah. He lost Tommy last year in a fight. That's why his face is scarred," Scarlett spoke a hint of hurt in her voice.

Lena looked back at the stone then up at the sky. She closed her eyes for a second then when she looked back down at the stone, she held her hand out. Blue mist rose from the palm of her hand and just as her eyes changed to an electric green, she spoke.

"Sor drachon du."

The blue mist sprung from Lena's hand and shot into the earth in front of the stone. As the mist faded, a white, silver mist began to slip through the earth and it hovered juster above the stone.

"Tommy?" a voice called out.

Lena and Scarlett snapped their heads to look behind them. As they did, they noticed Scar walking up to them. He approached the stone and looked at his younger brother.

"Drake. I have missed seeing you," the ghost boy spoke.

"I have missed you too mate."

The two girls walked away so they were out of hearing shot and let the two brothers have a moment alone.

Lena watched as the two boys laughed along with each other and smiled. Then an idea popped into her head.

"Scarlett, can you bring someone back from the dead?" she questioned.

"Yeah, of course."

"Are there any consequences?"

"No. What's all of this about Lena?" Scarlett questioned.

Lena closed her eyes and searched for the spell that would bring Tommy back to life. Scarlett watched, concerned about why Lena had the sudden urge to know about this spell. Lena opened her eyes and smiled. She ran over to Tommy and Scar (Drake) and began to talk.

"Tommy, how would you like to be able to hug your brother and hang around with him again?"

"I would love to," Tommy spoke.

"Scar, how would you feel about having your little brother back?"

"I would love that more than anything Lena, but there is no one powerful enough to do that, that is still alive," Scar spoke, a hint of pain lingering as the words left his mouth.

"Don't be so sure about that," Lena spoke as she stepped back.

"What are you doing Lena?" Scar questioned as he, Tommy and Scarlett watched.

Lena closed her eyes and raised her hand towards the ghost boy. A green mist rose from her hand along with dark blue sparks. They shot into Tommy's ghostly figure and as the raven-haired woman opened her eyes, they changed colour again as she spoke.

"Dawnson zo zine." As the words left her mouth, the mist and sparks created a whirlwind around the ghost.

The three magical folk watched as Tommy's body began to change. The ghostly figure that was once so see-through, had magically begun to grow the boney structure of its body. The three magical folk watched as crimson red liquid rose from the ground and into Tommy's now boned structured body. Muscle and veins began to form over the bones and then creating the finishing touches, flesh began to cover the bloody, muscly structure that was able to stand firmly on the ground.

Tommy stood six feet from the ground. He had red eyes and flame like hair like his brother. Scar looked at his brother in disbelief and fell to his knees. Tommy walked over to his brother and knelt down to his level. Scar placed his hand on Tommy's shoulder and a tear fell from his eye.

"You are really here," Scar spoke as he hugged his brother, letting more tears fall down his cheeks.

"Yeah, I really am back here with you," Tommy spoke back, allowing his tears to fall as well.

The two brothers stood to their feet and wiped their eyes. Scar walked up to Lena and hugged her tight.

"Thank you so much. You don't know how much this means to me, to us." Scar pulled away and smiled.

"Of course," Lena smiled back.

***

As the magical folk arrived back at the temple, a letter magical appeared in the sky and floated down towards Lena. As the letter reached Lena, it hovered in the air. Lena took the letter and opened it up.

After reading the letter, she immediately looked at Scarlett.

"We need to go to Brunuhville. Alexa needs me. Something terrible has happened."

Scarlett nodded. They said their goodbyes to Tommy and Scar and Lena began to open a portal. When the portal was ready, Lena and Scarlett walked through and the portal closed behind them.

***

The queens and the princes were sat in the hall room having a game of chess with Bear when a blue and purple portal opened up. The five of them jumped up, magic ready at their hands. Lena and Scarlett jumped through the portal and noticed everyone readying their magic.

"Hey no magic, no magic, it's us," Lena spoke.

They all calmed down and placed their hands at their sides. Bear ran to Lena and hugged her tightly.

"I thought you were never going to come home," he mumbled.

"I will always come home to you Bear," Lena spoke as she hugged him back.

As the two pulled away, Alexa jumped on her best friend, smothering her in a teddy bear hug.

"I am so glad you are safe."

"Always, I am the most powerful witch to ever live, except you of course," Lena laughed as Alexa pulled away.

"I literally just received your letter. Explain to me what has happened," Lena spoke.

They all sat down at the table and Alexa began to explain what had happened to Elsie and Kohana.

Just as they finished up talking, the hall doors opened, revealing Leonard, Kohana and Elsie. Elsie and Kohana ran to Lena and Lena inspected the two wolves. She stood to her feet and closed her eyes, searching her mind for the spell to change the two wolves back to their animagus state. Lena opened her eyes and held her hand out to the wolves. Black and red sparks emerged from Lena's hand as the raven-haired woman's eyes changed colour but this time instead of changing to electric green, they changed to black, as she spoke.

"Dar zender ru ender."

The sparked shot into the two wolves and began to swirl around them. Lena let go of the energy and fell to her hands and knees, drained from the power. Alexa ran to her best friend's side and Bear did the same. They all watched as the wolves stood.

"Kohana, Elsie, try and change back," Alexa spoke.

Elsie and Kohana looked at each other and sighed. They closed their eyes and suddenly pink and blue mist appeared around them. Everyone watched as their bodies began to change back into their human forms. Elsie and Aria looked at each other and smiled. They both walked over to Lena and hugged her.

"Thank you so much!' Elsie spoke.

"Yeah, you don't know how good it feels to be back in this form again," Aria laughed.

"You are most welcome," Lena spoke as she stood to her feet.

Elsie and Aria walked out of the hall with Leonard to go and show Jasper that they have changed back as Lee and Felix headed to their rooms to bed as the night was getting on.

"I think we should head to bed too. Especially you Lena, you are drained," Shinara spoke.

Lena nodded and allowed her queens to help her to her room while Bear trailed behind her.

***

That night, Lena found it hard to sleep. She felt a dark magic around Brunuhville. She tried to ignore it but it was becoming a fight for sleep. Bear noticed how restless his friend had become and jumped on the bed so he could keep her safe. Shortly after, Lena was just about to fall into a deep sleep when there was a loud crash from inside the castle and Lena felt the dark presence once again.

Lena and Bear jumped out of bed and ran down the hallway where they were met with Alexa and the rest of her pack.

"What the bloody hell was that?" Jasper spat.

"I'm not sure but whatever it was, it has unsettled my dragons," Alexa spoke as she could hear her dragon's screeches.

"Look after them Smok," she spoke through her mind.

"Of course, Alexa. They are safe with me."

The pack walked down the hallways of the castle on guard until they reached the throne room where they heard smashing and crashing emerging from the room. Sam suddenly appeared and readied himself along with the others.

Sam threw open the doors to the throne room and they all burst in but stood still at the sight they saw before them.

"Miss me?"

8

The Magical Graveyard

Link was sat on Alexa's throne and everything in the throne room had been smashed and blown apart.

"Link," Lena spat through gritted teeth.

"Aha, Lena, it's so good to see you. I heard that you had moved here. You really shouldn't have," Link laughed.

Lena readied her hands and her eyes turned black. Scarlett and Alexa placed a hand one each of Lena's and she calmed down. Alexa looked her brother dead in the eye and smirked. remembering that there are more powerful creatures in this room that Link.

"So, what brings you to my home?" Alexa questioned.

"Oh, you know sightseeing, sister killing, throne taking. The usual," Link smirked.

Suddenly black mist began to appear in three spots by Link. out from the mist, Angel, Spike and Sparrow appeared and Leonard gritty his teeth and clenched his fists.

Link noticed Leonards actions and laughed.

"Oh you didn't really think that I would come alone did you?"

"That just shows that you are a coward," Alexa sniggered, catching her brother's attention.

"I thought you guys were dead?" Leonard spoke.

"Aha you thought wrong," Spike laughed back.

Alexa walked forward towards her throne, where her brother sat and smiled. She turned to looked at Shinara and Lena and winked. The two women knew what she was up to and motioned for everyone to walk out of the room.

***

Alexa looked back to her brother and saw a look of pure evil in his eyes, a look that she knows all too well.

"Poor little Alexa, all alone now to fight me and lose," Link chuckled.

"Of course, but it only seems fair if you lose your goons as well. One against three, that seems like an unfair fight to me. But then again, you will be the one that will need back up, not me," Alexa replied as she walked around her throne room confident in herself, which she knew would get her brother's back up.

"You have it all wrong sister, you will need the back up. You are fighting the most powerful dark elf to ever live," Link spat.

Alexa chuckled as she faced her brother once again.

"Suit yourself," And with that, Alexa raised her hand and directed it at her brother as a fireball left her hand, hitting Link in the chest and making him go flying through the air.

Link hit his back against a wall and fell to the ground. He stood to his feet and a look of anger lingered over his face.

"You've had it witch."

***

When they walked out of the room and closed the throne room doors behind them, Lena and Scarlett walked down the hallway, a little way away from the rest of the group, that were arguing over what was going on as bangs and crashes were heard from outside of the throne room. As they closed their eyes, a dark mist fell over the two witches, allowing dark, powerful magic to consume them. They held one of their hands out towards the wall that was directly opposite the thrones and held onto each other with their free hand. When they opened their eyes, they had turned a midnight black. They twisted their hand slightly and spoke.

"Daxen cand zint du fort."

Lee and Felix noticed what Lena and Scarlett were doing and noticed they didn't have enough power to go against Link through a wall, so they ran over to them and placed one of their hands on theirs and held their other one up towards the wall, speaking the incantation.

A silver mist emerged from their hands and disappeared through the wall. Once the mist was gone, there was no sound to be heard from the throne room. Everyone looked at each other unsure whether to stay outside or go in. Suddenly the throne room doors opened and Alexa walked out. Everyone else rushed into the room but everything was back to the way it was before Link had turned up.

"What happened in there?" Leonard questioned.

"Yeah mother? What happened? You don't have a scratch on you," Lee said.

"Well thanks to you Lena and Scarlett and you two Lee and Felix, the magic you produced, was strong enough to cast Link and his followers outside of the castle wall. I am unsure where but I know they are gone," Alexa explained.

"I wouldn't be so sure about that," Lena muttered under her breath.

Alexa gave her a concerned look but Lena just smiled back. The group decided to walk back to their rooms to finally go back to sleep. Lena stayed behind with Scarlett. She leant against the wall and sunk down to the floor and held her knees to her chest.

"You don't need me to stay here anymore Lena. You know everything you need to know," Scarlett spoke.

"So that means you are leaving?" Lena questioned, her voice shaking.

"I need too. Sky-guard needs me back."

And with enough being said, Lena clicked her fingers and a portal appeared in front of them.

"I am only a letter away Lena if you need me." And with that, Scarlett was through the portal and it closed behind her.

And once again, Lena was alone. This feeling came all so naturally to Lena. After her parents died at the hands of Link, after she was adopted by the family that was meant to love her and now someone that made her remember her mother, she was more alone in this world than she had ever been. Tears began to roll down the raven-haired woman's cheeks as she bowed her head to her knees.

"Lena…" A voice called out.

Lena lifted her head and looked around her, trying to figure out where that voice had come from but there was no one around.

"Lena…" It called out again.

Lena stood to her feet and looked around the space she was in. No one was there. She was sure that she was going crazy but there it was. A silver lining flowed through the hallway and as it reached her, a light blue ball of light hovered in front of her face.

"This way Lena…" There it was again.

Lena looked around one last time but this time, the ball of light followed her. She turned back to the ball of light and looked closely at it. A face of her mother appeared in the ball and it looked like she was smiling. Lena closed her eyes and shook her head. She thought she was just tired but when she looked again, her mother's face was still there.

"Mother?" Lena questioned.

"This way Lena…" The voice spoke again as the ball of lift began to drift slowly in the direction of the castle doors.

Lena knew for sure that it was her mother talking to her. Lena clicked her fingers and from mid-air, her hooded robe fell into her hands. She placed her robe over her shoulders, zipped it up and placed the hood over her head. She followed the ball of light out of the castle and down the steps towards the village. As she walked through the village, she watched as the sleeping village came to life with pixies and fairies, flying around and showing off their beautiful colours.

She followed the blue light through the village and it led her to a bridge that went over this beautiful pound that could be mistaken for a lake, but it in fact lead into the lake that ran through the great forest. On either side of the pound, there was an island. One island had a seating area of benches around the outside of the island and in the middle of the island, there were a couple of chess tables with wooden chairs. On the other side, there was a great old tree that stood slightly taller than the other trees around the kingdom.

The raven-haired woman carried on walking until she came to a graveyard. The graveyard was big but spacious. There were not many gravestones there, but the ones that were there, ranged from baby to adults. A long the edge of the graveyard, there were mausoleums that held each generation of the Snow family that lived before Alexa. Also doted around in the air, slightly above the mausoleums, were white balls of light, that lite up the graveyard at night.

Lena followed the blue ball of light to the end of the graveyard, where it hovered above two stones. Lena looked down at the stones and noticed that they were her mother and father's graves. The ball of light sunk into one of the graves. Lena held her hand out to her mother's grave and closed her eyes.

"Sor drachen du," Lena spoke as she opened her eyes and a red mist flowed from her hand and into the grave.

A blue mist emerged from the grave and hovered just above the grave. Lena looked towards the ghostly figure and a tear fell from her eye.

"Mother."

"Yes darling."

Lena fell to her knees and cried.

"I never thought I would see you again. Lena cried as she looked up at her mother's ghostly figure.

"Lena, I may not be here in the flesh but you can always call for me. I heard your cries earlier. I knew you felt alone," her mother spoke.

Lena's mother floated down and sat on top of her grave. Lena crawled forward towards her mother and sat next to her.

"I wish I would hug you," Lena spoke.

"You can, search your mind for the spell."

Lena closed her eyes and searched her mind. A few moments later, Lena's eyes shot open, but instead of being the beautiful green jobs that they were, they were now electric blue. Lena looked at her mother and spoke.

"Thap twick." A faded pink mist swirled around Lena's mother and then shot into her ghostly figure.

Lena watched the magic do its job and even though her mother still looked ghostly, her body was more solid than what it was. Lena leaned into her mother as she was embraced by a cold hug but it was warm in a sense.

The mother and daughter stayed like that for the rest of the night. As the sun started to rise, Lena's mood seemed to have dampened.

"Don't worry my love, you can come back and see me whenever you want to. Thanks to your spell, my body will like this for eternity," her mother whispered.

"I don't want to leave you just yet," Lena mumbled.

Her mother sighed and tightened her embrace around her daughter's body.

"We can stay until the sun is fully risen and then I have to go back to your father."

Lena had forgotten all about her father that night. She really had enjoyed her mother's company.

"Can you bring father with you tonight please? I would love to see him," Lena questioned.

"Of course, darling."

Then they both fell silent, watching the sun rise.

***

Lena woke to a cold sensation on her face. When she looked around she noticed that her mother was gone. She looked to the sky and squinted at how bright the sun was. She went to stand to her feet when she noticed something on the ground shimmering. When she looked closer, she noticed that it was a ring. She looked at the ring and smiled. The ring itself was gold and dotted around the ring were emerald stones. Lena placed the ring on her finger then smiled to her feet. She then noticed a slip of paper stuck on to the stone. Lena picked it up and read what it said.

> *My dearest daughter,*
>
> *I know that we had to cut the meeting short but I am glad that we got to see each other again. I have missed you dearly but you are doing so well. I am sorry for the family that took you in. I wish I had never left you. I will see you tonight and I will bring your father.*
>
> *Your mother.*
>
> *Ps. Before I left you, I kissed you forehead. But it wasn't just any kiss, this kiss has given you the power to speak to me ad Alexa through your mind.*

Lena smiled as she folded the paper up and put it in her robe pocket and began to walk back up to the castle.

As she got to the castle, she decided to go and pay the dragons a visit. She walked down the corridors of the castle until she was met with the door to the dragon caves. She walked down the steps and saw that Smok was the only dragon in the caves and he was asleep. Lena went to walk back up the steps when Smok began to wake up.

"Don't leave young witch," Smok spoke through his mind.

"I am sorry for waking you, I just came down here to have some alone time before I went to grab some food."

"Please, stay. I heard you coming so I decided to get one of the guards to bring down some food for you," Smok replied, moving a plate into show.

Lena sat down next to Smok and began to eat.

"How was the meeting with your mother?" Smok questioned.

"It was nice. I really have missed her," Lena replied.

"Take Alexa with you next time. It would be nice for her to see her parents too."

Lena nodded and finished her food.

Just as she finished, the three dragons flew in with Alexa, Lee and Felix. As the boys climbed down from their dragons, they ran to Lena and hugged her. Alexa jumped down, allowing her dragons to feast on their breakfast.

"Hey, where were you last night?" Alexa questioned as she walked over to her best friend.

"It's a long story. Could we talk over a walk in the gardens?" Lena questioned.

"Of course."

Lena and Alexa made their way up the steps into the castle and to the gardens, allowing themselves some privacy.

Lena explained about seeing her mother the night before and how she had spent all night with her talking and just enjoying each other's presence after fourteen years of being apart. Alexa's heart warmed to the way her best friend was feeling, but also felt a twinge at her heart strings. The queen's face dropped and the raven-haired woman had noticed.

"Alexa, I'm sorry," Lena placed a hand on her best friend's

shoulder and gave a half-hearted smile. "Mother told me to bring you along with me next time."

"Why?"

"Mother will bring your parents too, so you can see them," Lena spoke, a bit more cheerful than she anticipated.

"Okay, I will come. But what am I meant to say to them? It's been fourteen years," Alexa spoke, almost in a whisper.

"I didn't really talk much. I cried at first, but then we sat there and enjoyed the night." Lena smiled.

***

That night after dinner, Alexa had said good night to her two boys and her wife and followed Lena out into the kingdom. The village was quiet. Magical creatures were out, making themselves known and showing their colours off as Draco, Spitze and Zepter were out flying. Alexa smiled as she carried on walking until she noticed a small bridge in front of her. The same bridge that Lena walked across the night before. Alexa looked at the sight before her in awe. She thought she had seen everywhere around the kingdom but she knew she would of remembered a place as beautiful as this in her kingdom.

As they carried on walking, they came to the entrance to the graveyard. Lena didn't notice it before but the entrance to the yard was a tall, metal gate that was intertwined like vines that were connected to metal fences that were the same as the gate, that stood tall around the edge of the graveyard. They walked through the entrance and slowly walked to the far end of the yard. Lena slowed herself as she noticed Alexa had fallen back slightly.

"Are you okay?" she questioned.

"I… Er yeah I'm okay." Alexa smiled slightly.

Lena came to a halt when they reached their parent's graves. Alexa looked at her mother and father's graves and knelt down in front of them. She placed a hand on her mother and then her father's as silent tears escaped her ice blue eyes. Lena watched her best friend closely, remembering the feeling she had when she came here just hours ago.

Lena held her hands out to her father and mother's graves and closed her eyes.

"Sor drachen du," Lena spoke as she opened her eyes and a red mist flowed from her hand and into the grave. She waved her hand over to Alexa's parent's graves, allowing the red mist fall into their graves.

Alexa hung her head towards the ground and wasn't aware of the blue mist that emerged from the graves and hovered just above them. Lena then closed her eyes again and spoke *"Thap Twick."* A pink mist swirled around the four ghostly figures and emerged into them.

Lena hugged her mother and father and the three then turned to look at Alexa, who still had no idea what was happening. Alexa's mum reached her hand out and placed it onto her daughter's shoulder. Alexa lifted her gaze and her eyes widened in shock but also happiness. Alexa looked at her mum and dad and silent tears began to fall once again but this time, she wasn't afraid to be seen as weak. her body fell into her parents and they hugged her tight. Alexa hugged them tight back, so tight that she was scared that she would lose her parents again.

Lena and her parents sat down and smiled at the the sight of the dead king and queen and the alive queen. Alexa pulled away and the three sat down as well, next to Lena's family. Alexa was still in shock. Lena placed an arm around her friend and smiled.

"Tamara, Leo, it's great to see you again, even if in these circumstances." Lena smiled.

"Like wise child," Tamara spoke, then looked at Lena's parents. "I see that your daughter is getting stronger with her powers, Emily and Daxim."

"Awe, yes she is, and we are so proud of the woman she is becoming." Daxim smiled.

"As am I," Alexa spoke up, shifting slighting in her dad's embrace.

Lena looked over at her and smiled.

"I thought she was dead for so long, after everything that had happened but then when she reached out to me and told me everything that had happened, I was so glad that she was still alive. I'm glad that I get to share my home with my best friend once again," Alexa smiled, allowing more tears to fall.

***

The two best friends and their parents spent hours talking and catching up. The parents telling stories of the spirit world and their daughters telling stories of their adventures throughout the different dimensions.

Lena noticed that the sun was rising and knew it was time to they had to say farewell. Lena placed her hand on Alexa's and smiled weakly.

"It's time to say goodbye."

"Okay," Alexa sighed and then looked back at her parents.

She gave her mum a hug first.

"I have missed you so much mum," Alexa cried.

"I have missed you too. We are always here." She placed her hand on her daughter's chest, above her heart. "And you can come and see us whenever you want to."

"I love you."

"I love you too darling. Always." Tamara kissed her daughters head and allowed Leo to have his farewell hug.

"I have missed you so much kiddo," he spoke as he stroked Alexa's hair.

"I have missed you too dad. Will I ever get to see you again?" she questioned.

"Of course, you will," Leo spoke, pulling out of the hug and looking into Alexa's eyes. "Listen, I have had this for years and it is time for you to have it." He reached into his ghostly trouser pocket, drawing out a ring. The ring was a gold band and had sapphires and rubies placed around the gold band. Leo handed his daughter the ring and she smiled.

"This isn't just any ring. When you want to talk to me or your mum or are in any kind of trouble and need some help or guidance, whisper *dalence du kinde* into the ring and we will be here for you. I promise," Leo spoke.

Alexa hugged her dad one last time and stepped back towards Lena.

"We will see you soon," Tamara spoke.

"We love you," the two couples spoke in unison.

And just as the sun had reached just above the graves, the girls' parents were gone. Alexa sighed and the two girls turned on their heels. Lena put her arm around her best friend's shoulders and pulled her close.

"Thank you for this. It was nice to finally see them again after so long," Alexa spoke.

"Anything for you." Lena smiled.

The two girls walked back to the castle, close to each other.

***

Later that morning, everyone had seemed to go their own way and spend time with the other people they love.

Shinara and Shadow were walking through the gardens. This was the first time in months that the two women had their sister time. After Shadow had betrayed Shinara to walk on the dark side, Shinara has not been ready to talk things out. Until today.

As the two women walked through the gardens, Shadow decided to sit down by one of the water fountains. With Shinara following her sister's actions, they sat there in silence for a while, neither one of them knowing what to say. They both exhaled and rambled some words that neither one of them could understand. They both laughed a nervous laugh and smiled at each other.

"Go first. You have probably held back a lot of words that you are wanting to say to me," Shadow said.

Shinara smiled. "Not really. You have always been the one to follow the wrong crowd because it seems cool. I just didn't think that you would carry it on into adulthood."

"I know it was stupid. I don't even know what I was thinking. I even made Elwin fake that test for me so you could be like me," Shadow confessed.

The queen smiled and placed a hand on her sister's thigh. "I kind of gathered that. I'm a ice elf. I had one of the greatest professors help me before me and Alexa got together."

"Have I told you how happy I am about you two?" Shadow questioned.

Shinara shook her head then smiled. "I know you are though."

The two sisters hugged then stood to their feet. They walked through the gardens laughing and joking with each other until Jasper and Ray rounded a corner and bumped into them.

"Ah Shadow! Just the woman I was looking for," Ray spoke making the older woman smile.

Since Ray and Shadow had met, they had been getting closer and closer to each other. Shinara had noticed this and smiled to herself.

"Me and Jasper are needed. I will see you later." Shinara kissed her sister's cheek and walked off with Jasper at her side.

"Are we needed?" Jasper questioned.

"No. I just know that my sister needs something good in her life." The queen smiled and carried on walking back to the castle.

Ray and Shadow walked around the gardens and found

themselves within the village and outside of Ray's home.

"I was wondering if you wanted to come in?" Ray questioned, hoping his nerves wouldn't get the better of him.

"I'd love to." Shadow smiled and she took his hand, allowing him to enter his house with a beautiful woman attached to him.

***

The day soon faded into the evening. The beautiful light blue sky began to fade into the midnight blue night sky. Stars began to appear as the people of Brunuhville began to turn the lights on within the homes, allowing the night settle in around them.

Lee and Felix were standing on the second-floor balcony that hung over the castle gardens, looking out into the night sky, spending quality brother time together, when snow began to fall from the sky.

"Is that?" Lee began.

"Snow?" Felix finished as the two boys looked at each other.

"Yes, it is, boys," Lena spoke as she was leaning against the balcony door frame.

She walked over to the boys, slipped in between them and put an arm around each of them.

"Beautiful, isn't it?" she questioned.

"It sure is Auntie Lena," Lee spoke.

"What are you doing in here anyway Lena?" Felix questioned.

Lena laughed and clicked her fingers. Three blankets appeared on the floor of the balcony and she smiled.

"I wanted to show you boys something and teach you how to do it."

The boys and Lena sat down on the blankets. Lena crossed her legs and closed her eyes, clearing her mind and letting the energy from the earth travel through her. She lifted a hand up level with her eyes and opened her eyes. As she concentrated on her hand, she twisted it slightly then as her eyes changed to an electric green, she spoke,

"Es Ther Ra…" Then she clicked her fingers, allowing a silver lining to flow from her hand.

The boys watched in amazement as the light from their aunt's hand turned into a silhouette of an eagle. The two brothers and Lena watched as the eagle soared through the air and as it landed on top of Lena's shoulder, it faded into a mist.

"That was amazing!" Lee spoke.

"Right, now it's your turn."

Lena began to teach the boys how to summon a guardian, which didn't take too long as the boys were very fast learners.

Felix closed his eyes, clearing his mind and letting all of the energy from the earth travel into him. He lifted a hand up level to his eyes and opened them. As he concentrated on his hand, he twisted it slightly and spoke,

"Es Ther Ra…" Then she clicked his fingers, allowing a silver lining to flow from his hand.

The silver lining turned into a silhouette of a wolf and ran around in the air, catching and playing in the falling snow. The wolf ran onto Felix's shoulder and faded into a mist.

Now Lee's turn.

Lee closed his eyes, clearing his mind and letting all of the energy from the earth travel into him. He lifted a hand up level to his eyes and opened them. As he concentrated on his hand, he twisted it slightly and spoke,

"Es Ther Ra…" Then he clicked his fingers, allowing a silver lining to flow from his hand.

The silver lining turned into a silhouette of a dragon and flew around in the air, burning and playing in the falling snow. The dragon flew into Lee's chest and a blue glow emerged from him.

Lena's eyes widened in shock and then closed her eyes, searching for an answer to why this happened.

After a short time, she opened her eyes and smiled.

"What just happened? That didn't happen to you or Felix," Lee panicked.

"There's nothing to worry about. It just means that your magic is like mine. Your magic is connected to the old religion," Lena explained. "Not everyone can possess it. Magic grows with how time wants it to but mine and your magic sticks to the old ways."

Lee smiled and closed his eyes again. He lifted a hand up level to his eyes and opened them. As he concentrated on his hand, he twisted it slightly but then his eyes changed to an electric red and then spoke,

"Es Ther Ra…" Then she clicked his fingers, allowing a silver lining to flow from his hand.

The silver lining turned into a silhouette of a dragon and flew around in the air, burning and playing in the falling snow. But this time, the dragon landed on his shoulder and faded into a mist.

"I need to go and write a letter, boys. I will see you at dinner." And with that, Lena stood to her feet and left the boys' room.

She walked down the corridor and entered her room to see bear curled up on the bed. She walked over to her desk by the winder, that overlooked the gardens and pulled out her quill, paper and ink.

"You were gone a while. What happened?" Bear questioned.

"I was teaching Felix and Lee some magic and just found out that Lee maybe in possession of magic from the old religion," Lena explained.

"You mean like you?" Bear asked as he walked closer to Lena.

"Yes. I need to asked Scarlett about this." And with that, Lena began to write her letter to Scarlett.

***

The snow began to thicken as it landed on the ground. Felix, Lee and Lena were sat in the hall talking when Shinara and Alexa entered the hall. The two queens sat down, one a seat away from Lena, leaving the seat for Bear and the other opposite.

"Lee what's wrong? You look like you have seen a ghost?" Leonard spoke as he and Bear took their seats at the table along with Elsie and Aria.

"Nothing. Why?" he questioned.

"You just don't look yourself," Aria spoke.

"I'm fine, I promise." Lee smiled and food began to be served.

***

Scarlett was sat in her study when a letter fell onto her desk. She opened it up and began to read.

Scarlett,

You said you were only a letter away and right now, I am in need of your guidance. I was teaching Lee and Felix how to summon a guardian when Lee's guardian went into his chest and a blue glow emerged from him.

I searched for an answer and the only answer I could come up with was that he has the same magic as me.

I really need your help Scarlett.

Lena.

Scarlett began her letter back to Lena straight away. She knew the answer from just reading the letter.

After writing the letter, she sealed it with her wax and stamp. She clicked her fingers and the letter was gone.

***

Lena was almost finished with her meal when a letter began to float down from the ceiling. She reached up and grabbed it. Noticing the hand writing, Lena stood from the table and left the hall. She walked out into the snowy, cold aired filled gardens and sat down on one of the benches. She opened the letter and began to read.

Lena,

I am glad that you wrote to me about this. Yes the answer you found is correct. Lee possesses magic from the old religion but if he has only just realised then he needs a lot of training, like you did.

I can come and help but I think that you are more than capable to teach him. You will have to tell Alexa and Shinara. They are his parents after all.

Hope everything goes well.

Scarlett.

Lena looked to the sky and allowed the falling snow to land on her face as she let out a long sigh.

"What's wrong Lena?" a voice called from behind the raven-haired woman.

Lena turned to the voice to see Alexa standing there.

"I need to tell you something," Lena stated.

Alexa sat down and placed a hand on her best friend's shoulder.

"Of course," she smiled.

Lena took a deep breath and began to explain everything that had happened in the last hour or so.

***

"So you are telling me that my son takes after you?" Alexa questioned.

"Yeah. I was hoping you would be alright with me teaching him how to use it and control it?" Lena asked.

"Of course. I want you to help Lee. You may get a bigger bond with him too. Just don't leave Felix out. He's very distracted at the moment and he won't talk to me. Maybe you could get it out of him," Alexa sighed.

Lena smiled and stood to her feet.

"Let's go in. It's cold and I have a long day ahead of me tomorrow."

And with that, the two best friends walked back into the castle.

9

The First Christmas in Brunuhville

The snow fell freely from the white blankets of clouds, that hung high in the grey, winter sky. A thick, white blanket that covered the kingdom land was at least eight inches high, but was gradually building up as the snow began to fall heavier from the sky above. The castle was coated with a thin layer of snow over the tops of the roofs. A thin layer of ice shimmered over the top of the sea, but it wouldn't stay frozen for long as the dragons will be out hunting for their food.

Alexa stood at her bedroom balcony, watching the people of her kingdom play in the snow. Some building snowmen and snow-women, others making snow angels but then she spotted the funniest sight. Just outside of the castle gates, she noticed a group of kids with balls of snow within their hands. The closer she looked, she noticed this group of kids were girls and they were ganging up on Lee and Felix. The two boys were backed up against a brick wall and Alexa couldn't help but laugh at her sons. The group of girls threw the snow at the boys and laughed with joy. Lee and Felix looked at each other and smirked. When they looked back to the group of girls, the girls looked confused at what the brothers had just done. Seeing that their work was done, the boys made a run for it towards the castle. They laughed together, thinking they had made their great escape, but the laughter soon died down when the brothers heard the sound of girly laughter behind them getting louder and louder. They boys looked at each other and before their brains could come to terms with what was happening, snow was being pelted at their backs. The boys ran faster until they reached the castle doors. They turned to look towards the group of girls and they all began to laugh in sync.

"Same time tomorrow?" one of the girls questioned.

"You bet!" Lee spoke enthusiastically.

The girls walked off laughing as the boys laughed as they walked into their home. The boys closed the door, placing their backs onto it and slumping down towards the tiled floor. Lee and Felix looked at each other and laughed, noticing that they were both well and truly covered in snow. They were laughing so hard that they didn't realise that Alexa and Lena were standing right in front of them.

"I see that you two had fun," Alexa announced, making the boys give their full attention to their mother.

"Of course." Lee managed to breathe out from all the laughing.

Lena chuckled at the two boys then clicked her fingers. A purple mist danced around the boys, cleaning all of the snow off of their clothes.

"Christmas is in a couple of days' time. I told Sam that we will help make some decorations. Sam has already started along with the rest of the castle staff but I thought, once you two have sorted yourselves out, that you would join your mum, me and the rest of the family in making this a special year," Alexa spoke, hoping that her two boys would help out.

"Of course. We will be down soon. Meet you in the throne room," the boys shouted as they ran through the castle.

***

Shinara and Shadow were out within the castle gardens, placing decorations on the now snow-covered trees and bushes, while Sam and some of the other guards carried a large black fir tree into the castle. Awaiting the tree, Lee and Felix sat impatiently in the throne room. The brothers began to play a game of cards when suddenly the doors to the throne room creaked open, showing Sam in front of a fir tree, that was hovering just above the floor.

As Sam and the other guards placed the tree upright, Leonard, Elsie, Aria and Lena came walking into the room. Leonard clicked his fingers and several brown, taped up boxes appeared in front of the tree. Lee and Felix ran over with the biggest grins plastered on their faces. Leonard looked down at the two boys and smiled.

"Let's get this decorating started," Elsie cheered.

"I second that," Aria smirked.

With the click of Lena and Leonard's fingers, the boxes untaped themselves and the decorations began to drift out from the boxes and place themselves onto the tree. Lee and Felix watched in admiration at the magic being displayed before them.

It didn't take long for the tree to be decorated but there was just one thing missing. Lena walked over towards the two boys and bent down, her mouth level with Lee's ear.

"En Dawsar," she whispered as the lights began to shine multi colours.

Lee smiled then noticed that there was nothing upon the top of the tree.

"Lena, where's the dragon that goes on top of the tree?" Lee questioned.

Leonard rubbed his hands together and as he opened them, he blew out some sort of green dust. The dust danced around the tree until it reached the top, to where it just hovered.

"Drachen," Leonard mumbled and right before everyone's eyes, the green dust transferred into a beautiful, golden dragon, that stood a top of the tree.

***

After a couple of hours, Alexa walked into the throne room seeing that the tree was completed. She looked over to her boys to see that they were messing around with Lena and Leonard. Lee was summoning guardians with Lena, while Felix was learning how to manipulate dust with Leonard. Alexa smiled until she felt two arms snake around her torso.

"They look so happy, don't they?" Shinara spoke.

"They do. It's a shame that Link wants to destroy everything and everyone I love," Alexa sighed.

Shinara hugged her fiancé a little tighter. Alexa relaxed into her grasp and sighed contently.

"I'm sorry love. A lot has been playing on my mind." Alexa turned around and kissed Shinara.

As the two women pulled away, Alexa noticed Kohana and Elsie in their wolf form, running towards the castle doors. Alexa smiled then turned to everyone.

"Hey guys, who wants to take a break and go and play in the snow?" Alexa called out to her family.

Everyone smiled and followed in the wolves' footsteps.

As everyone got to the castle doors, they all laughed at the sight before them. As the snow came down heavier, they could see the wolves running and jumping around in the snow while catching the snow in their mouths. Lee and Felix ran into the snow and began to throw snowballs at each other. While the boys' backs were turned, Shinara swirled her fingers over a patch of snow, gradually turning into two snow balls while Lena began to gather snow in the air above the two boys.

With a click of Shinara's fingers, the balls flung towards her son's backs. As the boys spun around, everyone laughed.

"Mother!!" the boys shouted.

Everyone laughed, hiding the slight mutters coming from Lena's mouth.

"Denston." And with that, the snow that hung above the boys, fell onto their heads, covering them in a thin, white blanket.

"LENA!" the boys shouted.

Everyone carried on laughing and then began to have a snowball fight.

***

After a long two days, it was finally Christmas in Brunuhville and throughout all the dimensions. Christmas carols, music, sounds of Christmas were heard through every dimension as the snow fell.

Lee and Felix ran down the hallways within the castle until the came to a halt outside of the throne room. As they burst through the doors, they saw that there were no presents under the tree.

"What the? Where's all the presents?" Felix questioned.

The brother's heard a click of fingers behind them and they turned towards the sound. Their eyes widened.

"Don't try and scream. Look around, you are all alone," the voice spoke.

"What the hell Elsie?" Lena questioned as she stood behind the shapeshifter.

Alexa walked in with Shinara at her side. Their eyes widened, but Alexa's soon turned to a frown as she knew what was going on.

"Boys, get behind me," Alexa called out as her son's ran behind their mums.

"What the hell are you doing Elsie?" Alexa questioned, a hint of anger in her voice.

"Oh, don't act like you didn't know. Jasper never saved me. I double crossed him," Elsie began as she walked around the throne room. "I overheard you telling that guard to keep an eye on me. I'm just better at acting than Link is. I also had the help from someone as well. I'm really sorry Shinara." Elsie clicked her fingers, opening a portal. But the person that came through wasn't to their surprise.

"Oh of course. That's why you wanted to get our sisterly bond back. How could I have been so stupid?" Shinara spoke, annoyed with herself.

"It wasn't hard to fool Constantine and Brook. They might be smart when it comes to their jobs and magic but anything else, they are quite dumb. Do you really think I wanted to get a bond that we never truly had back? You must be mad," Shadow sneered.

"You're mad more like," Lee muttered under his breath, hoping no one would hear him, but someone did.

"You what?!!" Shadow shouted.

She launched herself at the boy but Lena clicked her fingers, creating a forcefield around the Snow family. Shadow was thrown back from the forcefield and landed in the Christmas tree. As she fell to the floor, the tree came tumbling down on top of her. Shadow flung the tree off of her, causing the decorations to smash into tiny, little pieces and the golden dragon to disappear into thin air.

Shadow stood to her feet and dusted herself off. She pointed a finger at the family and sneered.

"Fine, have it your way." Elsie swirled her fingers then clicked them, opening a portal.

"But Link is always watching." And with that, the animagus and the dark elf were gone.

Everyone looked at each other and sighed. Alexa looked around and then smiled.

"Come on guys. Let's not let this ruin Christmas. Let's clean up and get this party started," Alexa chimed.

Everyone began muttering incantations, cleaning up the mess the two women had created.

***

After cleaning up all the mess, the tree was finally put back up and the presents were put under the tree. Blankets and pillows were placed on the floor of the throne room floor. Everyone was sat around the tree waiting to open their presents.

Leonard clicked his fingers and piles of presents began to place themselves next to who they belonged to. Everyone began to open their presents.

Lee was given a red suit that was made from the rarest of dragon scales, a ring made from the purest of gold in the shape of a dragon, silver dragon beads to decorate his long blonde hair that he had decided to keep growing out, a few bands to hold his hair in place and two-thousand gold from his family and friends.

Felix was given a suit the same as Lee but his was purple, the same ring, hair gel and two-thousand gold from his family and friends.

But to the boys' surprise, they were given a present between them. Lena handed the boys a small, black box. When the boys opened it, there were two gold chains attached to a two headed dragon pendent. Lee picked up the first chain and one of the dragon heads was pulled up with it. Felix took the other half and they both placed the chains around their necks.

"This is so you know that if you ever part ways, you will always have each other," Lena spoke, smiling at the two boys.

"Thanks Lena," the boys chirped.

Alexa and Shinara were given different types of clothes. Some leather (mainly for Alexa), some summer wear, some winter, all different colours. Gold and silver jewellery and ten-thousand gold for themselves and their family.

Leonard was given different coloured suits and clothes, most of it being leather and a cloak and beads for his husky form.

Lena was given two cloaks, one purple, one red, an emerald-green suit, a ring made from the purest of silver with green dragons engraved within, and a crown, made to look like silver vines intertwined with emerald crystals dotted in a pattern.

Kohana (Aria) was given purple, white, green, blue and red suits, gold and silver wolf hair beads and a black cloak for her human side. For her wolf side, she was given a cloak for the cold and some beads for her fur.

Ray was given two-thousand, five-hundred different materials for his craftsmanship.

***

After opening their presents and having some festive fun, the day was almost over. Alexa, Felix and Lee were out on the dragons, flying around as the snow falls, while the rest of the family were inside the castle, helping the staff create the best Christmas dinner they could ever think of.

As the mother and sons arrive back at the castle, four Christmas dinners appeared in front of the dragons.

"Merry Christmas guys. Enjoy," Alexa spoke.

The dragons screeched and began to eat their food as the three walked back up to the castle, the smell dinner roaming through the noses.

As they reached the throne room, the doors immediately opened. Tables and chairs were placed around the room, decorated with the most amazing Christmas decorations, golden cutlery, plates and goblets were placed in front of every seat.

Everyone took their seats and suddenly, food appeared in their places on the tables. Everyone began to fill their plates with food and laugh and joke with each other.

From the events of what happened that morning, it was like nothing had even happened. No one spoke of it, they just moved past the negativity so their day wouldn't be ruined.

***

Christmas day went by amazingly for the kingdom of Brunuhville. Everyone was happy. No one had heard or seen Shadow or Elsie since that day and even though that was a relief, something just didn't seem right about the whole situation.

Six days had gone by and it was now 3020, but the snow still fell heavy from the white sky above. A new year and a new start for everyone. Including Link and his followers. But no one wanted to think about the next plan he had installed for them, but the thought always managed to linger in their minds.

But meanwhile as the thoughts ran through every Brunuhvillian's mind, Link was well and truly coming up with a plan. Since Elsie's and Shadow's encounter with Alexa, Link had been doing some extensive research on how to create a new world along with the help of the Lotz family. Every dimension that Link has been to, he has been trying to take over that land but it has always failed. So he thought that he would take matters into his own hands.

After Caity's letter to him, Link had to get an extra pair of hands that hated his sister just as much as he did, to help him build a world and army to finally take his sister out, once and for all.

But thanks to the new year, new me idea, Aria, Jasper and Ray were in the basement of Ray's hut, trying to make a portal to a dimension they had never been before. They have been doing this since new year's eve and they still had no luck creating the portal.

Days went by and the trio still had no luck. Aria was frustrated. She wanted to prove that she could do magic and not just an animagus.

The trio were sat in the basement of Ray's hut, still trying to make this portal. Piles of books and loose paper were covering the floor. The trio tried to figure out what they were doing wrong, but everything they were doing, they were doing right.

Aria was so frustrated that she stood to her feet with her fists clenched.

"That's it! I've had it.!" she screamed.

"Aria calm down. We will find a way," Ray spoke.

But Aria wasn't listening. She lifted a hand and swirled it around. She closed her eyes and then muttered something.

"Danson du."

Suddenly, a purple and blue portal opened. The trio jumped up in excitement and hugged each other.

"Time for an adventure boys?" Aria questioned.

"Hell yeah!" Ray smiled.

"Let's do this!" Jasper grinned.

The three held onto each other's hands and stepped into the portal. But something was wrong. As the trio disappeared, electrical sparks began to shoot all around the portal and the portal began to change colour.

There was something wrong. Terribly wrong.

10

The Unknown Land

In a dimension far from any other dimension, there was a land unknown to others but to the novices and mages that lived there. Very few people lived there but to the ones that did, had the magic, that was made from none other than dust. This type of magic was rare. The people of this land could change into a spirit animal, commonly known as a Metamorph. On every single one of these very few people, laid a tattoo that indicated what type of spirit animal they would turn into. A mystical animal that was within the land, guards over the people. When trespassers walked into the land, the guardian did not look a kindly eye upon them. Trespassers had not left this land and they were never seen again.

As the portal opened, Jasper, Ray and Aria stepped onto a ground that looked as if it had never been touch.

"Where are we?" Ray questioned.

"I have no idea. But we have found a new dimension," Aria spoke.

"We should have told someone that we were going," Jasper piped in.

"Oh, you're such a spoil sport. Let's go and explore," Aria said as she walked off with Ray at her side.

"This is so stupid," Jasper muttered as he followed behind the two.

As they walked on, the trio looked around themselves, taking in the sight around them. The grass was rich green in colour with beautiful-coloured flowers dotted here and there. The trees stood tall into the midnight blue sky that hung above them. Within the trees, there were treehouses made from the trunks of the trees. Each treehouse had a different symbol carved into them. Some had dragons, others had wolves and then there were some that you couldn't make out. It looked as if that the people that lived there, lived in the trees. The grassy meadows were untouched.

As the trio carried on walking through the grassy meadows, they noticed a circular patch in the middle of one meadow. The circle was created by trees and in the centre, there were two trees that intertwined together, leaving a slight hole in the middle at the bottom of them, slightly above the ground. Within this hole, there was swirling, clear water that was enchanted to hover in the air.

***

As the trio walked through the meadows, something was watching them. Something was not happy that they were there. Rustling of trees and bushes were heard all around them. Jasper looked around then stopped as his eyes focused on two bright, yellow eyes, hiding in the bush. As if the eyes noticed, they disappeared and green mist floated up into the night sky.

"Guys, did you see that?" Jasper questioned.

"See what?" Ray huffed as he turned to look at his friend.

"Over there in that bush, there were yellow eyes and green mist."

Aria and Ray looked over to the bush but saw nothing.

"Jasper, just keep your mouth shut. There's nothing there," Aria spoke as Ray and herself turned back and carried on walking.

"I think he's going mad," Ray whispered.

Jasper heard what his so-called friend had said and decided to take his own path.

"I'm not mad. I did see something," Jasper muttered to himself.

"I will find those eyes. I'll show them." And he carried on walking away from his so-called friends, that hadn't even noticed he was gone.

As he walked his own path, the sound of trees and bushes were heard rustling all around him. Jasper began to feel extremely uneasy. As he walked deeper and deeper into the unknown land, strong gusts of wind whipped around Jasper, making his balance unsteady. But Jasper wouldn't let this stop him from finding those eyes.

He carried on walking until he found himself back at the intertwined trees. He walked closer to the hovering water and looked into it. Green mist was seen in the depths of the water and Jasper smiled.

"I knew I wasn't mad. Come out and show yourself," Jasper spoke.

As Jasper turned around to look at the green mist, he saw the very same yellow eyes that peered at him through the bushes some time before. As he starred deeply into those yellow eyes, he felt his head go fuzzy.

"What are you doing to me?" Jasper questioned as he placed his hands onto his head.

Jasper's vision began to go blurry as he fell to his knees. As he looked up, it was as if the green mist he once saw, had duplicated. As his vision darkened, the green mist flowed closer to him.

"What are you?" Jasper whispered as his head hit the ground and everything went black.

***

Aria and Ray found themselves walking around in circles. They had walked past the same broken tree, the meadows began to look the same but then they realised that they were outside the tree-houses. The bushes and trees around them began to rustle, making the two very uneasy. As the two began to look around them, they both noticed something that they couldn't believe. Ray looked to the right of him to see two blue eyes staring at him and as if the eyes had noticed, they disappeared and yellow mist was seen drifting up to the sky. Aria looked to the left of her and saw two green eyes staring back at her. As she looked deeper into them, they disappeared and blue mist was seen drifting up towards the sky.

"Bloody hell! Jasper was right," Ray spoke.

All of a sudden, the yellow and blue mist glided down towards the two and hovered just behind them. A gust of wind whipped the two around, making them looked into the two pairs of eyes that were boring into their souls.

"What are you?" Aria questioned, curious about the mist in front of them.

Ray began to hold his head as he began to feel dizzy.

"Aria, I don't feel so good," he spoke as he fell to his knees.

Aria looked at her friend in shock, then changed into her wolf form. Kohana began to growl at the mist until she fell to the ground, landing hard on her stomach. She changed back into her human form but when she tried to stand to her feet, she was knocked back down. As her head hit the ground, everything went black. Ray looked over at his friend until it was almost hard to see.

"Well, this can't be good."

***

The people of this village heard all the commotion of their land. The guardians were restless and they knew it.

A young woman ventured out onto the balcony of her tree house and looked out towards the intertwined trees. The woman's hair was dark brown with a hint of red in it with brown eyes as dark as her hair. From the top of her shoulder, just under her neck, to the tips of her fingers, laid a snakeskin tattoo. The woman wore a beautiful black blouse, that was tucked into a knee length black frilled skirt. Her hair was still down from the sudden morning wake.

"Peyton Slade, get your sorry ass in here now," a man called from inside the house.

"Yes Dad," she huffed as she turned on her heels and headed into the house.

As she walked in, a slightly older man, her dad, Jefferson, with jet black hair with bright blue eyes stood by a fireplace. From the top of his neck to his hips, laid a snake scale tattoo, just the same as Peyton's. Jefferson wore a pair of smart black jeans with a white shirt tucked into it. Over the top of the shirt, he wore a red and gold checked waist coat along with a black tie around his neck.

Just as Jefferson finished buttoning up his waist coat, a woman with auburn red hair with blue eyes, who was dressed in a stunning red and black dress, walked out into the room the man and Peyton were stood. The woman also had a snakeskin tattoo but hers was around her ankle.

"Ah, Peyton, do me a favour and help your sister out," the woman spoke.

"Of course, Dahlia." And with that, Peyton walked out of the room and towards her step sister, Alice's room.

As she walked into the room, she noticed Alice was still led in her bed. her blond hair sprawled out all over the pillows. Peyton looked at her step sister and sighed. She pulled the covers off of her, earning herself a few grunts from the sleeping woman. She walked over to her step sister's drawers, pulling out some clothes and placing them on a chair.

"Dahlia said you need to get up," Peyton spoke as she grabbed Alice's shoulders and pulled her up.

"No, she didn't. She told you to help me dress," Alice smirked. "And is mother to you."

Peyton looked at Alice then slapped her, leaving a red mark on Alice's cheek.

"I'm telling mother."

"Go ahead. I don't care what you say to Dahlia."

Alice ran out of her room and straight to her mother. Peyton ran her hands through her hair, until she felt a hand on her shoulder. She looked up to see her dad, smiling down at her.

"What happened this time?" Jefferson questioned.

"Why did you have to marry that monster? She and that little monster spawn have ruined my life. Can't you see Dahlia is only with you because you are the leader of this place," Peyton rambled as tears began to fall from her eyes.

"Oh, hunny." Jefferson pulled his daughter into his side, stroking her hair to sooth her. "Things will get better love. I have just got word from the guardians that there are some unwanted visitors here," he smirked, knowing how much his daughter loved torturing the unwanted guests.

Peyton looked up into her father's eyes and a devilish look appeared within the depths of her eyes. The two got up from the bed, walked through the house and out onto the balcony. As Peyton looked out below at all the people of the village gathering to hear about what the guardians had done and what their leader had to say about all of this and began to think back to all the times the guardians found trespassers in their land and how she was always allowed to torture them.

***

FLASH BACK

It all started nine years ago, when Peyton was only twelve. She had just finished learning everything she needs to know about being a metamorph. She was always left in the dark when it came to family problems.

The Slade family were the leaders of this unknown land. They were kind, fair but they would always seek out justice for the ones that they loved and cared about.

The Slade family consisted of Mr and Mrs Slade, Jefferson and Harley, and their twelve-year-old daughter, Peyton. This family were what everyone wanted to be like. Everyone idolised them. The Slade family had been leaders of this land for generations. And with each generation, they lived up to each family member.

The Slade's were out on a walk one day. The sun was shining, the birds were chirping. Everything seemed normal. Peyton was showing her parents how well she was mastered becoming a metamorph and her parents couldn't of been more proud of her.

As they were walking through their land, strange noises were heard. As the noises began to get louder and louder, Jefferson began to feel on edge. He knew that the guardians would be on to this strange situation already, but he was always on edge when his family were around.

Just as things began to calm down, Harley was knocked down to her knees. Jefferson and Peyton looked around seeing that no one was there, but suddenly an arrow was shot from one of the trees, hitting Harley in the chest, causing her to fall dead instantly.

Peyton began to cry uncontrollably. She ran over to her mother's lifeless body and hugged her tight. Jefferson stood staring at his wife and daughter, as if he was in a daze. But something suddenly clicked inside of him and he screamed. His screams were heard all over the land. People left their homes to see what had happened, and what they saw, broke every single heart.

The trees and bushes began to shake uncontrollably and different colour mist were seen darting around everyone. It wasn't until a loud thud was heard that everyone began to pay attention to what the mist was doing.

Everyone went silent.

"Guardians! Appear," Jefferson called.

Three different coloured mists appeared from the bushes with an unknown man. They dropped the man to the ground, causing him to moan. A few men tied up this man against a tree and Jefferson just scowled at him. As the man began to wake up, Jefferson backed away slightly.

"Who are you?' He questioned.

"What? Where am I?" the man questioned.

"Answers me! Who are you?"

"The name is Remus. Now let me go!" Remus spat.

"Why should I let you go when you killed my wife? How did you get here? Where are you from?"

Remus looked at Jefferson and sneered.

"I am a human! Nothing magical about me. I just know my way around a magical being. It's amazing what happens when you threaten someone's family," Remus laughed.

"You know what to do," Jefferson said as he looked at a few men in the crowd around him. "Oh, and let Peyton have the final kill. I know she would like that." And with that Jefferson walked off, letting the men and his daughter take care of this human.

FLASH BACK ENDS

***

Peyton and her father made their way down in amongst the people to see what everyone was going crazy about. As they got to the end of the crazed crowd, Jefferson and Peyton noticed three bodies, two male and one female, laying in front of the guardians.

Peyton took one look and then looked at her father.

"I know what we should do with them."

"And what is that my love?" Jefferson questioned.

"Send them to the Underworld. No one will care for them after," Peyton sneered.

Jefferson looked at the guardians and smirked.

"You heard the girl. Take them to the Underworld." And with that, the guardians picked up the three friends and took them down to the Underworld.

***

As Jasper, Aria and Ray's eyes began to flutter open and their vision became more clear, they realised that they was no longer in the unknown land, but yet it was like a dream world.

"Where the bloody hell are we?" Ray spoke as he sat up.

"I told you we should have called someone or went back home," Jasper spat.

Aria stood to her feet and looked around her while the boys argued. She noticed that they were in an invisible cage.

"You are meant to be grown men, not children. Now shut up and help me look for a way out," Aria spat as she held her hand out to the side of her to show the boys that they were stuck.

"This is weird," Ray spoke, looking around.

"We wouldn't be here if you had both listened to me!" Jasper sneered.

Ray and Jasper began to argue with each other again so Aria carried on looking for a way to get them out.

"I'll do it alone then," she muttered.

Just as Aria started looking around, a loud bang and talking were heard. Aria, and the two boys backed up towards the back of the cage but they were zapped by some sort of electric force.

"Ah you are awake. About time," a dark figure spoke.

"Where are we? What do you want from us?" Aria shouted.

"You're in the Underworld of course. Oh, and you will see very shortly." And with that the figure walked away.

***

As the figure walked away, another figure came out from the shadows. In a cage next to the three Brunuhvillians, another man stood, weak and fragile. Aria walked over to the other side of the cage to get a better look at the man, while Jasper was shouting off his mouth and Ray looked like he was in his own world.

"The Underworld? I thought that was a legend?" Jasper questioned.

He then placed his back against the cage and gained another zap.

"How comes the front of the cage doesn't zap you but the back keeps zapping us?" Jasper shouted at Aria.

***

Back at the Brunuhville caves, Link, Elsie and Shadow were planning sweet and evil. After months of research, Link had final come up with a plan that will finally be able to help him stop Alexa.

"Are you sure about this?" Shadow questioned.

"You question all of my plans. What is my usual answer?" Link spat.

"I'm just making sure. All of your other plans have never gone to plan."

Just then, Link had spun around so fast and pinned Shadow against a wall by her neck, that even Link was shocked by his own actions.

"You speak out of line again and I swear I will end you," he spoke as he got closer and closer to her face, making sure that the young elf felt every breath and spit on her face.

Elsie changed back into her wolf self, walked over to Link and began to pull him away from Shadow by his coat. As Shadow fell to the ground and held her neck, Link flung his coat to the side, making Elsie go flying across the room. Link looked over to where Elsie landed and smirked.

"Same goes for you mutt. I will end you."

Link went back to his bed, where all of his plans were scattered. He began to look through them all when he noticed one plan he had not done yet.

"Before we get started, there is just one plan that I need to do first," Link spoke before he clicked his fingers and a portal opened.

Elsie and Shadow looked at him and gulped. He knew what he was going to do and now was his chance. Link stepped through the portal and landed just outside the kingdom walls. Link spotted someone walking towards the gates. He clicked his fingers and the person dropped dead. Link walked over to the person and saw that it was an elderly man.

"No one would suspect and old man." And with that, he placed his hand over the man's body. Tiny particles began to float up into the air and with a click of Link's fingers, the particles shot onto Link and he became the old man.

"Show time."

He walked into the village and begins to look around making sure his plan went well. As he carried on walking through the village, he noticed Leonard walking towards him. Just as Leonard came close enough, Link fell to the ground. Leonard came running over to see what the problem was.

"Sir, are you alright?" he questioned.

"Oh, you are so kind," Link said as he looked up.

Link pulled a dagger, cloaked in poison, out of his cloak and stabbed Leonard. The animagus held onto where he was stabbed and looked the old man in the eyes.

"Link…" Leonard breathed out.

Just then Sam and a couple more guards noticed Leonard on the floor and ran over to him. Link made a run for it and made his way through the village, finding a way to get into the dragon caves.

Sam and the guards took Leonard into the castle and into the throne room. Alexa and Lena turned to see Sam carrying Leonard and ran over to him. Sam placed Leonard on top of a table so Alexa could see him.

"Oh, Leo. Who did this to you?"

"Link… But he has stolen someone else's identity. He's in the kingdom," Leonard said with his last breath.

Alexa began to cry and looked up at Sam. "Find him." And with that Sam was gone.

***

Link was still on the run through the village, trying to find a way into the castle. But it became a bit harder now that Alexa had a search party after him. As Link got closer to the back of the castle, he noticed that the castle was on a cliff. Link looked to His right and saw two dragons fly out from a cave.

Link clicked his fingers, creating a portal that opened in front of him. He stepped inside, landing inside the dragon caves. He noticed that one of the dragons was asleep. As he stepped closer, Spitze began to wake up. Spitze turned to face Link and began to breathe fire at him, but Link protected himself.

"You are just as stupid as my sister," he spoke as he pulled the dagger out of his cloak.

Spitze began to breathe fire again but this time, Link turned the fire the other way and pushed it towards the dragon. As the fire began to burn through Spitze, Link saw his chance to stab the dragon, making him die faster.

As Link stabbed Spitze, he saw the poison take over the dragon's body, making Spitze weak. The dragon fell to the ground dead. Link clicked his fingers and the fire had stopped. He then placed his hand onto the dragon and began to mutter and incantation.

"Dawnson zo zine…" And with that, the dragon came back to life but there was something different.

The dragon had holes in its body and wings where Link had burnt him but he moved as if he were still a fully alive dragon. Link climbed onto the dragon's back.

"Now take us home. We have some more work to do." And with that, Spitze flew him and Link back to the Caves.

***

As Ray and Jasper walked around the cage to figure out how to get out of it, Aria couldn't take her eyes off of the weak looking man on the other side of the cage.

"What's your name?" she questioned.

The man just looked at her but no answer.

"I'm Aria, formally known as Kohana. These two are Ray and Jasper." Aria pointed two her friends, who were still looking around.

The man, again, just looked at her, but still no answer. There was something strange about the man to Aria. She didn't understand why he was here, why her and her friends were here and why this man couldn't talk. Suddenly the dark figures came back through the dream like room and stood in front of the cages.

"Don't try and escape these cages. You won't be able to. They are designed to keep trespassers in," one said.

"What do you mean trespassers? We never did anything wrong," Ray shouted.

The figures took down their hoods and revealed their true identity. The man figure, who has been talking to the Brunuhvillians, had a face of a snake, his skin scaled with green and yellow snake scales, his eyes red as blood with the pupils in the shape of diamonds. the other, had the head of a fox, his skin laced with red and white fur, his eyes blue as ice with pupils in the shape of stars.

The snake man looked at Ray and sneered.

"Oh, you didn't, did you?" he spoke.

"So, you didn't teleport to the Unknown Land through a portal?" the fox man questioned.

All three looked incredibly guilty after the words they had just heard.

"You stepped on land that you were never meant to step on."

"I tried to stop them!" Jasper piped up. "I went alone in the end."

"We know Jasper. That is why we will let you go," the snake man spoke.

"Nice one Jasper. You got them to let us go," Ray cheered.

"No Ray. Not you. Not Aria. Just Jasper. He tried to find a way out of that land, you and Aria did not. Which results in you staying here," the snake man continued.

The fox man opened the door to the cage, allowing Jasper to be set free.

"You traitor Jasper," Ray shouted.

The fox and snake man escorted Jasper out of the dream like room and back up to the Unknown Land. As they reached the grassy meadows, the snake and fox man came to a stand still.

"What will happen to them?" Jasper questioned.

"They will become weak and fragile. They will be lost in time. When you leave this land, you will no longer remember them or where you have been," the snake man spoke.

The fox man opened a portal and stepped aside for Jasper to walk through it.

"Thank you," he spoke.

The two men bowed slightly, then looked up.

"Now, never come back." And with that, Jasper walked through the portal.

***

As Link and Spitze landed back in the Brunuhville caves, Link noticed Shadow and Elsie standing there waiting for him.

"You said you were only going to kill Leonard, not a dragon as well," Shadow snapped.

"And? Your point is?" Link questioned as he walked away. Link snapped back at the women and smirked. "And the dragon will help me in the next step of my plan," he finished as he walked off.

The two women looked at each other and gulped. They knew what Link was up to but now knowing what he was capable of, they did not want to be a part of this. But that was now an issue. Even if they tried to leave, they knew Link would end them.

As Link walked into his room, he closed the door behind him and locked it. He walked over to his bed and crouched down, reaching underneath. As he pulled his arms out, he placed pieces of paper onto his bed. He searched through all the paper until he came across an old looking scroll. As he rolled it open, a smirk plastered itself onto his face.

"Now this is what I was looking for," Link spoke to himself as he looked at the scroll that held the incantation to creating a new world in a new dimension.

Link looked at all of his belongings and smiled.

"Dreka," he spoke, making all of his belongings pack themselves away.

Link picked everything up, unlocked his door and into the caves. He saw Elsie and Shadow standing by the edge of the caves, talking. He wandered over to them and smiled.

"Come on girls, we have a new home to create." And with that, with the two women on Link's heels, they wandered off into the nearby field that Spitze was waiting in, to create their new home.

As they reached the field, Link placed all of his belongings onto Spitze's back, except for the incantation scroll. The three friends huddled around each other and began to say the incantation.

"Set the sun in the West and rise the moon in the East, cheat codes create a wrong direction, mist or magic, dark or light, set me a new tight flight to a new dimension I call home."

Multicoloured mist began to surround the magical folk, getting thicker and thicker, until it was too hard to breathe.

"Link… What's… Happening?" Shadow coughed out, struggling

for air.

"I have... No idea," Link replied.

And just like that, the three friends and the dragon were gone and so was the mist.

11

The Start of Sweet Revenge

Multicoloured mist appeared in a burnt-out crop circle in the middle of a destroyed meadow. Three smoked figures emerged from within the mist along with a loud roar as the dragon landed. As the smoke and mist began to fade, Link, Shadow and Elsie looked around to see where they had landed.

Destroyed meadows laid on the ground, broken and burnt trees stood barely alive and within the distances, a castle that was centuries old but looked as if not touched, stood tall.

Link looked over to the castle and a smirk plastered itself across his face.

"Now this is what I am talking about," Link spoke.

"You mean, you created this?" Shadow questioned.

"Yes and no. I mean, this dimension was lost until I…" Link looked at Shadow who seemed to have an annoyed expression on her face. "I mean we found it. Now this will be our new home. I just have some work to do," Link spoke as he climbed on top of the dragon's back. "You two go and explore. I will see you shortly." And with that, Link flew off into the distance, making his way to the castle.

Elsie and Shadow watched as Link flew off and then looked at each other.

"Well, I guess this means we get to see what this new home of ours is like then," Elsie spoke.

The two women walked off in the direction of the castle, ready to enjoy their first day in their new home.

***

As Link climbed off the dragon's back, he noticed that he was in a graveyard. He looked around at all of the graves and smiled to himself. He walked over to the front row of graves and held his hands out towards them all.

"Sor drachen du," he muttered as black mist fluttered from his hands and shot into every single one of the graves.

Link looked at all of the graves and noticed that transparent ghostly figures rose from them. As he looked around at all of the figures, he noticed that they were all men or boys. And then something clicked within him.

"Hello, my fellow men and boys. I know you do not know me so let me introduce myself. My name is Link Snow. I am a dark elf. I have two friends with me on this land, Shadow and Elsie. We have come to save you, but I also am in need of your help. You see, my sister, who is in another dimension, is after me and has threatened to start war against me. I have no army, it is just us three." Link looked around at everyone and noticed that they did not look impressed.

Link then closed his eyes and raised his hands slightly. "Dawnson zo zine." Mist flowed from his hands and into every single ghostly figure in front of him.

"Now, is that better?" he questioned.

"What makes you think we want to help you?" one shouted.

"Yeah, dark elves are the reason we were dead in the first place," another snapped.

"I am nothing like them. I promise you that," Link said as he crossed his fingers behind his back.

The figures in the graveyard looked around at each other and then back at Link.

"We will help," a man spoke up.

Link looked at them all and smiled.

"Thank you. First things first I…" He began but was cut off by a man standing in front of him.

"No need to tell us what to do. We have been here before," he began. "Come on lads, suit up and onto the training fields," he spoke as they all walked off past Link and to the castle.

Link watched as the men and boys walked off into the castle and he smirked.

"But first things first. let me just cast a spell over you guys so you belong to me," he muttered.

Link closed his eyes and began to mutter to himself. "Vandoor."

White mist began to fill the area around all of the men and boys that were walking into the castle, making it easier for Link to control their minds.

"And just one more thing," Link spoke to himself. "Pictok."

Black sparks shoot into all of the kingdom people's bodies, altering their body time and manipulating their brains to make them think that Link was their king.

"This is going to be fun." And with that, he too, walked off into the castle to stake out his new kingdom.

As he walked through the castle doors, whispers were heard all around him. No matter how hard he tried to listen to them, he could never make them out. He narrowed his hearing down so he could hear only one whisper. As he focused on the voice, he followed it through the castle, where the voice got louder and louder, almost deafening, until he reached two tall, wooden doors, where the voice became silent. As Link looked at the door, he looked down at the key holes, a key with a skull head at the top of its body, hung loosely within one of the key holes. Link grabbed the key and looked at it closely.

"Strange. I have never seen a key like this before. I wonder if there are any more," he muttered to himself.

One of the kingdom people noticed Link looking a little strange and walked up to him.

"Sir, are you alright?" a man spoke as he raised his right hand to his head to salute his king.

"Yes," Link spoke as he looked puzzled at the key.

But he wasn't the only one who was hearing strange whispers and voices.

As Elsie and Shadow were walking through one of the meadows, they began to hear the same whispering as Link did.

"What the bloody hell is that?" Elsie spoke.

"You hear it too?" Shadow questioned.

Elsie turned into her wolf self and began to narrow her hearing so she could focus on the voice and that was when she heard it.

"Find us where the secrets lie, through kingdom dawn and kingdom rise, secret keys for secret doors."

Elsie changed back into her human self and looked at Shadow.

"The voice said Find us where the secrets lie, through kingdom dawn and kingdom rise, secret keys for secret doors," she spoke.

"What do you think that means?" Shadow questioned.

"There is only one way to find out," Elsie spoke as she turned into her wolf self.

Elsie began to follow the voice with Shadow at her tail. They began to walk through the meadows until they reached a forest that was completely different to the burnt-out meadows. This forest was as if it was never touched. There were no scorch marks, no broken or burnt trees, everything was new and fresh.

But then Shadow began to hear another voice, speaking the same words Elsie had repeated earlier.

"Elsie, follow that voice, I'll be back soon," Shadow spoke as she began to follow the other voice.

As Shadow followed the voice through the forest, she came to a halt at a beautiful lake. But there was something different about this lake. As Shadow bent down to her knees and looked closer at the water, she noticed that the reflection in the water was completely different to what was actually around her. Around Shadow, there were trees and bushes, but within the water, there was also a waterfall, falling from a high slope on top of a hill. As Shadow moved closer to the water, the voice began to get louder.

"Oh, screw this," she spoke as she stood to her feet and jumped into the water.

But it was as if she had never jumped at all. As she landed into the water, her whole world had flipped upside down, literally. She was standing in the water but it was as if the water was the sky. But the sky was underneath her along with treetops and birds flying.

"These secrets don't make it easy to find them," Shadow muttered. "Fliptop," she spoke, making the world around her turn back to the way it should be.

As the world became upright, Shadow listened out for the voice. Shadow began to follow the voice until she came face to face with the waterfall. Shadow thought about it for a while until the voice became deafening. She knew she had to walk through the waterfall to find the secret.

"Oh great," she said as she walked through the water. But she never got wet.

"Strange," she muttered.

Shadow looked around to see that the waterfall was hiding a cave. Within the cave, different coloured crystals lit up the dark space. Shadow followed the voice all the way through the cave. Finding herself at a dead end, she noticed the voice had stopped. She looked around herself until she saw a shining object on the floor. As she picked up the object, she noticed it was a key with a slanted "L" as its head.

"A key? This better be something better than just a key." And with that, she made her way back to the lake and jumped back through to the other side.

Back in the forest, Elsie was still sniffing around and listening to the voice, finding it hard to find out what this voice was leading her to until she reached an old, slanted Oak tree that stood taller than the other trees within the forest. Elsie began to walk closer to the tree until the voice stopped. She looked down to see something shining within the dirt she stood on. Elsie began to dig through the dirt until the shining object became into view. Elsie turned back into her human self and picked up the object to find that it was a key with an "S" for its head.

"Nice. I wonder what this unlocks," Elsie said as Shadow came into view.

"Look what I found!" the two women said at the same time.

They both showed their keys and smiled.

"I wonder what these do," Elsie spoke.

"Let's go and show Link! He might know." And with that, the two women ran off into the direction of the castle to go and show Link what they had found.

***

Meanwhile, back at the castle, Link was sat in his throne room inspecting the key he had found. Every turn of the key, there was a different ringing sound that was heard, as if the key was trying to talk to Link.

Elsie and Shadow came running in through the doors and ran straight up to Link.

"You wouldn't believe what we just found!" the girls spoke.

"A key by any chance?" Link questioned.

"How did you know?" Elsie questioned as both her and Shadow looked back and forth to each other.

"Because I found one too," Link spoke, holding out the key he had found.

All three looked at each other and then the keys.

"They must go to something," Elsie said.

Link took all three keys into his own hands and looked at the girls.

"They should but right now I just want to relax. You two can do the same. The kingdom people will be around soon to give us our dinner. I will be in my room if you need me," Link spoke as he stood to his feet and walked off through the castle to his room.

Shadow and Elsie looked at each other confused until they heard a noise just outside of the throne room. As they walked outside of the doors, they saw what seemed to be a person but they were undead.

"Hey, you," Elsie called out.

The person turned around to look at the two women and walked over to them.

"Ma'am? Is the something wrong?" he questioned.

"Did Link bring you back to this plane?" Shadow questioned.

"Yes, our king did. He also brought the rest of this kingdom back as well. Is that all Elsie, Shadow?" he spoke.

"Yes, thank you." And with that, the man walked away.

"What is he up to?" Elsie questioned.

"I have a feeling, but let's see what he has planned first," Shadow spoke as the two women walked through the castle and to their rooms.

As Link made his way through the castle, another voice was heard, but this time, he could make out what the voice was saying, and it sounded like a cry for help. All Link could hear was "Help me. I am stuck. Where am I?"

Link followed the voice through the castle, walking down halls and corridors that he hadn't paid any attention too just yet, along with rooms that he had never see within a castle before. Link found himself at a dead end, but he could still hear the voice crying out for help.

"How am I meant to help you when I am stuck at a bloody dead end?" Link shouted.

Just then, the bricks from the wall in front of Link began to move, creating a beautifully structured door in front of him. Link looked at the door and smiled.

"Now that is what I am talking about," Link smirked as he walked towards the door, one hand out to push the door open.

As he walked through the door, he wasn't too sure of where he was. Everything was dark. Suddenly, flame torches were lit and Link could finally make out his surroundings. Where he was within the castle, was a long, dark, winding passageway. The walls were black brick with metal railings placed upon the walls.

Link walked down the passageway, listening to the same voice asking for help, getting louder and louder until he reached a dark and gloomy T junction.

"Great. Now are you going to show me a sign?" Link questioned.

Just after he questioned the voice, flame torches lit up down the right side of the T junction. Link walked down the passageway until he reached a jail gate. As he went to open it, one of the keys flew out from his shirt pocket and into the lock, unlocking the gate. Link carried on walking down the path until he came to a cave like room. As he looked around the room, he saw a man huddle in the corner, still breathing, shallow but still breathing. He walked over to him and clicked his fingers, making a goblet of water appear in his hand. Link crouched down next to the man and helped him drink it.

"Thank you, Link," the man said.

"How do you know who I am?"

"Who doesn't? You have lied to this whole kingdom, just to get what you want. Now you want me to help you," the man spoke.

Link looked closely at the man to see that he had a bandage wrapped around his head, covering his eyes. He was wearing a red shirt with a black collar and chain, black jeans and black boots.

His hair was bleach blonde.

"Are you…"

"Blind? Yes. You are not the smartest dark elf I know. Now get me out of here," the man spoke.

Link helped the man back up to the castle and into his throne room, so he could have a real meal and drink. Link called Shadow and Elsie in so they could meet their new guest. Elsie and Shadow came walking in and sat down at the table in front of the man. Curious, Elsie began to talk.

"Hi, I am…"

"Elsie. Yes, I know. And you are Shadow. I am Sora. The old King of this Realm. Now may I eat in peace please?" Sora spoke.

"Yes, of course," Link spoke.

The three went to turn away but was stopped.

"Link, those keys that you have found," Sora spoke.

"What about them?"

"May I have them?" Sora asked.

"Whatever for?" Link questioned, anger in his voice.

"Once I have finished my meal, I would like to show you how to use them. They are, of course together, the master of death," Sora spoke.

Link handed over the keys to Sora, then walked out of the room with the two women, allowing Sora to be at peace. But what Link didn't realise was that Sora was blind but his hearing was exceptional. Just as Link and the women walked out of the room, Link began to explain his plan.

"So, the plan is, I will send a storm throughout the dimensions hitting all of the kingdoms, destroying them. Once the storm is in play, we will make our way to Brunuhville, where our fight will begin," Link explained.

"The first and last fight Alexa will see," a voice called out from behind the three.

"Ah, Caity, you have arrived," Link spoke as he turned to see Caity standing with Ripp behind him.

Link walked over towards the two. He kissed Caity's hand and shook Ripp's.

"My army is awaiting you command," Ripp spoke.

"Samuel," Link called out.

A man came rushing to Link's aid.

"Yes, sir?" he questioned.

"I would like you to get both armies together and begin their training. We have one short week to prepare for this war."

"Right away, sir." And with Link's command, Samuel rushed off, obeying his master's commands.

Sora heard every word that the dark elf had spoken and was furious.

"Sky-Guard must hear about this." And with a click of his fingers, a grey mist emerged over Sora. Once the mist had disappeared, it left no trace of the man that once sat there.

Link walked back into the throne room to see if Sora was finished, but to his dismay, the blind man was no longer there.

"AAAHHHHH!!" Link shouted.

Everyone came rushing in to see that Sora was no longer there.

"He tricked me! I will have my revenge!" Link spat, storming out of the throne room and straight to his own bedroom.

***

Within a meadow in Sky-Guard, the very same mist had appeared. After vanishing, Sora began to walk through the meadows and straight to the gates of the Tower of Magika. As he walked up to the gate, he sensed a familiar face. After walking slightly closer, he sensed that it was his old best friend, Scar.

"Scar my old friend," he called out.

Scar turned his head to see Sora making his way towards him. He rushed over with his brother, Tommy, to give him a hand.

"Oh Merlin, Sora. Where have you been? After the dark elves had attacked, I didn't hear or sense a trace from you," Scar spoke as they made their way through the gate.

"There is much to discuss. May we go somewhere private?" Sora questioned.

Scar and Tommy clicked their fingers and all three apparated from the ground floor, up to where Scar's office laid. Tommy helped Scar seat Sora down in a chair and walked out of the room, locking the door behind him. Scar took a seat opposite Sora and looked at him pitiful.

"Don't give me that look. You know I can see the future," Sora laughed.

"Sorry Sora. It has been so long. What happened to you? After you left the Old Religion to become the king of your kingdom after your father, I thought I had lost you," the man questioned.

Sora took a long breath and sighed.

"When the dark elves attacked, they had killed all of my men. I was alone. No friends, no family, alone. I was face to face with the master of all dark elves. There was a battle down in the caves. He was at the brink of death, I was still going strong. But something had changed. His eyes turned black and his skin turned pale. This was something I had never seen before. As if he were infected by something."

"You mean by a vampire? But they are just myths," Scar spoke.

"We may think they are myths by all of the stories we have been told, but from what I saw, they may be real. Tell me how does a dark elf stay in reign for so long and never die? how do they always win wars? This master had the teeth of a vampire, the markings around his eyes were as if someone had drained the blood from him and inserted infected blood back into him," Sora spoke.

Scar began to look through all of the scrolls and books in his office to see if there was any truth about these vampires, while he listened to the rest of Sora's story.

"After he had turned, all he did was look me in the eyes. Nothing less, nothing more. He just looked me in the eyes and said nothing. I felt my lungs collapsing. I was struggling for air. Then suddenly everything went black, but I was still breathing. I felt myself dying by the second. If it wasn't for the curse that you had place upon my kingdom, I would have been dead. But one thing stayed the same. I am still blind. But I can see the future more clear than before." Sora began to fiddle with his hair as he carried on talking.

"So where have you been all this time?" Scar questioned.

"Your curse had a flaw. When the curse was released, my kingdom, my people and I, were forgotten. My kingdom no longer existed, until now. That is why I am here. Alexa Snow is in grave danger."

Scar suddenly stopped what he was doing and looked at Sora.

"What do you mean?"

"That brother of hers. Link. He brought my people back to life but made them think that he is their king. He is building an army with Caity and Ripp Lotz on his side. He plans to kill Alexa."

Scar looked at his feet and then back up.

"I am glad you have come home and told me this. I will let Alexa know right away. you are safe now Sora," Scar spoke.

Scar sat down at his desk and began to write a letter to Alexa to tell her what was going to happen. After writing the letter and sealing it, he clicked his fingers and the letter was gone.

After looking at the mess that Scar had created while looking for information about vampires, he decided to clear everything up as there was nothing to be found. As he clicked his fingers, the books and scrolls began to place themselves back to where they belong, until Scar noticed something. Scar reached out and grabbed a book with the title "Vampire Lore" on the front.

As the rest of the books and scrolls went back to where they belonged, Scar sat down to read through this book. Scar flicked through the pages until he landed on a page he never knew existed. Sora heard Scar's heartbeat increase and suddenly became worried.

"What is it Scar?"

"I have just found something," Scar muttered.

"Go on."

"You were right. Vampires are real. They are not just a myth. Vampires and dark elves have been working together for centuries. Vampires have been turning dark elves so they can do their bidding during the day. They call them Sun Walkers."

Just then, the door swung open, revealing Alexa and Lena.

"Tommy!" Scar shouted.

"Sorry Scar, but you know I can not say no to the queen," Tommy muttered.

"Very well. So you have received my letter?" Scar questioned.

"Yes. What is going on?" Alexa questioned. She then looked down to see Sora sat in a chair.

"King Sora. I am ever so sorry to disturb you," Alexa spoke.

"No need Alexa. I am the reason you are here. I know your brother is going to try and kill you," Sora spoke.

Sora explained to Alexa what Link's intentions were and how he was going to try and go through with them. Alexa stood to her feet and looked between Sora, Scar, Tommy and Lena.

"If it is war he is after, then it is war he shall get."

***

After landing back in Brunuhville, Alexa and Lena made their way to the throne room. As they got to the throne room, Alexa commanded Sam to bring all of the kingdom people to the gardens at once. Sam obeyed and made his way to tell everyone the command. Alexa sat in her throne and placed her head in her hands. Lena walked up to her friend, kneeled down and placed a hand on her friend's knee.

"There is no need to worry Alexa. Link will fall and you shall rise," Lena's voice rang softly.

"I hope you are right."

Shinara came running into the throne room as Lena stood to her feet, giving the couple the space they needed.

"I just heard Alexa. Are you okay?" Shinara questioned.

"No, I am angry. I am done playing games. He murdered mum and dad, he murdered Leonard and now he plans to kill me." Alexa stood to her feet, her fists held tightly in balls. "I will show him who the real ruler is." And with that, Alexa made her way to the gardens.

As she walked out into the gardens, she noticed that everyone was there, waiting to hear what their queen had to say. Alexa walked up to the front, looked everyone in the eyes and sighed.

"I know it is late and I know that you have some important things to do but this can not wait. As you all know, my brother is trying to kill me and take over this kingdom and I will not have it, but something has changed."

Whispers were heard all around the gardens.

"My brother is making his way to start a war with me. In one week, he will be here. I know this is not fair on any of you and I am truly sorry that I ask this of you, but I am in need of more manpower. My army may be big but with Link, it is just small. I know I ask a lot, but I am asking for your help. I will forever honour you in my heart. I will recognise you as a Knight or Dame of Brunuhville."

From all over the gardens, men, women, boys and girls all cheered and stepped forward with one arm in the air.

"I will."

"Me too."

"For Brunuhville."

"For our queens and princes."

Alexa's heart warmed with joy as she watched male and female of all ages step forward with pride wanting to join Alexa in her fight.

"You all warm my heart. Those of you who wish not to join, I will make sure that you will have a safe place to take shelter in my castle. FOR BRUNUHVILLE!" Alexa chimed.

"FOR BRUNUHVILLE!" the whole kingdom shouted after their queen.

Now let the preparation commence.

After Alexa's speech, she went back into the castle and into her secret room. She sat down at her desk and pulled out everything she needed to write her letters to Sky-Guard and Smoke Tower. She started off with her letter to Smoke Tower.

> *Dear Dany,*
>
> *I am writing to you in utter emergency. I wish I was writing to you for a better situation but I am in complete despair and in need of your help.*
>
> *My brother is on his way t0 commence war with me and knowing how close our families were, I am asking for your help. Is there any chance that you could spare some men? I will be forever in your debt.*
>
> *Yours kindly,*
>
> *Alexa Snow.*

After sealing the letter, she clicked her fingers and the letter was gone.

"Now time for Sky-Guard," Alexa muttered to herself.

She pulled another piece of parchment in front of her and began to write.

> *Dear Scar,*
>
> *I know I have only just pulled away from you only hours ago, but after the news, I am in need of your assistance. Would you kindly spare some of your men for this war? I would be forever in your debt.*
>
> *Alexa Snow.*

After sealing the letter, she clicked her fingers once more and the letter was gone.

Alexa made her way down to the training grounds, where she saw Sam training his army for the war ahead. A sound was heard from behind Alexa. She turned around to see two portals open at the same time, with Sky-Guard and Smoke Tower waking through them.

Dany walked up to Alexa and gave her a hug.

"We are at your beck and call Alexa," she spoke.

"We will fight with you like we did with your parents," Jofree spoke.

"As will we Alexa. Your fight is our fight too," Scar spoke.

Alexa smiled at the three and looked at the armies behind them.

"Let's get the training on the roll."

The two armies walked over to Sam and they began to train for the battle ahead.

***

Six days had gone by and Link's storm was on its course to

Brunuhville and Sky-Guard. Link and Caity sat in the throne room, watching through the portals to see that the storm was working as a charm.

Ripp watched over Link's and Caity's armies, making sure that they were training hard and fast. Elsie and Shadow watched from a far. They knew what Link's intentions were but they never thought that Link would actually go through with it. And they never thought they would be a part of it either.

Back in Brunuhville, the Brunuhville, Sky-Guard and Smoke Tower armies trained night and day, not once stopping for a break. They knew the war to come was important. It was life or death. But even knowing that, never stopped them.

It wasn't long until the storm had hit Brunuhville. When the sky turned dark and the first drop of rain hit the ground, the kingdom went still and silent. Alexa and Shinara stood in the kingdom village and look up at the sky. Thunder and lightning were heard and seen throughout the kingdom and everyone knew that nothing good would come from this.

Lena made her way into the village and joined the queens in their silence. Alexa looked at the two women and then to the ground.

"I'll meet you back in the castle later. I need to see my dragons." And she was gone.

Alexa made her way through the castle and down to the dragon caves to see that Smok, Draco and Zepter were watching the rain.

Smok turned his head to see Alexa watching them.

"Your grace, is everything alright?" the dragon questioned.

"Where is Spitze?" the queen asked.

"We are not sure. He hasn't returned for a few days. He'll show."

Alexa made her way over to the dragons and placed a hand on each of them one at a time, along with resting her head one theirs.

"I am scared, Smok," Alexa's voice quivered.

"I know you are. As are we all. But you will triumph. Link does not stand a chance."

"With you three by my side, I will always win," Alexa spoke.

"We will fight by your side until the days for us have run out," Smok spoke.

Draco and Zepter both looked at their mother and screeched.

"I am glad that you will. And as will I with you too."

Alexa left the dragons in peace and made her way back up to the castle to find her sons. As she looked through every room, they were nowhere to be seen, until she heard laughter in the throne room. As she walked in, Lee and Felix were sat on their thrones playing a game of cards. They both looked up and saw that their mother was upset.

"What's wrong mum?" Lee questioned.

"You know how much I love you both?"

"Of course, as do we to you. But you are not going to die mother," Felix spoke.

Alexa hugged both of her boys as a tear rolled down her cheek. She pulled away and made her boys look her in the eye.

"If I am to die on the battlefield, I need you to promise me something."

"Of course, anything," they both said.

"Look after your mother and this kingdom. Grow up to be the best men that you are meant to be." Alexa began to cry.

Lee hugged his mum while Felix whipped away her tears.

"We will make you proud mother," Felix spoke as he hugged his mother.

Alexa pulled away from her sons and looked at them.

"There is one last place I need to go." She kissed them both on the head and walked out of the room.

Alexa made her way through the kingdom and to the magical

graveyard. As she walked through the gates, she walked straight up to her mother and father's graves. But as she knelt down, she remembered that Lena was not there to help reveal them. Tears began to fall and the droplets landed on the patch were her parents were laid to rest.

"Oh mother, father. I don't know what to do. I feel as if I have failed you. Link is making his way to Brunuhville as we speak and I still have no idea whether I will die or if I will lose someone dear to me." Alexa sobbed. Her eyes puffy and swollen. "I can not do this alone. I wish you were here. I need you," she choked out. "What I would give to see you one last time, but that time may never come," Alexa sighed. She bent over and kissed both graves and stood to her feet.

"Wish me luck."

12

Their Last Wishes

The skies throughout the dimensions never faded from the grey colour and rain still poured down on everyone and everything. Alexa and Shinara looked outside of their bedroom window and watched as the rain began to fall heavier by the second.

"Link is on his way, isn't he?" Lee questioned as he walked into his mother's room.

"Yes, yes he is," Alexa said as she ushered her son over to her and draped an arm around his shoulders.

Felix and Lena walked in seeing the three tense. Felix went over to Shinara and hugged her tight while Lena looked at the four and sighed. As she walked over to Alexa, she placed a hand on her shoulder.

"Everything will be fine. Nothing can stop you from reigning over this land," she smiled.

Alexa looked at her friend and smiled back, placing a hand over hers, the slight feel of electricity being felt in the process.

"I know. I'm not scared. I'm angry. This will be his last battle. He will never hurt us again." And with that, Alexa looked out towards her kingdom, ready to face her brother for what she thought would be the last time.

Down below in the kingdom courtyard, Sam and his army were training hard for the upcoming battle, but what they didn't know was that Link wasn't that far behind and he had a few tricks up his sleeve.

***

As the last day went by and the rain never stopped. Everyone in

Brunuhville was on edge and they had every right to be. Sam and his army had been non-stop training, including the help from Smoke Tower and Sky-Guard that Alexa had kindly asked for. Dany had kindly helped by giving her army and horses to Alexa, while Scar gave every man and woman he knew that was willing to fight, including himself to Alexa, both knowing that Link wouldn't stop at anything until Brunuhville was his.

But time was cut short as a dragon's roar and horse's stomping were heard across the entire kingdom. Alexa and Dany looked out from Alexa's bedroom window to see that Link and his army had finally arrived.

"The time has come," Dany spoke, placing a hand on her friend's shoulder.

Lena walked in and looked straight out of the window.

"Let's show your brother who we really are," Lena spoke.

Alexa smiled at her best friend and then turned on her heal, heading towards the door.

"Let the war begin." And with that, she was gone.

***

As the queens, princes, king, princesses and armies of both Brunuhville and Smoke Tower made their way to the barrier between Link and them, everything became silent. A deafening silence. Alexa made her way to the edge of the barrier and clicked her fingers. Smok, Draco and Zepter flew down and stood behind Alexa, screeching, allowing their presence to be known.

Link smirked and allowed himself to do the same actions. As he walked towards Alexa, he smirked. Clicking his fingers, Spitze flew down from the sky and landed next to Link.

"Missing something, sister?" he laughed.

Alexa looked behind to see that there were only three dragons, not four.

"What did you do?" she spat through clenched teeth.

"Oh, you know, poisoned your beloved Leonard, killed a civilian and also killed your dragon and brought him back to life to reign on my side," Link smirked.

Alexa jumped onto Draco's back as Lena did so to Smok and Lee to Zepter, flying back to where the army stood, waiting for war to commence. As they flew over the army, it was a sight to be proud of. Sam, with all of his pride walked back and forth in front of his army, giving a spectacular speech, men on foot with swords stood first in ten rows, men on foot with bow and arrow stood second in ten rows, men on horseback stood third in thirty rows and lastly men and women from the Old Religion stood tall in fifteen rows. This army stood at two-hundred-thousand men and woman.

Alexa flew down slightly and looked at every single man and woman that stood before her.

"I know this is not what you had signed up for, but I know that you are all strong, brave, proud and full of pride. I want you to take all of that onto the battlefield and show Link that this is what you are fighting for," Alexa shouted, earning cheers from the army.

"So, who's with me?" Alexa shouted.

"YEAH," he army called back.

"I said, WHO'S WITH ME?" Once more, Alexa shouted.

"YEAH," the army called back louder, showing Alexa that they would stand by her side until their very last breaths.

"NOW LET'S WIN THIS WAR." And with that, Alexa flew off into battle, with the army charging and roaring behind her.

Link saw what was coming towards him and climbed onto his dragon's back. He turned to look at his army, that compared to Alexa's was small. His army stood at just sixty-thousand men, with dark elves, animagis, horses, along with the help from Stone Grave that Caity happily gave to Link for her own sweet revenge.

As Link looked at his army, he shouted.

"I want to win this. I want my sister dead and that throne to be mine. You all signed up for this, now make it happen." And with that, he flew off into battle with his army behind him.

Let the battle commence. But deep within Sky-Guard, where only a few stayed behind to look after the land, Link had sent a few of his followers there to retrieve something that only a few knew about. Not even Link should know about the ancient scroll that tells the undying truth of the dark elves.

Spike, Sparrow and Angel snuck through the Tower of Magika's doors, making sure that no one would see them. Two guards were walking up and down the ground floor of the tower. Spike and Sparrow decided to slip up, taking a guard each. Both moving ever so slowly, not to be detected, they slowly pulled their daggers from underneath their cloaks and held a firm grip around them. As the guards moved so their backs were against the two dark elves, Spike and Sparrow took their chance. They lunged forward towards the guards and plunged their daggers into their necks and sliced across, leaving a gruesome gash in their necks.

After dealing with the guards, the three men made their way through the tower, looking for the library. They came across a large metal gate with yet another guard walking left to right in front of it. Angel clicked his fingers, causing him to change his identity to one of the other guards that they had just murdered. Angel went walking up towards the other guard, dagger held lightly behind his back.

"You, sir. You are needed at the main doors," Angel spoke.

"Yes, sir," the guard spoke, making his way past Angel and towards the main doors.

Just as the guard turned his back towards angel, Angel plunged his dagger into the man's back three times, making sure that the man was no longer breathing. After Angel had turned back into his normal self, the three men opened the gate to see that they had found the library. The three split off, Spike taking the upstairs right, Angel taking downstairs and Sparrow taking the upstairs left.

After a few minutes of looking through all of the bookshelves, well not looking, throwing, ripping and burning what they were not after, Sparrow had finally found the scroll they were after.

"Lads, I have found it," Sparrow called.

Angel and Spike wandered over to him and saw that he was correct in saying that he had the scroll Link was after.

"Now let's get back to the battle."

But before returning back to the battle, the three men decided to set fire to everything they set their eyes upon, causing bricks and wood to turn into rubble as it fell to the ground.

Back in Brunuhville, dragons soared through the sky, blowing fire at the opposing army down below, causing masses of explosions and men to fall to the ground either injured or dead. Arrows flew through the sky, near misses or injuring the men as they plunged into their bodies. Men on horses galloped into battle, swords in hand, stabbing, slicing, beheading their enemies.

The sound of swords clashing against each other as men and woman, boys and girls fought against each other, explosions and buildings crumbling as magic was thrown at every chance that was possible. Buildings and nature burning as each side lost control of their magic.

As Link and Alexa watched over their armies, Link began to fall into anger while Alexa began to feel slightly prouder by the second as Alexa's army still held their front strong, never letting Link's side through their hold.

As a man on horseback came riding near Sam, Sam pulled his sword into both of his hands, igniting the fire throughout the blade. As he the horse came closer, Sam pulled the sword behind him and swung, slicing one leg off of the horse, causing both man and horse to fall to the ground. The man stood to his feet, sword in hand, glaring at the man that just threw him off of his horse.

Both the man and Sam looked at each other, deep in eye contact and then;

CLASH.

Sam's sword clashed with the mans. Sam bounced on the balls of his feet, as did the man, readjusting their grips on their swords. Not afraid of what the other may do, with each swing, neither would back down.

Kohana ran and tore into every horse, man and woman leg that she could get her teeth into. Many soldiers falling and not being able to get up. To the ones that couldn't stand, Kohana ran towards them, mouth fully open and teeth dripping in saliva, she bit into them, tearing limb from limb until there was no more.

Shinara, Dany and Jofree stood face to face with Caity and Ripp, swords in hand, magic at the ready and anger plastered all over their faces. Caity took a swing at Shinara, but poorly missing as the sword was too heavy for her. Shinara fore swung towards Caity, catching her arm. Jofree and Ripp lunged towards each other, the sound of metal clashing against each other. Ripp took the chance to strike Jofree but Dany jumped in the way, shouting.

"Thorstruck." Purple sparks flew from within Dany, piercing through Ripp's clothes and body.

Ripp stood and looked at Danny and Jofree.

"It's over, Ripp." And with the click of Dany's fingers, Ripp fell to the floor as a crumble of dust.

Caity saw what Dany had just done and lunged herself towards her, but as quick as a wolf, Shinara threw her sword towards Caity, cutting her head neatly off of her shoulders.

"That's for my wife, you bitch."

Overhead, Lena flew through the sky on top of Smok with Lee on top of Zepter slightly behind, burning through the crowd of Link's followers, making sure to not hit their own people.

Link watched as Lena and Lee fight and cheer with their dragons, with a small thought that crossed his mind. Link closed his eyes, his fists bunched up into balls. As he opened his eyes, he looked straight at Zepter and Lee, his eyes changing black, he lifted his hands up towards the boy and dragon and whispered.

"Thorstruck." Black sparks shot out from Link's palms, as fast as light, travelling through the sky, hitting Zepter in the side.

Just for a moment, everything went silent and still. A slight parting in the clouds opened up, allowing the rays from the sun to pass through and light up the space around Zepter. But then things began to fall into slow motion. Zepter and Lee were falling to the ground. Lena looked over to Lee with a smile on her face, soon disappearing when she noticed that Lee was falling to his death.

"Smok fly after him," she screamed.

Smok and Lena flew down as fast as they could to catch up to Lee and the dragon. Soon reaching them, Lena grabbed hold of Lee's arm and pulled him over to sit on top of Smok. As soon as Lee was safe, they watched as Zepter fell through the sky and plummeted to his death.

Alexa watched as another one of her dragons fell to their death. The ground shook as Zepter landed with a cloud of dust around him and rubble thrown everywhere as the dragon's body landed on part of the castle.

Alexa screamed. The battle had stopped. Everyone looked up to see Alexa destroyed over what had just happened. Alexa looked up at Link and her eyes changed to a blood red and her blood began to boil beneath her skin.

"THE BATTLE WILL NOW STOP!" Alexa screamed. "LINK! THIS IS OUR FIGHT! I WILL NOT HAVE NO MORE BLOOD SHED!"

"HAVE IT YOUR WAY SISTER." And with that, everyone took shelter and watched from a distance the battle that would now take place.

Alexa and Link flew down to the ground and jumped off of their dragons. Alexa walked up to Sam and held out her hand.

"My sword please Sam."

Sam placed a gold-plated sword, with dragon heads on the handle and flames engraved throughout the blade. She looked at the blade and tapped it, allowing the magic of the sword to come to life, causing bright orange and red flames to take hold over the blade.

Link walked over to one of his followers and took hold of his sword. He too tapping it, but there was nothing magical about this sword.

"Where's the flames?" Link spat.

"There is none. This is an ordinary sword."

"Oh, bloody hell! Do I have to do everything myself?" Link clicked his fingers and tapped on the sword, allowing flames to override the blade.

"Now this is a fair fight," Link smirked as he looked Alexa in the eyes.

"Nothing is fair about you Link," Alexa spoke as she ran towards Link, clashing their swords together.

Alexa dodged as Link threw a back swing towards her, allowing her to swing a fore swing at him. Taken by surprise, Link staggered back, maintaining his balance on his feet, Alexa waved her sword in figure of eights as she danced around her brother. Link lunged forward but missed, causing the people fighting for Alexa to cheer as they witnessed Alexa's stealth moves. But again, Alexa danced around the dark elf, Link lunged forward, but missed.

Link began to get angry. His eyes turning black and his grip around the sword getting tighter and tighter.

"This is no time for games sister," he spat.

"And who said I was playing?" Alexa spoke as she made her way to the back of Link, slowly but accurate, she strikes, stabbing Link in the back of the ribs and slicing his arm. Link screeched in pain, holding onto his back and then his arm, dropping his sword in the process. Link looked at his sister and then at the sword. He staggered to pick his sword up, but when he did, his face was greeted by the harsh touch of his sister's fist, causing him to fly back and land on his back.

Link tried to stand, blood dripping from his face, arm and back. By the time that he had stood to his feet, Lena and Shinara were by Alexa's side.

Alexa, Lena and Shinara knew they had to end this now. All three of them held hands and closed their eyes. As they muttered an incantation, magic began to swirl all around them. Link had noticed this action and began to throw fireballs at the three women, but it was no use. The magic just bounced off of the women.

The women opened their eyes and looked Link straight in the eyes. The three women held their hands out towards Link and sparks began to shoot towards him, hitting him in the chest. Link fell to the floor, lifeless. With caution, the three women went to walk over to him but something was wrong. The women stood at a halt when they saw that link was still breathing. With every rise and fall of Link's chest, the women readied their magic. Link shot up to his feet and smirked at the women.

"Did you think it was that easy?" he spat.

Red and black magic began to swirl from his hands.

"Now it is your turn to die by my hands." And with that, Link shot red and black sparks towards Alexa.

Before Alexa knew it, Shinara had pushed her out of the way and took the shot. Shinara fell to the ground, struggling with each breath to hang on to life. Alexa ran to her wife, falling to the ground next to her and scooping her up in her arms. Tears began to fall from both of the women's eyes.

"Hang on love. Please. You have to stay with me. I can't lose you now," Alexa cried.

"You're alive and that's all that matters to me," Shinara choked out.

"Shush, save your breath," Alexa began. "Smok I need you," Alexa spoke in her mind as Lena walked over to the women and placed a hand on Alexa's shoulder.

Shinara looked up at Lena and smiled. "Lena, look after my wife and children for me. I know you will make me proud."

"Of course," Lena replied.

Shinara looked back up at her wife and placed a limp hand on her face.

"May we meet again." And with that, Shinara took her last breath, falling lifeless in her wife's arms.

Alexa screamed through her cries, causing sparks to fly out from her body and hit Link in the chest, causing him to fall backwards to the ground. Elsie and Shadow saw what had happened and ran over to him.

But that wasn't the only thing that had happened. While Alexa screamed causing magic to erupt from her body and hitting Link, her magic also created a dimensional bang, causing some of the dimensions to collide and become as one with others.

Seconds later Smok arrived and saw that Shinara was no longer on this plane.

"Your grace, I am sorry for your loss." And with that, Smok picked her up and flew off.

Lee and Felix came running over to their mother and noticed that she had been crying.

"Mother, where is mum?" Lee questioned.

Alexa just looked up at her sons and shook her head. Lee fell to the floor screaming and crying, while Felix cried into Lena's arms. Lee's screams were heard all over the kingdom, causing everyone to stop what they were doing and huddle around the royal family.

***

It had been a week since the batter had commenced and the kingdom were getting on as if nothing had happened. Except for Alexa. After losing Leonard before the battle, she thought she could handle another death but she couldn't. Alexa was beyond broken after Shinara had jumped in front of her and saved her from Link.

Alexa was sat on her bed, holding a piece of Shinara's clothing when there was a knock at the door. Alexa turned around to see Dorian standing in the doorway.

"Sorry your grace, but the ceremony will be starting shortly."

"Of course." Alexa stood to her feet and followed Dorian down to the magical graveyard.

As they reached the gardens, everyone in the kingdom was standing there to give their loved ones the best send off. Lee and Felix walked over to Alexa and hugged her tight, making all three of them start to cry. Lena walked over with Sam and gave a half-hearted smile. Alexa pulled away from her children and sighed.

"Let's get this over and done with." And with that, they all sat down, allowing Maester Logan to start the ceremony.

"We are gathered here today for such unfortunate events. To say goodbye to the ones who fell in the great battle," Logan began.

Alexa zoned out. She looked around and saw people crying, holding on to their loved ones that were still here and then she looked at her sons and her best friend. Lee and Felix were hugging each other, crying at the words that were falling from the maester's lips and then Lena. She looked calm but an emotionless calm. Lena didn't know what to feel. Yes, she was close to Leonard and Shinara but she had not spent most of her life with them unlike Alexa.

Alexa looked back at Logan and zoned back in.

"Now, I would like to hand you over to our queen for a few words before we reveal our tribute to the fallen."

Alexa stood to her feet and walked up to where Logan was standing. Logan gave her a quick hug and then went to sit down. Alexa sighed and then looked out to her people.

"What a year it has been. I really don't know where to start. Everyday I have looked out onto all of you and watched how you all get on with your lives, with no worry or care at all. I wish I could be like you all. I feel as if this is all my fault. You have lived without a queen for so long and when I come back home and become your queen, nothing but terror has roamed over this kingdom," Alexa began, but was interrupted by her people.

"It's not your fault."

"Don't blame yourself."

"You have lived up to your mother and father."

"Thank you for your kind words," Alexa smiled. "But, of course, we are not here for me to talk about myself, but to talk about our loved ones that have fallen pure to the hands of my brother. Firstly, let me talk about Leonard. This man has been by my side since the day I was born. He helped me cope with my parents' deaths, taught me everything I need to know about magic and my powers, taught me the ways of a dragon lord but also, after my father died, he was the best father figure I could of asked for. And how did he die? By the hands of a monster that couldn't even show his face!"

"And For Shinara, my amazing wife and mother to my two handsome boys. Where do I begin. Not only was she my wife, but my best friend. Yes, we had our disagreements but we stood by each other's sides. She was the most beautiful soul that I had ever met and I couldn't thank her enough. I know it has been a week since I lost Shinara and three weeks since I lost Leonard, but I will never stop loving, missing and caring for them. I miss you so much. And to the people who gave their lives to fight by my side against my brother, I thank you and will forever be in your debt," Alexa finished.

Alexa looked around and saw her people crying and smiling at the words she had just spoke. She walked back to her seat and allowed Logan to finish off.

"Now, to show tribute to the fallen, Dorian, will you do the honours?"

Dorian walked over to several cloth covered objects. He took hold of the cloth and pulled it away, revealing two statues, one of Leonard and one of Shinara and scattered behind the statues were gravestones for everyone that had fallen by Link's hands.

Everyone walked over to their fallen loved one's gravestone and began to smile and cry. Alexa looked around at everyone and smiled.

"At least I have done something goods," she muttered to herself.

"You do nothing but goods," Lena spoke as she placed a hand on her friend's shoulder.

***

Link was teleported back to the caves by Elsie and Shadow. Even though they weren't keen on everything Link had done over the past year, they still deeply cared about him, or it was just the fear of Link ending their lives that made them care for him. Suddenly Link jumped to his feet, surprising the two women.

"Why are you so surprised? You know no one can kill me."

The two women began to worry and began to run away. As they tried to leave the caves, Link clicked his fingers, causing a forcefield bubble to capture the two women in.

"Please Link, don't hurt us!" Elsie shouted.

"What makes you think that I was going to hurt you?" Link questioned with a smirk.

Link clicked his fingers, snapping Elsie's neck.

"Please Link! I have always been loyal to you!" Shadow trembled.

"Oh is that what you think you have been doing?" Link began.

"Elsie was loyal to me, but you had to get inside her head."

"I would never!"

"What did I say about speaking out of line?" Link spat. "Well, all things, good or bad, have to come to an end." And with that, Link clicked his fingers and snapped Shadow's neck.

Link walked over to both of the girls and one by one, he placed a warm hand on to their cold bodies and absorbed both of their powers.

Link stood tall, smoothing out his leather jacket. As he began to make his way out of the Brunuhville caves, he flicked the collar of his coat up and smirked.

"Now this is where the real fun begins."

***

The End. Or is it?

Irish To English Translations

"Tine." -- And the dragons blew fire.

"Iasc." -- And the dragons got some fish.

"Smután mairteola." -- And the dragons got a beef chunk.

"Sruthán." -- And both the dragons blew fire and burnt the wood.

"Drachen Lord." -- Dragon Lord

"Is mise an Tiarna Dragon, geallaim duit tú a chosaint, agus ní ligfidh mé do dhochar teacht gar duitse, mo mhuintir." -- I am the Dragon Lord, I promise to protect you, and never allow harm to come near you, my people

"Eitilt." -- Fly

"Téigh abhaile." -- Go Home

"I Alexa Snow, ar dtús de m'ainm, banríon Brunuhville agus tiarna an Dragon." -- I Alexa Snow, first of my name, queen of Brunuhville and the dragon lord.

"Dearbhófar an ríocht seo agus daoine na ríochta a chosaint go dtí mo anáil dheireanach." -- Vow to protect this kingdom and the kingdom's people until my last breath.

"Chun lá bainise Dragon Lord agus Snow!" -- To the Dragon Lord and Snow's wedding day!

"I Alexa Snow, an tiarna Dragon, swear chun tú a chosaint agus grá duit don chuid eile de mo shaol." -- I Alexa Snow, the dragon lord, swear to protect and love you for the rest of my life.

"I Shinara Ondovir, mhionnaím tú a chosaint agus grá duit don chuid eile de mo shaol agus suí le do thaobh chun an ríocht seo a chosaint." -- I Shinara Ondovir, swear to protect and love you for the rest of my life and sit by your side to protect this kingdom.

"I Lee Snow, a dheimhníonn go gcosnóidh mé an ríocht seo le mo chumhacht go léir go dtí go dtarraingeoidh mé anáil anuas." -- I Lee Snow, vow to protect this kingdom with all my power until my last drawing breath.

"I Felix Snow, a dheimhníonn go gcosnóidh mé an ríocht seo le mo chumhacht go léir go dtí go dtarraingeoidh mé anáil anuas." -- I Felix Snow, vow to protect this kingdom with all my power until my last drawing breath."

Teacht -- Come

Fada beo na prionsaí -- Long live the princes

Spells

Es Ther Ra -- Summon a guardian

Sor drachen du -- Summon the dead

Dawnson zo zine -- Bring the dead to life

Dar zender zu ender -- Change someone's being

Daxen cand hint du fort -- To banish someone

Thap twick -- To make a ghost more solid

Dalence du kinde -- Call upon a loved one

En Dawsar -- Turn lights on

Drachen -- To transform dust/mist to what you want

Denston -- To make something fall

Danson du -- To open a portal

Dreka -- To pack things away

Vandoor -- To mind control

Pictok -- To manipulate time

Fliptop -- Making something upside down, upright

Thorstruck -- Killing spell

Acknowledgements

A massive thank you to Grace Jolly…
The artist for the cover of my book.

A massive thank you to Sharmayne Gelston...
This book would not be what it is now if it was not for her.

Printed in Great Britain
by Amazon

66716138R00173